Close the Door
on Murder

Close the Door on Murder

John Creasey
as
Jeremy York

David McKay Company, Inc.
Ives Washburn, Inc.
New York

CLOSE THE DOOR ON MURDER

COPYRIGHT © 1948 BY JOHN CREASEY

This revised edition copyright © 1971 by John Creasey

Originally published in Great Britain

First American Edition, 1973

Second Printing

LIBRARY OF CONGRESS CATALOG CARD NUMBER: 72-87141

MANUFACTURED IN THE UNITED STATES OF AMERICA

Close the Door
on Murder

CHAPTER I

MINE HOST OFFERS A WARNING

Alec Dane hunched his shoulders and pulled the brim of his hat over his coat collar. Rain streamed down his mackintosh, and the wet ends of his trousers flapped about his ankles. He took little notice of the cottages on either side of the steep hill on which the village was built. Behind him was the garage where he had left his car, ahead, the *Marrigay Arms*; he had no immediate interest in anything between those two points.

The inn was at the foot of the hill, and in front of it the yard was a morass of muddy gravel. Rain splashed from the eaves of a narrow porch. The inn itself was square and squat, built of drab grey stone. The windows were small, dark squares, like the empty eye-sockets of a pale-faced troglodyte.

In a half-circle at the top of the flat, newly-painted board were the words *Marrigay Arms*, and at the bottom the succinct statement: *'Prop'r; Abel Buller.'*

A gust of wind swept down the hill, making Dane's mackintosh billow forward and tipping his hat over his face. Grabbing a wooden post with his right hand, he pulled himself on to the step, and stood breathing heavily, his face only a foot from the door. He turned the handle and pushed.

The passage ahead of him was long and narrow; the dark floor-boards shone, reflecting light from an electric lamp hanging from the ceiling. It was a surprise to see anything so modern in this village.

Dane took off his hat, shook the water from it on to the porch, then hesitated, not quite knowing what to do. He was about to take off his coat when a man appeared from a room half-way along the passage.

7

The new-comer might have been modelled on one of the inn's barrels; he was short and of great girth, with a thick chest and powerful shoulders. He wore a green baize apron, and was drying his hands on a towel.

'Good afternoon,' said the visitor, anxious to create a good impression. 'Will my mack be all right here?'

'Better in the kitchen, poss'bly,' said the barrel-shaped man, coming forward and taking the coat. 'Will ye be wanting lunch?'

'If I'm not too late,' said Dane. He was surprised by the man's voice, soft, gentle and rich in its broad Limshire vowels.

'There'll be something,' the man said, and pointed to a door. 'Dining-room's there.'

Dane moved on to the dining-room. He was feeling dispirited. Two hours driving through the relentless rain, finishing with a flat tyre! He had left his car at the garage, after having driven ten miles on the 'flat' which had probably cut the inner tube to ribbons. Now he smiled with pleasure at the sight of a log fire in a huge brick fireplace. There were half-a-dozen small tables laid for luncheon or dinner. On the walls were some old sporting prints, giving the room a friendly touch.

He ordered a pint of beer and sat wondering why anyone had given such a village the lovely name of Marrigay – and whether the people he had come to see had taken their name from the village, or the village had taken its name from them. Little though he had seen of the place, it was nothing like the picture he had formed in his mind – of a picturesque hamlet in a picturesque county, miles from the main roads, in the hinterland of England where progress had stopped and life went on much as it had for centuries. Of course, he had been a fool to conjure up such a vision. Nothing stopped progress. But at least he might have met with thatched roofs and not the bleak stone-walled, slate-roofed cottages which he had glimpsed on his way down the hill.

Buller himself brought in piece by piece, a fairly well-

8

cooked meal. Over the final items he showed a disposition to linger.

'If ye'd like another drink, 'tis near closing time,' he remarked.

'Will you have one with me?' asked Dane.

'Why, now, that's kind of ye,' said Buller. 'The same again?'

Comfortable and well-fed, Dane took out a pipe and was lighting it as Buller put his beer down beside him.

It was evident to Alec Dane that mine host was curious about him; but then, he might be curious about anyone who passed through the village, especially on such a day as this. That thought made Dane glance at the window. He could not see the rain falling, although a gust of wind smote the house and made the window rattle.

'The rain has stopped, seemingly,' remarked mine host.

'That's fine!'

'Have ye far to go?'

'I want to drive back to London tonight,' said Dane.

'London, is it? London, eh?' Buller spoke as if of a legendary place, in a vague world outside his ken. 'I didn't see your car,' he ventured.

'I left it at the garage,' said Dane, mildly amused by mine host's ill-concealed curiosity. 'I suppose you have a lot of visitors in the summer,' he went on.

'No,' said Buller, after a pause, ' I wouldn't say that. Mind ye, we've had a tidy few this last few weeks.'

'Ah,' said Dane.

'From London, most of them,' Buller told him.

'I suppose so,' Dane took his pipe from his lips and had another drink, then smiled broadly into Buller's face. 'Yes, you're right,' he went on, 'I'm another newspaperman come to attempt the impossible.'

Buller did not smile; he had not once smiled since Dane had seen him.

'You don't know a way of achieving it, do you?' asked Dane.

Slowly, Buller shook his head.

'That I don't,' he said, "tis none of my business but I won't say I'm not interested in what goes on at the House, now. 'Tis Marrigay House and part of the village when all is said and done. It isn't only the folk from London who would like to see the Colonel,' he went on, 'time was when he would come into the village friendly-like as his father did – aye, and *his* father before him – and it's been a disappointment to all of us. Aye.' He finished his beer. 'Young man,' he said, 'ye won't take a word of warning from me amiss, I hope.'

'I'll be grateful for it,' said Dane.

'Then don't take your car to the House,' said Buller, 'not into the drive. If ye go by car, leave it outside by the gates. And when you're inside, have an eye open all the time for the dogs.'

'Ah,' said Dane again. 'I've heard about those dogs. Did the Colonel bring them home with him?'

'That he didn't,' said Buller, 'they were new to him, I've no doubt, as they are to all of us. Aye. They're rare wild.' He was speaking slowly, as if with a great effort. 'None of us can understand what happened at the house. It's changed so much since Mr Marrigay died, and his poor wife – '

He broke off, shaking his head.

Dane did not know what prompted him to say:

'I knew Mr Marrigay, and I used to know the Colonel. That's why I'm hoping I shall have better luck than the others.'

'Well,' said Buller, 'maybe you will, maybe you won't.'

He picked up Dane's tankard, as if to intimate that he had gossiped enough, and Dane stood up.

'You've been very helpful,' he said, gratefully, 'and I haven't enjoyed a lunch like that for a long time.'

On the way out he gathered up his coat and hat and stepped into the porch. There were blue gaps in the grey clouds and the water had stopped dripping. He stepped gingerly across a puddle, reached the road and turned left, away from the garage and the village. He knew where Marrigay House was to be found; half-way up the hill leading out of the village, set back off the road and half-hidden by trees.

10

He pondered over Buller's warning.

He had told Buller that he was seeking the impossible, and the innkeeper had agreed, accepting the situation without surprise. It would take a great deal to surprise Buller, reflected Dane; yet obviously Colonel Marrigay's attitude had hurt the innkeeper – and, possibly, most of the villagers. In his slow way, Buller had conveyed a great deal.

Half-way up the hill, the road steepened. Why anyone had built the village on the slope instead of along the valley near the *Marrigay Arms* was incomprehensible; but there it was, with the church on the west, the gilt hands of the clock on the short Norman tower glittering in the sunlight. To the north the sky was still a leaden grey, but here was brightness and beauty – which he had been told to expect of this part of Limshire. Lovely, lonely country . . .

He smiled as the words passed through his mind. The Editor of the *Gazette* had used them only that morning. Dane was not on the staff; he was part-owner of a large London suburban newspaper, but sometimes became 'special representative' of a national daily. He knew Cameron of the *Gazette* fairly well, and had called on him soon after nine o'clock. Cameron had been pleased to see him, but too busy to pay him much attention until he had mentioned Marrigay. Then Cameron had flicked down the handle of the talking box on his desk and said:

'Don't disturb me until I call again.' He had looked up sharply. 'What do you know about Marrigay?'

'I used to know Peter. Not only as a cricketer.'

'Where'd you meet him?'

'At school.'

'Know him well?'

'Not to say well,' Dane had admitted. 'He was in the Sixth, I was three years younger. Apart from county matches, we met at Old Boys' dinners and the annual *Past versus Present* match.'

'Why the hell didn't I think of you before?' Cameron had said. 'You can name your own fee for an interview with Peter Marrigay. Think you can get it?'

11

'I can try.'

'Today?'

'Yes, but why – '

'There's always a hurry,' Cameron said. He slapped his desk with the flat of his hand. 'Preposterous business! Man returns to England after wandering for nearly six years in Burma having escaped from a prisoner-of-war camp, and he won't see a soul, won't say a word, just shuts himself up in that damned house and keeps a guard on the gates and dogs to drive off anyone who climbs over the hedge. If he were a nonogenarian who'd never been heard of that wouldn't be news, but Peter Marrigay – personally, I think he's mad. His family knows he is but won't admit it. Always unsteady, wasn't he?'

'Erratic,' murmured Dane.

'Call it erratic,' Cameron had agreed. 'That's the trouble with these brilliant men, always liable to crack up. Well, go and see what you can do – but mind those damned dogs!'

As Dane reached a gateway near the top of the hill, a dog barked and startled him out of his reverie. He looked beyond the gate, to a man who was walking towards it along the drive, with a huge Alsatian lurking sombrely at his heels.

Dane touched the gate as the man drew up. The dog stopped dead, glowering at Dane.

Now that he was here and saw for himself that there *was* a man and a dog on guard, Dane's optimism wilted. The house could just be seen through the dripping trees, the sunlight reflected on the windows.

Next moment, he saw Peter Marrigay.

CHAPTER II

PETER MARRIGAY

Marrigay was wearing an old raincoat and gumboots. Dane saw his face, there could be no possible mistake. There were the sharp, handsome features, the hooked nose, the incredibly bright, hawklike eyes.

'May I ask your business, sir?' asked the man at the gate.

'I would like to see Colonel Marrigay,' said Dane, pitching his voice high.

Marrigay, hearing his name, looked towards him. There was no sign there of recognition. The Alsatian, hair bristling the whole length of its back, raised its fine head and bared its teeth.

'Have you an appointment, sir?'

'No, but – '

'I'm sorry, sir, the Colonel can see no one except by appointment.'

'Oh,' said Dane, absurdly.

Marrigay had turned and was walking sharply up the drive. Suddenly an idea flashed into Dane's mind. He threw back his head and shouted, much to the astonishment of the guard.

'Howzaaat!'

Marrigay swung round on his heel.

'Hallo, Peter!' called Dane.

Across his mind had flashed a vision of a green field and men in white flannels, himself behind the sticks, appealing for a catch or leg-before-wicket with his head thrown back and the curiously piercing yell startling somnolent fieldsmen and spectators alike.

Marrigay stared at him with a growing interest, and Dane waved.

13

'Out?' he called, raising his forefinger.

Marrigay came forward, smiling. Dane had a curious impression that the smile was strained. The guard stood back a pace as Marrigay reached the gate; but the dog did not move.

'There can't be two men with a voice like that,' said Marrigay. 'It can only be Alec Dane.'

'I'm glad you haven't quite forgotten me,' said Dane.

'Who could?' asked Marrigay. 'All right, Lem,' he said in an aside, and the guard unlocked the padlock which secured the gate. 'What on earth have you been doing with yourself?' asked Marrigay, 'you've lost stones!'

'Two and a quarter, to be exact,' agreed Dane. 'The Army was a hard life.'

The gate swung open and he stepped through, forcing himself not to glance at the Alsatian, although out of the corner of his eye he saw its hair still bristling and its great teeth bared. 'Lem' closed the gate and spoke to the dog, which did not move.

Marrigay put out his hand.

'The Army hasn't made you any more handsome,' he remarked, 'you need a double chin to look your best.' He smiled again, and this time the impression of restraint was missing. 'You've carried me back a few years, I'd almost forgotten a yell like that. Still playing?'

'When I can get the time,' said Dane.

'For Wessex?'

'Of course.'

Marrigay chuckled.

'The faithful Dane! I'd almost forgotten. You needn't worry about the dog,' he went on, seeing Dane cast a glance downwards, 'he'll be all right so long as Lem tells him to behave. Let's go up to the house.' He began to walk up the drive, taking long swift strides. He had not altered much, thought Dane: he seemed to be in a hurry, as he had always been – working, playing, doing whatever came his way with a tremendous gusto which obviously drew heavily on his store of nervous energy. As a bowler, he had been capable of taking half-a-dozen of the best wickets in the land in a row, as a

14

batsman, capable of knocking the fastest speed merchant and the most guileful slow bowler off his length. As in cricket, so in other things, he was a man whom everyone expected to be inconsistent, yet who played with remarkable consistency.

The house, like the *Marrigay Arms*, was built of grey stone. Creeper softened the harshness of outline. A wide porch, with two square pillars tapering towards the top, protected the front door from the weather. The steps leading to the porch were still wet, and a pool of rain water had gathered on one side of them.

'Come in,' said Marrigay.

He strode before Dane into a large, square hall. Huge pieces of old oak furniture stood against the dark panelled walls. A door on the right stood open. As Dane followed Marrigay past this, he glanced into the room and saw an old lady sitting in front of a blazing fire, with some needlework in her hand. Dane caught a glimpse of her face, the expression, startling him, was one of infinite sadness.

Marrigay flung open another door.

'Make yourself comfortable,' he said, 'I'll be back in two shakes.'

The room was small, the walls half-panelled in light oak. On brackets stood some of Marrigay's trophies – two mounted cricket balls, scored and marked from use, probably those with which he had twice taken all ten wickets in a First Class county match; there was a bat, with a chip off the shoulder; probably the bat with which he had scored a century in each innings against Australia. But all the trophies were not the spurs of cricketing fame; golf and rowing had made their contribution. The room, book-lined, a Chinese carpet stretching from wall to wall, was obviously Peter Marrigay's especial sanctuary.

Dane wondered what he should say.

Before leaving Cameron, he had told the editor that he would try to persuade Marrigay to make a statement for the newspaper, but that he would pass nothing on without Marrigay's permission; Cameron had made no demur. But even though he had made that proviso, Dane was not too happy about the coming interview; perhaps the best way to handle the situation would be to tell the truth. Marrigay was capable of flying into a rage if he thought that his caller was trading on an old acquaintanceship for the sake of a story.

Marrigay was gone a long time.

Dane stirred the logs in the fire with his foot. He could not forget the sad face of the old lady; in its way, he thought, it was a lovely face – pale, with large eyes; he remembered her thin, veined hands.

Someone came running down the stairs. The footsteps drew nearer. Dane stood with his back to the fire, looking towards the door, conscious of a strange, inexplicable excitement. The haste of those footsteps might account for it; they gave the impression that whoever drew near was bursting with eagerness.

The door was flung open and a girl appeared.

'Peter – ' she began, and then stopped short, catching her breath.

'I think he'll be here soon,' said Dane, slowly.

The girl was in her early twenties. Tall and slim, she had the same slightly hooked nose as Peter Marrigay, the same fine eyes and sensitive mouth. Her appearance fascinated Dane.

She murmured some inaudible, social phrase, and withdrew hurriedly; but not before Dane had realised that she was astonished at seeing him – astonished and, perhaps, puzzled.

Dane was left alone for another five minutes, remembering that it was no good being surprised by anything Marrigay did.

Was the girl his sister? Possibly, they were very much alike.

He heard footsteps approaching again, and Marrigay entered the room.

'Sorry I had to leave you. One or two little things I had to do. Sit down, man!' He pushed a chair in front of the fire, and picked up a poker, stirring the logs vigorously. 'You'll stay and have some tea, won't you?'

'Thanks,' murmured Dane.

'My dear chap!' Marrigay stood with his back to the fire

16

looking down at Dane.

This reception was curious; since manhood, they had only met on the cricket field and on 'great occasions, they could never have been called close friends, yet Marrigay undoubtedly put great warmth into his welcome. That made the coming 'confession' the more difficult for Dane.

'Well, life's full of surprises,' Marrigay went on, and the cliché suggested that he was trying to think of the right thing to say. 'Yes, full of surprises,' he repeated, then flashed: 'Do you share the popular view?'

'About what?'

'About me?'

'*Is* there a popular view about you?' asked Dane.

Marrigay chuckled.

'Not bad, for a newspaper Johnny,' he remarked. 'Yes – most people think I've gone crazy.'

He stood there, smiling, and Dane stared up at him blankly.

'You shouldn't look so surprised,' Marrigay said. 'The only people really interested in me today are editors and reporters. Most of my friends, after one half-hearted attempt to get in touch, stayed away, but the persistent Press never gives up trying. You *are* from a paper, aren't you?'

'Yes,' said Dane, 'but – '

'Oh, you won't run away and put words into my mouth unless I approve,' said Marrigay, 'the Great Dane wouldn't do a thing like that. Which particular rag do you represent?'

'The *Gazette*.'

'You used to report big matches for them, didn't you?' commented Marrigay. 'Yes, I remember. Alec Dane's Sports Commentary. On the staff now?'

'No,' said Dane. 'I've a share in a local weekly, this is a special.'

'By the editor's request! You know, it's a wonder someone didn't think of sending a cricketer-journalist down before,' went on Marrigay, 'although possibly they have. If I hadn't happened to be near the gate you wouldn't have got in. Why didn't you drop me a line?'

17

'Would it have served any purpose?' asked Dane.

Marrigay shrugged.

'Possibly – it would have depended on my mood. Had I been bright and sunny, as I am today, yes.' He chuckled again. 'As it was, I thought the rain would keep everyone away, and went nearer to the gates than I usually do. You forgot to bring a camera,' he added. When Dane did not answer, he went on more quietly: 'But I'm being shockingly rude. Forgive. You know, Alec, when I do think about cricket you crop up as often as anyone. I can see you taking fast ones on the leg, standing close up and tossing the ball back as nonchalantly as if I'd lobbed one into your hands. It's a pity you had to drop out so early, you're a 'keeper in a thousand. There – have I made some amends?'

'You haven't altered much,' Dane remarked. 'Mind if I get a word in?'

'Fire away.'

'I came down because, like everyone who ever knew you, I couldn't be more curious. I told the editor this morning that I would give him a story only if you agreed – that was the condition.'

'Justification accepted,' said Marrigay. 'If anyone gets past the defences, they deserve a story. Not that there's a great deal I can tell you, and that will have to keep.' He gave his quick, bright smile. 'You must meet my people before you get down to business!'

'Well – '

'Oh, I insist,' said Marrigay. 'You saw Joyce, didn't you? My sister. And probably my mother.' He sat on the arm of a chair and looked steadily at his visitor. 'I'll tell you one thing. *I* had some difficulty in getting into the house when I returned. I'd been given up for dead and they thought I was phoney. These defences are not wholly and only for my benefit.'

Dane made no comment.

'On the other hand, I'm quite pleased about them,' went on Marrigay. 'I think I was the wrong man to be wandering on my own for so long. Five and a half years without seeing

18

a white face – picking up the native language as I went along – never sure whether I was talking to a Burmese or a Jap - not good!'

'Pretty grim,' agreed Dane.

'All the same, it's no reason for behaving like a hermit,' went on Marrigay. 'I'm not the only man who had a rough time during the war. Thousands had worse. And one might imagine I'd be eager to get back among friends – seeing familiar faces, talking a civilised language – wouldn't one?'

'Loneliness affects people in different ways,' said Dane, cautiously.

Marrigay laughed.

'There speaks the diplomat! Anyone reading your reports on test matches knew that you ought to have gone into the Foreign Office. The man who never hurt another's feelings.' The bitterness in the words did not trouble Dane, he was interested only in Marrigay's story and his general manner, trying to pierce the shroud of mystery which still covered him. 'Be honest, Alec! Everyone, from the newspapers downwards thinks that it affected my head, and that my family is determined to keep that shameful fact from the world. Isn't that true?'

'Oh, a few idiots have made wild guesses, but –'

'At all events, you can tell your *Gazette* man that I am capable of making coherent and more or less intelligent conversation, can't you?'

'I can and will.'

'Splendid! Here's something else you can tell him.' Marrigay hesitated, took out a cigarette and lit it, and looked down at Dane with his eyes flashing. 'Wait for it, Alec! Now – you can say that I'm frightened. That's the simple truth. Peter Marrigay is hiding away from the public gaze because he's frightened. Got that?'

'Now look here –'

'Oh, but it's true,' insisted Marrigay. 'I hope it isn't an anti-climax. I have come to know the real meaning of fear. *Fear*,' he added, and caught his breath. 'A lot of people know

19

that now. Not the ordinary fear when your heart comes into your throat and you know that you or the next man is going to be blown to Kingdom Come. That's a healthy sign, it shows that you love life and hate the thought of dying – or being hurt,' he added, 'but the sneaking, creeping fear, which never leaves you, which is always at your heels, when odd noises make your heart thump and your knees like water, fear which stays with you day and night – the fear of hunger and thirst, of starvation, of madness – *that's* real fear, Alec.'

Dane sat quite still.

'And I've known too much of it,' went on Marrigay, 'so much that at times I thought it would drive me mad. I've known myself to be at the last gasp, raving in delirium, saved by some good Samaritan of a native who didn't give a damn whether I was white or yellow but saw a fellow creature in dire straits and rescued him – I've known that fear too often, felt it alone in that rotten, stinking jungle, the only water stagnant filth, sores on my body as big as your fist – look!' he added abruptly.

He bent down, and pulled up the leg of his trousers. In the centre of the calf was a huge scar, blueish in colour, red at the edges.

'That's probably put paid to my cricket,' he said, rather inanely. 'Some days I can hardly walk on that leg.'

'It's – grim,' said Dane, and cursed the uselessness of words.

Marrigay laughed.

'Grim – yes. But pleasant compared with some things. The nights were the worst, although it was bad in the day. But the nights – I still wake up in a sweat of fear, I scream the place down in nightmares, I give them plenty of reason to think I'm mad! And the truth is – I'm *frightened*, Alec. That's why I was so glad to see you this afternoon. At least –' he paused. 'When I saw you I was scared as I always am when I see someone I think is a stranger, and then you shouted and it brought something different, a breath from the days when I wasn't scared of my own shadow. How much is real – how much is mental – how near I am to being a psychopathic case,

I just don't know. Most of the time I don't greatly care. I – '

He broke off abruptly, swung round, and strode towards the door, pulling it open and glaring into the passage.

CHAPTER III

UNCLE NICHOLAS

Marrigay's words had gone deep with Dane; and the sudden movement had startled him. Now he saw Marrigay standing with a hand on the door, staring – and he wondered whether indeed Marrigay had lost his senses.

'So – it's you,' Marrigay said softly.

'Yes, my boy, me again – I'm always about, aren't I?' The newcomer's voice had a pleasing mellowness, but held a touch of mockery or malice in it – or so Dane thought. 'I hear you have a friend with you. I *am* glad.'

'Are you?' asked Marrigay.

'You know I am. But I shouldn't have come along just now, you'll have so much to talk over with your friend. I'll see you at tea, I hope.'

'You can come in,' said Marrigay.

'May I?' The unseen man sounded delighted. 'But if I'm interrupting – '

'No, come in,' insisted Marrigay.

Marrigay stood aside to allow a short, plump man to pass.

'This is Alec Dane, an old friend,' Marrigay said. 'Mr Lee – my Uncle Nicholas.'

Dane was already on his feet.

'I'm very glad to see you,' said Lee. 'It's a good thing that my nephew should meet some of his old friends again.'

Marrigay pushed a chair forward, and remained standing as the older man sat down. 'I promised Alec that he should

21

meet everyone before he left, so that he could get the proper background for a story.'

'Story?' echoed Lee.

'Alec is a newspaper reporter,' said Marrigay.

'A – reporter,' muttered Lee.

'Strange, isn't it?' asked Marrigay.

Undoubtedly Lee had received a shock, and for a while stared unseeingly at Dane. At last he sat upright in his chair, and took out a cigarette-case.

'No, no, why should it be strange?' he asked, nervously. 'You have a great many friends, Peter, and the press is an honourable profession. Strange? Certainly not! But – but, my boy, I really *mustn't* stay. I have so much to do – I only came along to ask if you'd seen my saccharine tablets.'

'Perhaps you left them in London on your last jaunt,' said Marrigay.

The old man looked hurt and rather sad.

'London – '

'Of course,' broke in Marrigay hastily. 'I was only joking.'

'I *do* wish you wouldn't joke about my visits to the Club,' protested Lee, still patting his pockets. 'Well, they'll turn up. Perhaps I'll see you again, Mr Dane.'

He got up, nodding and smiling. As the door closed, Marrigay looked at it with an enigmatic smile.

'Odd bunch, aren't we?' he asked.

Dane forced himself to chuckle.

'He seemed startled.'

'Oh, he was. Poor old chap!'

'He also seemed troubled,' remarked Dane.

'He always is! I shouldn't waste your sympathy on him,' Marrigay advised. 'He's an eccentric – with queer hobbies. If he can't get to the Archaeologists Club for its monthly dinner, he feels that the world is against him.'

'Well, why can't he go?' asked Dane.

Marrigay smiled.

'Occasionally my mother stops him out of sheer cussedness, I'm afraid. But when he's here, he hates anyone else to go out. As you've noticed, we don't go out often. But contrary to popular belief, I've been to Town with my sister since I got back.'

'Very secret journey,' commented Dane.

'Not really. Staying here got on our nerves, we – oh, forget it!'

Marrigay pulled his chair nearer to the fire. 'You know, I can never get warm now I'm back. It's a pity I didn't arrive in the summer, instead of the autumn. I hope we get some hot weather. I'm praying for it.' The words seemed to amuse him, and he looked at Dane quizzically. 'Have you duly noted that? I'm reduced to praying for what I want.'

'Even you couldn't make the weather,' said Dane inanely.

'The literal Alec! No. My uncle is rather like some of the rest of the family. Brilliant on his own subject, dull on most others. He's hot on mythology – especially Nordic. He can be interesting, too. But – '

He broke off, leaned back, and closed his eyes.

Dane sat watching him.

He had been prepared for the obvious signs of neurosis. And they were there. But there was something more, something odd and unaccountable. *Was* he frightened? Why had he sprung on his uncle so suddenly the news that a newspaperman had managed to get into the house? There had been something deliberate, mischievous, even malicious about it.

Now, Marrigay leaned back with his eyes closed; and Dane was able to study him.

His closer scrutiny showed him that Marrigay had, in fact, changed a great deal.

He was thinner than he had been, his cheeks were sunken, his hair flecked with grey; although that was not altogether surprising in a man in the late thirties. Nevertheless Dane had a curious impression that Marrigay was older, *much* older; and very tired.

Marrigay sat still for a long time, and Dane did not stir.

Suddenly, a dog barked.

Marrigay opened his eyes abruptly, and in a single, swift movement, reached the window. This time, Dane could not

23

restrain himself. He followed. The dog continued to bark – a growling, angry note.

It was getting dark. The window overlooked a stretch of lawn. Immediately opposite the window was a shrubbery; all this, Dane could just see. Someone was moving among the shrubs. The man Lem came into sight, peering about him cautiously. The dog, silent for a few moments, growled again.

Marrigay flung the window up.

As he did so, a man cried in a frightened voice:

'Keep him off! *Keep him off!*'

'Ruddy fool!' snapped Marrigay.

He climbed out of the window and began to run towards the shrubbery. Again Dane followed. He heard the growling of the dog, a gasping grunting noise, perhaps from the man, who did not call out again. Marrigay, running very fast, reached the shrubbery and disappeared.

'Get up, Thor. Up! Get up!' That was Marrigay's voice.

The dog was standing over a man who lay on his back. Marrigay had talked about fear; here *was* fear, for the man on the ground was afraid that those glistening white fangs would sink themselves into his throat. Lem appeared suddenly, carrying a hooked walking stick.

'Thor!' called Marrigay again.

The Alsatian backed slowly away but continued to growl. Marrigay put down a hand and gripped it by the scruff of the neck. Lem joined him and hooked the handle of the walking stick under the dog's collar; only then did the fallen man try to get up. He was breathing hard, and his eyes glittered insanely as he looked at the dog.

Marrigay asked evenly:

'What are you doing here?'

'I – I came to see – '

'Peter Marrigay?'

'Yes.'

'He's not available,' said Marrigay. 'Who are you?'

'I – ' the man hesitated, and then, his control breaking,

24

shouted: 'It's a crime, that's what it is – setting a savage beast like that on me!'

'The dog hasn't hurt you, has it?' asked Marrigay. 'It only brought you down. You should have known better than to force your way into the grounds.'

'I just climbed over a stile – '

'You didn't "just climb over a style",' contradicted Marrigay, 'the only stile here is wired so that no-one can get over it. You forced your way through the hedge. You can think yourself lucky the dog didn't tear you to bits.'

'It's criminal!'

'You're the criminal,' said Marrigay, 'you're trespassing. Not a very serious offence, perhaps. But allow Colonel Marrigay the privilege of doing what he likes in his own grounds, please.'

'If I ever see him, I'll tell him – '

'He won't be interested in what you think of him,' said Marrigay, crisply. 'Are you a reporter?'

'I – '

'*Are you a reporter?*'

'Supposing I am?'

'What newspaper do you represent?'

'The – the *Sunday World*.'

'Then you can return to London and tell the editor of the *Sunday World* that Colonel Marrigay will see no-one except by appointment,' said Marrigay. 'Now get off, while we hold the dog.'

Intense fear had gone from the stranger's eyes, but uneasiness was there. Dane noticed that his coat was frayed at the sleeves and the collar – and that his shoes were down-at-heel.

Marrigay turned to Lem and said impatiently:

'See him to the gates, will you? Go in and wait for me, Alec, please.'

Dane returned to the study, aware that Marrigay's words had been more of a command than a request. The incident had been disturbing, because beneath Marrigay's composure there was a hint – perhaps more than a hint – of taut nerves

25

and some devouring emotion. Yes, Marrigay was frightened –
but of what? Of someone who might break into the house?
Why? And there was another question, equally urgent.
Marrigay was exerting an iron self-control, but what would
happen if it broke?

* Marrigay was gone for some time and when he came back
he was breathless and on edge. He lit a cigarette and his hands
were unsteady. Dane noticed that his forehead was wet with
sweat. He stared into the fire as if seeing some unspeakable
picture.

At last he forced a laugh.

'Sorry, Alec. I did warn you. This is a good day for newspapers. Two got in where all the others have failed.' He added
apologetically: 'I don't class you with that little merchant.'

Dane smiled. 'I hope not!'

'Why so definite?' asked Marrigay quickly.

Dane said dryly: 'Isn't it obvious?'

Marrigay shot him an odd glance and looked as if he were
about to say something more, but at that moment a clock in
the house struck the half-hour.

'We'll have some tea,' he said, 'it's half-past four.'

Dane, hoping to draw him again, remarked:

'The *Sunday World* may be a gossip paper, but it pays its
staff well. I can't imagine it employing a down-and-out, even
to get your story.'

Marrigay said tensely: 'You don't think he's a reporter?'

'I don't think he came from the *Sunday World.*'

'Hmm,' said Marrigay. He put his hands on the back of a
chair and stared into the fire. 'You've had a pretty good
introduction to Marrigay House and its peculiar inmates,
haven't you? You now see something of the effect which fear
can have on normal people. We're all frightened, of course –
even Joyce.'

Dane said nothing.

'And Joyce is the last person in the world who ought to be
scared about anything,' Marrigay went on. 'She's led a
blameless life! Almost a Martha to my Mary!' He laughed,
without merriment. 'Tea will be ready – would you care to

wash before we go in?'

As he washed in a small cloakroom off the inner hall, Dane tried to make sense out of the situation. Most puzzling of all was Marrigay's extraordinary harping on fear. The effect of the stranger's visit had been fantastic.

The uncle had looked scared when he had been told that Dane was a newspaperman; and the old lady in the front room appeared to be unnaturally tense. The girl – no, she had only been astonished; but the effect of seeing a stranger had been to make her turn and hurry away.

The truth was that everyone he had seen had shown some indication of fear or alarm. He dried his hands slowly, thinking disquietingly of Marrigay.

What was the salient point to bear in mind? Obviously, the fact that Marrigay had said that all the family was frightened, that they had been frightened before his return.

Abel Buller's information returned to Dane's mind; the dogs had been at the house before the Colonel had come home.

The incident of the man who said that he was from the *Sunday World* had hardly been surprising in itself. Sooner or later someone determined enough had been bound to escape the vigilance of the watchman and his dogs. Dane wondered why he had been so certain that the fellow was not a newspaper reporter.

He'd got it!

The man had been within a foot of Marrigay, whom any newspaperman would have recognised on sight; yet this one had shown no sign of recognition and allowed himself to be misled by a simple bluff which would not have deceived a cub reporter.

Dane went thoughtfully into the hall.

'Oh, there you are,' said Marrigay, from the front door. 'I've been out to see Lem. Don't want more visitors! My mother's had rather a bad turn, I'm afraid, and has gone to her room, so we'll be a very small party for tea.' Still on edge, he led Dane into the drawing-room.

Joyce Marrigay stood up from a stool in front of an open

27

fireplace. There was no sign of Nicholas Lee. Marrigay said abruptly:

'My sister, Joyce – Alec Dane. Sometimes known as Great Dane! He of the lion-heart,' he added, and Dane thought that he was talking too quickly to cover his nervousness.

No one else was in the room.

'So sorry I ran out on you like that,' said Joyce with a stiff smile. 'The truth is that we're all rather on edge.'

'Nonsense!' scoffed Marrigay. 'What could be more humdrum – a pleasant room and a blazing fire and tea – ah! here's Leah with the tea.'

A little old woman came in, carrying a tray. Marrigay took it from her.

'Thank you, sir,' said Leah. She shot a quick, nervous glance at Dane, and hurried out.

The firelight flickered on the brightly polished silver.

'Milk and sugar?' Joyce asked casually; Dane found it oddly affecting to find anything approaching real normality here.

Marrigay said more calmly: 'Do push that chair a little nearer the fire, Alec.' He sat down himself, stretched out his legs and gazed into the dancing flames. 'Yes, just right – so peaceful, so nostalgic.'

'Pass Mr Dane some tea, Peter,' said Joyce lightly.

'Eh? Oh, I'm sorry. One loses the veneer of civilisation after too close a juxtaposition to nature's law.'

'You were always rather inclined to elbow other people out of the way, darling, weren't you?' asked Joyce.

'No, damn it!' protested Marrigay. 'Is that fair, Alec? And to come from this little chit – when I went away she was still at school.'

'I do remember some things,' said Joyce. She stood up, taking the bread and butter and jam to Dane. 'Mr Dane probably remembers a great deal more about you, doesn't he?'

'A mob of flannelled fools seldom worry about culture,' said Marrigay. 'One of the ugliest sights of pre-war days was

28

the battle-charge by thirsty teams upon a buffet for lunch or tea.'

'And you're so often thirsty,' murmured Joyce.

Marrigay threw up his hands in mock exasperation.

'That's one of the troubles with the modern young woman, she's been taught to be smart instead of serviceable.' He smiled at his sister. 'The truth is, Alec, that Joyce is the pillar of wisdom and strength in this benighted household. But enough of that – can you bear to be serious for a few minutes?'

'I think so,' said Dane.

'Good! Joyce and I have been into a huddle. We want a victim, and have selected you. You have only yourself to blame. Welcome though you are, you did come uninvited, and you probably expected something a little out of the ordinary. We are going to unburden ourselves. You are to be the first outsider to hear our curious story.'

Joyce looked straight at Dane, her steady gaze damping down the excitement which Marrigay's words had brought.

'Not for publication,' Joyce said, quietly.

'Yet,' amended Marrigay, 'and then probably only part of it.'

'That is understood,' said Dane.

'All right – we'll start from the beginning,' said Marrigay, and a harsh and ugly note sprang into his voice. 'The simple truth is that we have reason to believe that our father was murdered. When you've realised that you'll have some chance to understand the rest.'

CHAPTER IV

THE WEAKNESS IN THE STORY

Marrigay flung that statement out defiantly, with more than a hint of challenge. Dane's first reaction was of shocked surprise. He glanced from Marrigay to Joyce. She continued to watch him with that steady, calm gaze.

'Now tell us that we're crazy,' Marrigay cried with blazing eyes.

Dane put down his tea-cup, picked up a slice of bread and butter, and folded it carefully.

'Now look here, Peter,' he said, reasoningly, 'it's time you stopped assuming that I'm down here to pour ridicule on anything you tell me, and that I think you're a bit wrong in the head. You've a lot of friends – '

'I haven't a friend in the world,' Marrigay said shortly. Talk of murder had brought all his bitterness to the surface and now it was overflowing; what he had called his 'sunny' mood had faded.

'You've a lot of friends that you yourself have antagonised,' retorted Dane calmly. 'You were always up in the air one moment and down in the depths the next, and that doesn't encourage friends to stick very closely, you know. All the same, you've got them – and they're worried about you. I told no one except Cameron of the *Gazette* that I was coming down, but my real reason for coming is that general anxiety. Now I've seen you, I know you haven't altered much. This talk about you being off your head is all my-eye-and-Betty-Martin, you're just digging your toes in with an "attitude" the way you always did when anything put you off your stroke. But all who know you would agree about one thing – you aren't a liar. If you say you think your father was murdered, that's good enough for me.'

He finished, outwardly calm, inwardly agitated and wondering how his outburst would be received.

Marrigay watched him through lowered lashes.

Suddenly he laughed.

'I suppose I asked for that. You admit we've a starting point, anyhow. From it lead several obvious things. If we're right, who killed him? Why was he murdered? Uncomfortable questions, aren't they? And even before we ask them, there's another one: what grounds have we got for thinking it's true?'

'Well, what have you?' asked Dane.

'Oh, yes, this is your part of the show,' agreed Marrigay. He jumped up for Dane's cup. 'We have evolved a system of being perfectly casual about the whole business,' he went on, 'if we let it take possession of us all the time we'd be driven crazy.'

Joyce poured more tea.

Dane, remembering the Alsatians and the guard, thought he would hardly call their attitude 'casual'; but he made no comment.

Joyce began to talk in a quiet, thoughtful voice.

'You may know, Mr Dane, that my father died just twelve months ago – nine months before Peter returned. We'd given Peter up, of course, he was officially missing, presumed dead, and – but I don't need to go into that. My father was a remarkable man in many ways. He was sixty-nine – but healthy and fit. When he went down with gastric flu towards the end of last February, we didn't think much about it.'

Dane nodded.

'He had the usual symptoms and a temperature of a hundred-and-one. There was a snow-storm at the time, but the doctor came out fairly easily. He prescribed water and dry toast and some powder, called *Kaylene*, and said he would be all right in a day or two. It was snowing hard when I drove into Marston for the powder. Mine was one of the last cars to get through for four days.'

Again Dane nodded.

31

'The next day, my father seemed rather easier. He wasn't in pain, and his temperature was down a bit. We didn't give it much thought, we were so preoccupied with the weather. We're snowed up most years when there's a heavy fall, but last year it was exceptional. We couldn't get to the village, which itself was cut off, and when father's temperature suddenly rocketed, we were panic-stricken. He was in a great deal of pain, and there was nothing at all we could do. We couldn't even send a telegram or use the telephone. We spent the whole of that second night trying to help him, but he died. We assumed that father had got out of bed during the night, he was always impatient when he was laid up, and caught another chill on top of the first. We were all desperately upset, my mother particularly so. I needn't dwell on it,' Joyce went on, in a sharper voice. 'It was forty-eight hours before the doctor got through. He didn't seem surprised at my father's death. Afterwards, we realised that he himself was running a high temperature, and hardly knew what he was doing. He shouldn't have been out. He signed the certificate, saying the cause of death was a form of enteritis. Two days afterwards there was a quick thaw, and father was buried in the churchyard. My mother recovered enough to go to the funeral, but after that she collapsed again. It – it shocked us, because she was nine years younger than he, but within a month of his death no one meeting her for the first time would have been surprised to have been told that she was nearly eighty. Would they, Peter?'

Marrigay said: 'It gave me a shock when I saw her again.'

'And that wasn't all,' Joyce went on slowly. 'She was – frightened.'

No one spoke.

'She was frightened,' Joyce repeated in a hushed voice. 'First she locked her door at night – then she wouldn't sleep with her door closed, in case someone got in at the window. She wanted all the outside doors locked by day as well as night. And for some reason, she took a violent dislike to all motor cars. I suppose I've grown used to it and it doesn't seem to me as strange as it must to you. We had the doctor out, of course, and he called in a mental specialist, but they couldn't do anything to help her. One day in the late spring, we actually had a burglary. A man broke into the garage and took away some oddments and did a little spiteful damage. After that, we padlocked the gate and put barbed wire over the stile. We let the hedges grow high, and we bought the dogs.'

'All at your mother's request?' asked Dane.

'Yes,' said Joyce. 'We had to humour her. She was frightened whenever I went away; the result was that I didn't go. Mother's fear passed itself on to me – to everyone. I can't explain it. Except – that she told us one night that she was sure my father had been murdered.'

Marrigay interrupted:

'That was before I came back.'

'Several weeks before,' agreed Joyce. 'We were sitting in this room, late one evening, when she looked up at me quite normally and said: "You know your father was murdered, Joyce, don't you?"'

Joyce gripped her hands tightly together, and stared into the fire; the light from the flames flickered on her face. The tension in the room could hardly have been greater when that astonishing statement had first been made. Dane could not bring himself to break the silence, and Marrigay sat motionless, looking at his sister.

At last Joyce went on:

'Uncle and I tried to make her say what she meant, but she refused to give any explanation. That night, when I went into see her before going to bed, she was crying; she looked terrified. I became really frightened from that moment onwards. I tried to reason with her, but it was no use. She would only say again that father had been murdered, that she was afraid there would be other murders. I told myself that it was a delusion, that father's death had caused a mental breakdown. Now – I wonder.'

Marrigay moved restlessly.

Joyce looked at him, unseeing.

'Whatever the cause, it's turned this house into Hell!'

33

she burst out, startling Dane by her unexpected vehemence. 'As a family we were always rather odd, I suppose, but we were happy. Do you understand, we were *happy*! We'd grown used to the fact that Peter was gone; we were recovering from the worst of that when this happened.'

She stopped talking.

'Are you beginning to understand?' Marrigay asked Dane.

What could he say?

The truth seemed too obvious; that Mrs Marrigay was suffering from delusions and had contrived to pass them on to her son and daughter. Perhaps that was not surprising in Peter's case – and possibly Joyce had much the same temperament. It seemed to Dane that they were shying away from the verdict given by the mental specialist. But how could he say that?

He was saved from making any comment by Joyce's voice coldly continuing. 'The next thing happened in July. I was cycling down the hill into Marrigay. It's a perfect place for coasting, and I've always gone down that hill with the brakes off.'

Dane nodded.

'Well, that morning I pedalled out of the drive and started free-wheeling as soon as I'd turned into the road,' said Joyce. 'I was halfway down the hill, going so fast that I couldn't possibly stop quickly, when someone *threw* a piece of wood a few yards in front of me. I jammed on the brakes, but – the brakes just didn't work. I don't know how I managed to dodge that bit of wood, but I did. As I passed it I caught a glimpse of a man on the other side of the hedge. I thought nothing of it at the time, my whole mind being filled with the shock of discovering that my brakes were not working. Then, just as I reached the bottom of the hill, a dog ran out of a field and nearly had me over. Normally I would have applied the brakes gently, but as it was, I couldn't do a thing –'

She broke off, and caught her breath.

'There was a hole in the road,' Marrigay growled.

'A – hole?' echoed Dane.

'A sort of trench right across the road,' said Joyce. 'Not

very deep – two or three inches, and about a foot wide. I crashed. It's a wonder that I didn't break my neck,' she went on, 'but, apart from sprains and bruises, I was fantastically lucky.'

'Who dug the trench?' asked Dane, trying to keep his voice steady.

'No one ever found out,' answered Joyce. 'There's a policeman in the village, of course, but he was more concerned with calling me a reckless young fool for free-wheeling down the hill than with anything else. Of course, he made enquiries about the trench, but didn't discover anything. The village theory was that a few hooligans had gone out there after dark and dug it for a lark. But when I'd recovered from the spill, you can imagine what I felt like. I had to tell Mother, and her immediate reaction was pretty ghastly. And it wasn't any use blinking at facts, the trench was there *and* a man had thrown that piece of wood in front of me.'

Dane leaned forward and knocked out his pipe, deliberately avoiding her eyes.

'That seems a silly thing to have done,' he remarked. 'If the trench was already in the road, that was enough, surely? Why try to throw something under your wheels? After all, there was a good chance of you missing it, wasn't there?'

'I missed it by sheer luck,' said Joyce. 'It was a fairly long piece of wood, a dead branch which had been torn off a tree. It stretched half-way across the road, which is very narrow. It seemed to me that the man tried twice to bring me off, because if I'd come off before I reached the trench no one would have given thought to the trench itself.'

'You know, I can't believe that,' said Dane, judicially. 'A trench dug across the road in a small village would be a nine days wonder. And the local policeman ought to have done his damnedest to find out who dug it.'

Marrigay spoke quietly.

'I've no doubt he did. There's always been undeclared war between the Marrigays and that particular constable. He's a stranger to the district – although he's been here ten or twelve years now! – and he'd go all out to find what hap-

35

pened, but wouldn't tell us what he was doing.'

'Did you tell him about the piece of wood?' asked Dane.

Joyce shook her head.

'I was in bed for several days, and didn't give it much thought. Roger went out to get it, after I'd told him what had happened, but before I was about again, Pengelly, our handy-man, had chopped it up for kindling wood. It was a rotten branch, dry as a bone. And there didn't seem much sense in talking about it then, the trench was enough for the police to work on.'

'Did you ever make a formal complaint?' asked Dane.

'No.'

'Would you expect her to, in the circumstances?' asked Marrigay.

'Well, yes,' said Dane. 'If my neck had been in danger, I wouldn't have been satisfied to leave it to a hostile village policeman. I would have gone into Marston and told the police there, and worried them until they could explain what had happened. On the other hand –'

'We *were* in a pretty grim state of mind,' said Joyce. 'Nothing – nothing was quite normal.'

'Oh, it's easily understandable,' said Marrigay.

'But foolish,' murmured Dane.

'Now look here –'

'Of course, he's quite right,' said Joyce, 'it was foolish.'

'He'll soon be telling us that we've acted the fool all along,' said Marrigay, bitingly.

'Well, haven't you?' asked Dane, trusting his smile would rob the words of any offensiveness. 'Before we go any further, may I ask one or two questions?'

'Oh, go ahead,' growled Marrigay.

'Have you had Pengelly for long?'

'Oh, yes. He's been with the family for years as gardener and odd-job man,' Joyce told him. 'He's got a passion for wood-carving – he's quite good at it, too. Leah, his wife, runs the house for us.'

'I see. And were your sister and her husband here during the – the blizzard?' asked Dane, a little diffidently.

36

Joyce nodded.

'And the Pengellys were snowed up with you?'

'Yes.'

'What about Uncle Nicholas?'

'He was here of course – he's lived here for years.'

'Was anyone else at the house while you were snowed up?' asked Dane.

'What on earth has that got to do with it?' demanded Marrigay.

'My dear chap, it might have a great deal,' said Dane, quite unruffled. 'If your father was murdered, obviously he was poisoned, and anyone inside the house might have – '

Marrigay jumped to his feet. He had gone very white; and he stood over Dane with his fists clenched, glaring down at him. 'What the hell do you mean – it might have been some-one in the house?'

'Now, Peter – '

'Get out!' cried Peter, and moved forward swiftly, grabbing Dane's arms and pulling him to his feet.

CHAPTER V

MARRIGAY CALMS DOWN

Dane allowed himself to be dragged out of the chair without resisting, but when Marrigay tried to push him towards the door, he stood quite still anchoring himself against the side of his chair. Joyce jumped up and spoke, but Marrigay was still shouting, and the girl's words were drowned.

When he found that he could not shift Dane, Marrigay relaxed his grip, only to send a wild punch towards Dane's face. Dane fended the blow and Joyce stepped in between them.

'It's all right, Joyce,' said Dane quietly.

He did not know what made him use her Christian name; he hardly noticed that he did so. Looking over her shoulder, he saw Marrigay's wild eyes and pale cheeks, and felt sorry for the man.

'It isn't all right,' Joyce said. 'How shall we get anywhere if Peter behaves like a wild man when anyone makes a simple remark like that?'

'Simple!' barked Marrigay.

'Yes – and obvious. It's the main question in your mind and in mine, we both know it. What good does it do pretending that we don't?' demanded Joyce. 'If we're right and father was murdered and we're in danger, we've got to find out more about it. Supposing you'd behaved like that with a policeman?'

Dane said cheerfully:

'No policeman would have been ass enough to make the remark!' He sat down again, and smiled at Joyce. 'Is there any more tea, or is it cold?'

'I'll have some fresh made,' said Joyce, promptly.

'Did I hear you say fresh *tea*?' asked Nicholas Lee. He appeared in the doorway without any warning, startling Dane. Marrigay glared at his uncle, but Joyce seemed quite unperturbed.

'Yes, Uncle, come in,' she said.

'No, I'll have a cup in the Kitchen,' said Lee, shooting a nervous glance at Dane. 'I didn't know – '

He drifted out, gently closing the door.

'Will you have some fresh tea?' asked Joyce, as if nothing had disturbed them.

'No, thanks – let me have what's there,' said Dane. He glanced at Marrigay. 'You know, I spoke my thoughts aloud, Peter, but I reached an obvious conclusion. If this business goes any further, other people will reach the same conclusion.'

'It's a foul slander!' Marrigay's anger was still smouldering.

'Oh, don't be an ass!' snapped Joyce, handing Dane his cup. 'Are there any other questions you'd like to ask, Alec?'

'I suppose no one else was here during the blizzard period –

38

beyond the immediate family?'

'There were some friends with us on the evening that my father was taken ill for the first time,' Joyce said. 'Two friends from London. They went with me to Marston. In fact Arthur actually bought the *Kaylene.*'

'Arthur?'

'Arthur Bell,' said Joyce, with a quick smile, 'and his wife. They're close friends of Marjorie and Roger, and they'd all come down for the week-end. They came back with me but returned to London that night because the road was becoming very bad.' She looked at Marrigay. 'Give me a cigarette, Peter, will you?'

Marrigay, who was smoking a cigarette, drawing at it too quickly, handed her his case with a muttered apology. Dane flicked his lighter and held it towards Joyce.

'Thanks,' she said. 'You know, Alec, you're right – the question you asked was the obvious one. If Father died of poisoning it must have been given him by someone who was in the house that week-end. The thing is, would any one of the family or the friends who were here in July have dug that trench in the road? Or thrown that piece of wood at me? Only Uncle Nicholas, Marjorie and Roger as well as Mother and I were at the house then.'

'Any expert diggers?' Dane inquired lightly.

'Yes, there is one,' said Joyce, slowly.

'Uncle Nicholas is an amateur geologist as well as an archaeologist,' she went on more naturally. 'He keeps his tools in the garage.' She gave a wintry, unamused smile. 'His hobbies were always a bone of contention in the family. Father believed a man should have something more to do than amuse himself. It isn't as if – '

'Is there any need for this searching analysis?' asked Marrigay. 'Uncle Nicholas has the tools. But the said tools were in the garage – and still are. Anyone could have taken them out.'

'After first breaking in to the grounds,' Dane reminded him.

'The barricades weren't as strong then as they were later,' Joyce said.

'What about this fellow you saw through the hedge?'

'I only caught a glimpse of him,' Joyce told him. 'I'm sure I'd never recognise him again. There *was* a man, but that's all I could say for certain. We bought the dogs soon afterwards, and put up a big "Beware of the Dogs" notice on the gate. That was another queer thing,' she added.

'Why?' asked Dane.

'The notice was always torn down during the night,' Joyce said quietly. 'There isn't any doubt that remarkable things have happened here, you know.'

'No more attempted murder, I hope,' said Dane.

'I haven't *quite* finished telling you about the cycling incident,' Joyce said. 'When I was up and about again, I examined the brakes. They'd been cut – someone had nipped the cable right through.'

'Did you tell the policeman that?' Dane demanded.

Joyce shook her head.

Marrigay stood up abruptly, went to the window and pulled the curtains. Until then, light from a single chandelier had streamed into the garden. Dane wondered if Marrigay had seen anyone outside, but Marrigay turned back without any sign of alarm.

'Oddly enough, no one here took kindly to the thought that there was attempted murder, and no one wanted to make a scandal,' he said. 'I fully agreed with that point of view when I returned.' He was looking at Dane, and something of the tension had gone from his manner. 'I'd better weigh in with my part of the story. When I reached home, I was feeling as if I'd come back from the dead. After seeing no one for years, I was suddenly surrounded by people. I'd pictured white men as gods – and found them greedy, selfish, dirty little brutes, no better than yellow men. I began to hate the sight of them. That being my mood, I wasn't sorry that we'd barricaded ourselves in. It gave me the privacy I wanted, although I couldn't agree with Mother and Joyce, and I thought the whole affair was an exaggerated illusion –

resulting from shock. I was quite sure of that, until the day I first went out. I wanted some cigarettes and strolled towards the village,' Marrigay said. 'You've seen the copse. It's the place where Joyce's man was hiding. I walked through it. Thick, ánd overgrown, it had something of the fecundity of the jungle.' He gave a harsh, unexpected laugh. 'I reached the road; and it was then someone took a pot-shot at me.'

'Oh,' said Dane, helplessly.

'The bullet buried itself in a tree,' Marrigay said abruptly. 'God!' There was perspiration on his forehead and his hands were clenched. 'I'd been thinking what a change it was. The calmness of the English countryside. No Jap snipers. No snakes. No danger – and they shot at me. I travelled six thousand miles in a split second. I wasn't in that copse, I was back in the jungle. I just turned and ran hell-for-leather. Eh, Joyce?'

'I was in the garden,' Joyce said, 'when Peter came running, running . . . ' her voice trailed into silence.

'It was from that moment that *I* became fear-ridden,' Marrigay said harshly. 'And then, Lem came home.'

'I wondered about Lem,' said Dane.

Marrigay said: 'Lem is Pengelly's son.'

'Didn't he think the set-up rather odd?' asked Dane.

Marrigay laughed.

'Possibly. But a Marrigay still has some honour in his own country. The Pengellys have served us for generations. They're as loyal as you, Alec, but not so inquisitive. Lem was told we wanted the place protected, and that was that. He got on with the dogs all right – with Saturn especially. Thor's less tractable. You saw Thor, didn't you?'

'I did indeed.'

'Saturn will bring a man down, but he won't savage him – Thor would. That's why I went out in such a hurry this afternoon,' Marrigay continued, 'I recognised his bark, and it put the wind up me. Much though we dislike strangers in our midst, I don't want anyone killed by the dog.'

'I'm glad you've got that much sense left,' Dane remarked dryly.

41

Ten minutes earlier, the words would have sent Marrigay into a towering rage, but now he laughed.

'All right, Alec, we can take it!'

'But, oh, I'm so tired of it!' Joyce cried. 'It's no use grinning like that, Peter, I'm sick to death of it! Staying here all the time, huddled up as if each moment might be our last, afraid to go outside, never seeing people – it'll drive us all crazy before we've finished.' She stopped and Dane, understanding how she felt, only amazed that she should have allowed herself to be hemmed in for so long, watched her as she walked restlessly towards the window.

'The trouble is that if Joyce talks of going out, it upsets the old lady,' Marrigay said, very quietly. He spoke reasonably and normally, his spasm of rage quite gone. 'We're rather ruled by her, I'm afraid. But Joyce is right – we can't go on like this.'

Joyce turned from the window.

'That's why we decided to confide in you,' she said. 'We wanted an outsider's opinion. We're stifled by ourselves. The only people we see are Roger and Marjorie, and they can't be here all the time. For the rest – we've given up newspapers, and even the groceries from the village are left at the gates. Oh, but it's crazy! We're making ourselves freaks. Alec, what *do* you suggest?'

They watched Dane closely.

He sat deliberating, trying to decide what to say without risking another outburst from Marrigay.

'Well?' Marrigay's voice was harsh.

Dane said slowly: 'You won't take my advice when I give it.'

'Try us.'

'All right. Take down the barbed wire. Take the padlock off the gates. Keep the dogs under control. Let the tradespeople come and go. Tell the newshounds that you were ill when you returned, let them think that the reason for all this barricading yourselves in, and state of siege, was merely a need for privacy in which to recover from the strain of your experiences. That will satisfy them,' Dane went on. 'As it is news, you're news; one straight story, telling just as much as you want to, and that will be the end of the publicity.'

'You've rather forgotten – ' Joyce began.

'You're going to say that I've forgotten your mother. I haven't. But if you allow her fears and whims and prejudices to govern what you do, you haven't a hope of getting back to normal. Reason with her.'

'She's impervious to reason,' Joyce said.

'All right – don't *tell* her.'

Marrigay said slowly: 'That's an idea!'

'You say she never goes out, not even into the garden,' went on Dane, warmed and encouraged by the knowledge that he held their interest. 'She needn't know what's happening. If she finds out the truth – well, by then she will be so used to you being away part of the time that she'll probably think little of it.'

'Possibly,' agreed Joyce.

'What about your uncle?' Dane asked. 'What does he feel about this?'

'He's ruled absolutely by Mother,' said Joyce. 'She still has a strong personality, even though she's changed so much.'

'It's too strong,' said Dane, 'and you need to break her influence. Drastic advice, I know, but you asked me what I thought.'

'Now don't spoil it by apologising,' Marrigay said. 'But I haven't finished.' Dane hesitated, wondering how the next suggestion would affect them. 'One thing's all too apparent,' he went on cautiously, 'something strange *is* happening, the trench and that bullet weren't acts of God. So – go to someone who can get at the root of it.'

'Ah,' the exclamation came softly from Marrigay's lips. Dane ignored him.

'This looks like murder and attempted murder, and obviously you've grounds for suspicion. Tell the police. I don't mean your local Robert, but I think you might go into Marston and tell the Chief Superintendent there.' Neither of

43

them commented, and he went on: 'I know you're afraid that someone in or close to the family is responsible, but you'll never be happy until you find out. Probably only the police *can* find out. As a matter of fact – ' he broke off, abruptly.

'Go on,' said Joyce.

Dane shrugged his shoulders.

'I know a man in London who would revel in this problem. He – '

'Oh, Lord! Private detectives – ' began Marrigay.

'Oh, no,' said Dane, patiently. 'This chap's at Scotland Yard. He's a remarkable fellow, probably the best detective in the country. I've met him once or twice at newspaper functions, and an acquaintance of mine was once involved in an affair where Folly took charge of investigations.'

'Folly?' echoed Joyce.

'Odd name for a detective, isn't it?' asked Dane, smiling at his thoughts. 'Yes, Superintendant Folly, of New Scotland Yard. I'm sure he would give me an opinion if I were to tell him what you've told me. And he has a lot of influence, he would probably take it up himself with the local force. If I were you, I'd let me tell him,' he continued, more and more taken with the idea. When neither of them spoke he went on: 'You do want to learn the truth, don't you?'

Marrigay and Joyce looked at each other; and Joyce said quietly:

'Yes, Alec.'

'Consult him then,' agreed Marrigay, explosively. 'But don't tell anyone else, we don't want it to become gossip of the county!'

'It won't, through Folly,' Dane said reassuringly.

'And if you give our carefully contrived story to Cameron of the *Gazette*,' said Marrigay, with a harsh laugh, 'you won't have wasted your journey. But it's a bit late to return to London tonight, isn't it?'

'Oh, I shall be there by ten o'clock,' said Dane, looking at his watch. 'I – by jove, it's getting on, though. It's after half-past six.'

'Why don't you stay the night?' asked Joyce.

'And prove your courage,' said Marrigay, mockingly.

'Well – thanks,' decided Dane. 'If I can telephone to my home from here?'

'But of course,' Joyce jumped up. 'And now I must go and see how mother is.'

As the door closed, Marrigay smiled grimly.

'You've made a hit,' he said, his voice dry and a little surprised.

'Ass,' said Dane. 'Well – I hope you don't change your mind.'

'I don't think there is much danger of that, now the decision is made,' said Marrigay. 'Obviously matters couldn't go on like this, but – once you're caught up in them, it's surprising how difficult it is to get free. It's a relief to determine something tangible. It wanted someone with your practical common sense to make us see straight.'

Marrigay added quietly: 'As a matter of fact, Alec, I made a damned fool of myself, and I'm sorry. I've always blown hot and blown cold, as you pointed out, but since I've been back, and with this added strain –'

'Forget it,' said Dane, awkwardly.

'Now you want to put through that telephone call,' said Marrigay.

The telephone was in the hall. Shadows pressed darkly, the only light filtering from the landing. The house seemed very silent, and the inhumanity of the operator's voice startled Dane when it came through. He spoke briefly, and replaced the receiver. As he did so, he glanced up and saw a movement on the landing.

He stood quite still.

The movement was slow and furtive. Suddenly, he saw the eerie elongation of a shadow creeping up the wall. He stepped silently towards the stairs.

Uncle Nicholas was walking on tiptoe away from the landing.

Dane smiled wryly; but it would be foolish to start speculating. He was more than ever sure that the right man to handle this was Folly of the Yard.

'Finished?' called Marrigay from the door of the drawing-room. 'That's good. Joyce hasn't come down yet. Care for a breather before dinner?'

'That's a thought,' said Dane.

It was a clear, moonless night, and the wind had dropped. The stars were bright and seemed very close. Now and again the trees rustled in a light breeze. Somewhere a long way off an aeroplane droned and together they looked up and watched the tiny green light moving slowly across the sky. The trees of the copse rose straight upwards, the outlines dark arrows against the stars.

Suddenly, Marrigay stopped. 'What's that?' he asked sharply.

Dane listened. He heard nothing at first, and then, abruptly, the sound came to him of a man running across soft ground; soon he could hear heavy breathing.

CHAPTER VI

POOR SATURN

'That's Lem,' Marrigay said, positively.

Suddenly, Dane saw a dark figure running across the lawn in front of the drawing-room. Marrigay said again:

'That's Lem!' He raised his voice to a shout, and the man stopped running and turned around.

Without waiting for Dane, Marrigay jumped up the steep bank and hurried towards the lawn. Not until they were within a few yards of him, Dane a little behind Marrigay, could Dane be sure of the identity of the shadow.

'What's the matter?' Marrigay asked.

Lem fought for breath, he had run so hard and so far that

he was in acute distress. The pale starlight shone on his eyes and his swarthy face.

'Take your time,' said Marrigay.

The broad Limshire vowels broke harshly on to the night air. 'It's – it's Saturn, sir.'

'Well, what's the matter with him?'

'He's dead, sir.'

Marrigay did not speak, but Dane noticed the stiffening of his body. Suddenly Lem burst into halting, incoherent explanation. The dogs were fed together at half-past six, near the garage. After feeding Thor, Lem had gone to search for Saturn; he had found him lying near the hedge, quite dead, although still warm.

'Let's go and have a look,' Marrigay said at last. His voice was harsh and clipped. 'Unless you'd rather go back to the house, Alec?'

'No, I'll come,' said Dane.

It took them ten minutes to walk to the spot where the dog lay. The flash of the torch caught the open mouth, the tongue touching the long grass which half hid the body. The legs were stretched out, stiffly now, and the back was arched. Marrigay went down on his knees. He sniffed. 'Hand me the torch, Lem.'

Dane did not ask what he expected to find; for that was obvious enough. The bright light flashed to and fro, all three of them joined in the search without exchanging a word. It was Dane who found it – a large bone, with a little meat still left on it.

'Poor old Saturn,' said Marrigay, in a quiet voice. 'I think we ought to have that bone wrapped up, Lem. I'll tell you later what to do with it.' Marrigay stared down at the dog. 'Poor old Saturn,' he repeated. 'You'd better dig his grave here, Lem, and bury him.'

'Don't you think you ought to let a vet see him?' demurred Dane.

'Perhaps you're right,' said Marrigay abruptly. He turned to Lem, and gave orders that the body should be removed to a shed.

47

In the quiet of the night, the hoot of an owl sounded very clear.

'Well?' asked Marrigay at last.

'Poison, of course,' Dane said. 'Are you going to tell Joyce?'

Marrigay nodded gloomily. 'And we'll have to tell Uncle Nicholas. He'll miss Saturn tomorrow, if not tonight – he's fond of both dogs,' he added. 'He's the only man who's never had the slightest trouble with Thor.'

They fell silent.

It was an hour or more since they had left the house, and Dane was not surprised to find Joyce standing in the porch, peering into the garden. It passed through Dane's mind that if the sharpshooter who had once shot at Marrigay were anywhere near, Joyce would make a perfect target. The thought made him quicken his pace, and there was a rough note in his voice when he said:

'We'd better get indoors, I think.'

'Where have you been?' demanded Joyce.

Marrigay told her and Uncle Nicholas, who had appeared from the drawing-room, about Saturn's death. Both, at first, seemed too stunned to speak. Dane watched Uncle Nicholas closely. The man backed into the room, and ran his hand across his forehead; his fingers were trembling.

'You'd better have a drink, Uncle,' Marrigay said.

He poured out a stiff whisky and thrust it into the older man's hand.

Uncle Nicholas took a gulp of neat whisky and gradually a little colour returned to his round face.

Before dinner, Marrigay telephoned the veterinary surgeon who promised to come out at about nine o'clock. The waiting seemed interminable. Uncle Nicholas made a poor dinner. Joyce also toyed with her food, and Marrigay seemed disinterested. Dane, feeling a little callous, heartily enjoyed the casserole of beef and apple tart which followed. Conversation was strained and difficult until after dinner, when Uncle Nicholas, obviously making an effort, began to talk about the general situation; it appeared that he knew the

48

Marrigays had confided in Dane, and was anxious to find out how much they had told him. Marrigay explained that they had decided to stop barricading themselves in, and to live more normally. Uncle Nicholas nodded.

'Perhaps you are right. But I beg you not to tell your dear mother just yet. A shock – any kind of shock – might prove very serious. I don't like saying so, but – '

'We know it might do her harm,' Marrigay said sharply, 'and we don't intend to tell her. It is up to you to do the same.'

'Oh, *I* will,' Uncle Nicholas assured him, 'I really will, Peter, you need have no fear.'

'If Mother says anything to you, don't tell her the truth,' said Joyce. 'It'll be your fault if she does find out.'

'But she won't find out from me, Joyce. How unkind you are!' Uncle Nicholas looked as if he were on the point of crying. 'Poor, poor little Saturn,' he whispered brokenly, 'poor Saturn. To be – *murdered*!'

The door opened, and Leah appeared.

'It's Mr Cotterell, the vet, sir,' she announced.

'Oh, good,' said Marrigay, jumping up. 'You'd like to hear what he has to say, Alec, wouldn't you?'

But Cotterell had little to say. He grunted when introduced to Dane, commented in monosyllables as Marrigay told him what had happened while leading the way towards the shed where the dead dog lay.

He did not spend much time with the carcase.

'Hmm, yes,' he grunted. 'You may be right. Poison. Hmm. Does happen to savage dogs.'

He spoke without looking at Marrigay, and there was reproach, perhaps something stronger, in his voice.

'I'm anxious to find out what's happened to that particular dog,' Marrigay said equably.

'Hmm, yes,' said Cotterell.

The light in the shed was poor, and Cotterell switched on a powerful torch in order to make a closer examination. He grunted again when he had finished, asked for a sheet of newspaper, wrapped the meaty bone in that and a piece of sacking.

'Tell you in the morning,' he said. 'I'll take the dog, too. Ask Pengelly to wheel it down to my car.'

So the veterinary surgeon had left his car at the gates; that practice had evidently become a habit with the local people.

After his visit, there seemed no vitality left in any of them. Dane found himself nodding over the fire, Marrigay was silent, filled with his own brooding thoughts; and it was Joyce who jumped up suddenly, saying that it was time they went to bed.

Marrigay took Dane to his room.

The landing where Uncle Nicholas had been standing and listening was large and square. Five doors led from it, and Marrigay indicated one slightly ajar, from which streamed a dim yellow light.

'That's my mother's room,' he said. 'If you have to wander about during the night, don't make a noise – it will scare the wits out of her.'

'I'll be careful,' Dane promised.

Dane's room was the first along a side passage. A narrow flight of stairs at the far corner of the passage led to the second floor, where, he imagined, the Pengelly family slept.

In spite of his confusion of thoughts, he fell at once into a deep and dreamless sleep, seeing nothing, hearing nothing, of what might or might not be going on in Marrigay House.

The telephone bell rang a little after nine o'clock that morning. Marrigay, who was in the breakfast room with Joyce and Dane, went out to answer it. He did not stay long, and when he returned his expression was hard.

'That was Cotterell,' he said. 'The meat bone has definite traces of arsenic.'

His voice was strained, giving the impression that his thoughts were not of the watchdog's death, but of his father's.

Dane and Joyce walked down the drive towards the gates, which now stood open. From there Dane turned and waved to Marrigay. Near the drive, Lem stood with Thor on a lead; the dog watched Dane – and seemed still to be watching him after they had turned out of the grounds and started down the hill.

Joyce walked with a long, easy stride. She wore a comfortable tweed suit, and her sturdy shoes rang out.

It was good to be with her.

He felt a glow of satisfaction of a job well done. It had been folly for them to be jockeyed into a state of siege. The most remarkable thing about it was, thought Dane, that two such people as Marrigay and his sister had allowed themselves to behave as they had.

If Joyce felt any niggling doubt about the wisdom of the move, she did not show it. He hoped he had helped her to put in a healthier perspective a frail old woman and her nerves, and Marrigay, returned from the dead embittered and hostile.

'Very deep thoughts?' Joyce asked, suddenly.

He smiled, and jerked evasively out of his reverie.

'What about you?'

'I'm enjoying myself again,' said Joyce. 'And I don't think either Peter or I have really told you how much we appreciate – '

'Oh, stuff!'

Joyce laughed.

'Well, we do. I don't feel that I shall be worried – so worried, anyhow – if there is more trouble,' she went on. 'Why we allowed *this* to get us down I don't quite know. It's a horrid business, but we must get to the bottom of it.'

'And you will,' said Dane. He glanced at the wooded land on the left and saw the dark green of the pines with their pointed tops reaching towards the clear, pale sky, and remembered the story of the shooting at Marrigay.

'Where was Peter when he was fired at?' he asked.

'A little further down the road,' Joyce told him, 'near the stile. Hal*lo*! Lem and Pengelly must have been at it early

51

this morning, the barbed wire's down! She laughed. 'What a change you've brought, Alec!'

His name, on her lips, delighted him.

'You would soon have come round to it,' he said. 'I'd rather like to see the tree where the bullet buried itself. Do you know which one it is?'

Joyce pointed to one of a group of small oak trees.

'I'd like a closer look,' said Dane.

Nearing the tree he saw that the bark had been peeled back from a tiny indentation. There was little doubt that it had been made by a bullet, but someone had used a sharp instrument to widen the hole. The bullet was not there.

Joyce said slowly: 'That's very odd.'

'Has Peter been busy?' asked Dane.

'I don't think so,' Joyce said, 'and I know the bullet was there a week ago. *Someone's* been busy.'

The incident subdued her, but only for a few minutes. Near the bottom of the hill, Joyce stopped.

'The trench was here,' she said.

The marks were plain enough; the hole had been filled in and given a top layer of gravel, which had now sunk beneath the general level.

'I suppose you had the brakes mended,' he said, suddenly.

'I didn't, as a matter of fact,' Joyce told him, 'I haven't used the bicycle since.'

'Leave them as they are for a little while,' Dane advised.

'Might it help the police?'

'Possibly,' said Dane.

They passed the *Marrigay Arms*. A girl was washing the porch, and looked round curiously. The sight of Joyce seemed to startle her and she scrambled to her feet. Abel Buller appeared at a window, dark and forbidding.

Dane raised a hand and called: 'Good morning!'

'Hallo, Mary,' said Joyce. 'Morning, Abel!'

But neither the girl nor Buller replied. Joyce made no comment, and they walked up the hill. Furtively, people stood at their doors or at their windows, watching the couple; this was an event, and Joyce must know that she was creating a mild sensation, but she appeared not to notice it.

Dane's car was parked outside the garage, and no one was about.

'How I'd love a run!' exclaimed Joyce suddenly.

Dane said quickly: 'Well, why don't you come as far as Marston, do your shopping there, and let me run you back?'

Joyce's eyes brightened.

'I'll come to Marston and catch the twelve-forty-five return bus – oh, George,' she called, as a man came from the garage office, 'the twelve-forty-five still runs from Marston, doesn't it?'

'Why, yes, Miss Joyce.' The man was short and thick-set, and not unlike Abel Buller.

Soon, Dane was at the wheel with Joyce beside him. The road led up and down a series of hills, and at the top of each they could see the lovely Limshire country, the farmhouses and cottages, the narrow rivers running through the valleys. Cattle browsed by the way, lazy and slow-moving.

They reached Marston twenty-five minutes after leaving the village. It was a market town, not large enough to have encroached far into the fields.

The High Street was narrow. A church clock struck twelve as Dane slowly pulled up. He was reluctant to leave Joyce.

'This do?'

'Yes, it – '

Joyce broke off abruptly, and stared along the street.

Dane, puzzled at first, looked in the same direction. He could see nothing which might have attracted her attention.

Then he saw Cotterell, standing on the steps of a large stone building.

'Do you see him?' asked Joyce.

'The vet?'

'Yes, talking to – '

She broke off again, for Cotterell and his companion looked up and stared pointedly at them.

The man spoke to Cotterell, then turned into the building; and for the first time Dane saw the words over the arched doorway: *Limshire County Constabulary*.

Cotterell nodded curtly as he passed them.

'Who was it?' asked Dane.

'Inspector Ives,' Joyce told him. She hesitated, then rested a hand on his. 'Alec, if your friend Folly does take it seriously and there's an investigation, will you – '

She broke off.

'Will I what?'

'Well – Peter's so erratic, and Uncle's no use whatever in an emergency. I was wondering if you could spare a day or two.' She spoke with a rush, trailing into diffidence.

'Gladly.' Dane said simply.

Her hand pressed his.

'Oh, *thank* you, Alec! But I mustn't keep you now. Telephone a report as soon as you can, and come whenever you like.'

'I will,' promised Dane.

He opened the door for her, and she moved unhurriedly away.

It was several minutes before Dane drove off.

CHAPTER VII

'YOUR FRIEND FOLLY'

Superintendent Folly sat at a pedestal desk in his office at New Scotland Yard; sitting there reading some reports he contrived to look both dignified and ridiculous. That was because the desk was small and Folly large – large enough in stature and in reputation to be dubbed the Colossus of the Yard. Outside, the weather was dull, and a single lamp burned above Folly's sleek head.

His eyes were narrowed as he read, his small mouth pursed! One plump and well-kept hand was resting on the

54

desk, the other held a report. He was alone in the office.

Folly's desk was tidy, meticulously so. Two or three manilla folders, pens and ink and pencils and three telephones were mathematically placed.

One of the telephone bells rang.

Folly stretched out his hand and picked up the receiver. 'Folly,' he said, and waited. 'Who . . . I don't know him . . . My dear fellow, a great number of people *say* they know me . . . No, you must tell him to make an appointment to see one of the officials, strange and unvetted men cannot come along here asking for . . . ' he paused, although the operator had not spoken again, and then said slowly: 'What was his name ? . . . Dane . . . Dane . . . There is a cricketer named Dane, isn't there ? Well, bring him along. What are you waiting for ?'

He was reading when Alec Dane was brought into the office by a sergeant who entered as reverently as if the room were sacrosanct.

'Mr Alec Dane, sir,' he said.

'Ah, Mr Dane!' exclaimed Folly. He put down his report and held out his hand, with every appearance of being delighted. 'How are you ? Well, I trust – and looking forward to another successful season. Sit down – push up that chair nearer the fire, sergeant, and then you may go. Now, Mr Dane, how can I help you ?'

Dane said: 'I think I have a story that will interest you.'

Now that he was here, he wondered whether he had been justified in calling on the great man in person. During the drive from Marston, he had doubted whether Folly would really remember him, and often smiled at Joyce's cheerful: 'your friend Folly'. He had been kept waiting for some time in the entrance hall, and the importance of Folly had thus been impressed on him. Now Folly beamed at him, with the enigmatic beam of greatness, that gives nothing away.

'Ah, a story,' mused Folly. 'I am always interested in the unusual, the rare, the remarkable. Please continue.'

'I should tell you first,' said Dane, dryly, 'that it concerns a friend of mine who lives in the country – '

'What part of the country ?'

55

'Limshire.'

'What part of Limshire?'

'Near Marston,' said Dane, a little impatiently.

'Excellent! You have a friend who lives near Marston, in Limshire, and he is the victim – or imagines himself to be the victim – of some crime. Now we have a promising beginning.'

Dane felt the stirring of resentment; he wished to tell the story his own way; Folly just as vigorously wished, and intended, he should not.

'To be exact, he lives in the village of Marrigay,' said Dane, rather shortly.

For the first time, Folly showed interest. He did not speak, but rested his hands on his desk.

'I'm talking of Colonel Peter Marrigay. You may have heard –'

'I have read something about him, yes,' said Folly.

'I've just come from him.'

'You interviewed Marrigay? As a reporter?'

'As a friend.'

'Ah – admirable. And I must congratulate you. It could not have been an easy task.'

'How much do you know about him?' demanded Dane.

'As much as has been published, and perhaps a little more,' said Folly. 'Assume that I am reasonably well-informed about your friend. That I am aware he has shut himself up, for instance, cut himself off from the world, shall we say?'

'He's just re-established communication,' said Dane dryly.

'I *do* congratulate you,' said Folly, warmly. 'If, by that is implied – and I think it is – that it is by your own doing. Do continue.'

He no longer looked smug; and Dane, his exasperation slightly mollified, began to talk.

He had made no notes but on the journey he had gone over the story of the Marrigays time and time again, and was sure that he had forgotten nothing.

Not once during the recital did Folly interrupt. He sat staring at Dane, through narrowed, intelligent eyes, breathing softly. Twice there was a tap at the door, but Folly splendidly

56

ignored it, and the tapper crept away.

At last, Dane finished.

Folly stirred. 'Well, well!' he said. 'It *is* remarkable. I am grateful, Mr Dane. Have you ever paused to think of the remarkable multiplicity of temperaments? No two temperaments are *exactly* alike, if we could record them as we do finger-prints the task of the police would be so much simpler.

'A man might say thoughtfully how wrong the Marrigays were to have behaved like this, but that would be forgetting temperament – the stresses and strains of loyalty to Mrs Marrigay. Yes. But I mustn't bore you with such reflections. You won't mind if we go over some of the things you have told me together?'

'Of course not. I'm glad you're interested.'

'I should be a dullard indeed if I were not! This bullet, now – did the cuts on the trunk of the tree appear to be new?'

'Yes, rather new,' said Dane.

'You didn't think of running your finger over the cut surface, to see if there were any sticky dampness of the sap oozing out?'

'I'm afraid not.'

'Never mind. Miss Marrigay believes that the bullet was in the tree a week ago – in short, it had been left there for some weeks but was recently removed. A belated precaution. But perhaps not the most interesting feature,' went on Folly, pressing the tips of his fingers together. 'The "*Beware of the Dog*" was always pulled down, you say?'

'That is so.'

'Now *why*, I wonder,' mused Folly. 'It could hardly be more than a trifling nuisance to the people inside the house, but it *might* have been serious to anyone, not seeing it, who entered the grounds. Curious – in fact the whole story is curious, but you don't need me to tell you that. Now, Peter Marrigay – he is likely to be a little difficult, of course.'

'He's moody, certainly; always has been.'

'So. The thing is, Mr Dane, I cannot go down to this house in person at this juncture, I shall have to ask the Limshire people to make the preliminary inquiries. And I hope – I sincerely hope – that Colonel Marrigay won't object or cause difficulties. I shall try to make sure that the investigations are carried out in the most pleasant way possible, but – you tell me that the only occasion when Mr Marrigay really lost his temper was when you suggested the possibility that a member of the family had poisoned his father.'

'Yes.'

'So he is very conscious of his family – family pride is always a difficult thing to overcome, you know. However, that is a detail. Were they fond of their father?'

'Very.'

'Would you – be frank with me, please – would you advise exhuming the body *without* first consulting Colonel Marrigay?'

Dane said thoughtfully:

'No, I don't think so. Peter would fly off the handle when he discovered what had been done. He might be rather difficult, but I think I could manage him.'

'*You?*'

'Well, as I started all this, I'd rather like to be down there for a few days,' said Dane. 'It might help.'

'That's an excellent suggestion, really excellent,' enthused Folly. 'It would mean that on delicate matters we – the local police, I mean – could approach the Marrigays through a third party who is acceptable to them. Can you spare the time?'

'I can manage a week.'

'Good! Of course, we must act quickly – very quickly indeed,' said Folly, 'and when I tell Ives I'm sure he will want to exhume the body at once. Tomorrow, at the latest. Can you be down there again tomorrow?'

'Yes,' said Dane.

'You are being very helpful indeed,' said Folly, 'and I want to assure you that the police will do everything they possibly can to make this unhappy business both easier and safer for the Marrigays. And I hope that I shall be able to bear some part in the investigations myself,' murmured Folly. 'In fact I think that you can take it that the Yard will be consulted.

58

I – but just a moment!' Folly wagged his forefinger, and his expression altered. 'Dane, you scoundrel, you made me forget that you are representing the *Gazette* in this matter!'

Dane chuckled.

'You needn't worry about that. I'm going to tell Cameron part of the story, off the record, but the last thing I want to appear in the Press is a statement that the police are interested. We want to keep it a secret, don't we?'

'*Right* under our hats,' said Folly. 'I'm glad you take that view. Cameron is quite reliable, of course. All responsible newspapermen are. Yes. Oh, before you go – describe the down-at-heel man who claimed to represent the *Sunday World*, will you?'

'Don't forget that I only saw him in the dark,' said Dane.

'Do your best, that's all I ask,' said Folly. 'I won't expect the impossible!'

Dane did his best.

When Dane had gone, Folly sat for some minutes at his desk, looking into the fire. At last he picked up the telephone and put in a call to the Marston Police Station. Although Marston was not the county town of Limshire, Police Headquarters for the county were established there, and Folly had an encyclopaedic knowledge of the county forces. He had been sent by the Yard on various jobs to most counties, and possessed a remarkable memory – even those who took a poor view of the childlike vanity of the Superintendent agreed about that. As he waited for the call to come through, he recalled what he knew of Inspector Ives. A thorough man, and one who devoted all his energy to his profession. He lacked brilliance; but Folly did not demand brilliance, although he liked a man who possessed it, provided steadiness were linked with it. If Ives had talked to the veterinary surgeon, then he was the most likely man to have some knowledge of the circumstances. The police in Marston might know much more than the Marrigays imagined.

The telephone bell rang.

'Your call to Marston, sir, Inspector Ives is on the line.'

59

'Thank you . . . *Hallo*, Inspector!' boomed Folly. 'How are you . . . Splendid! . . . Yes, yes, I am as ebullient and unpredictable as ever, I fear, a constant thorn in the flesh of the ungodly and godly alike, ha-ha-ha! Ives, I've just had a visit from a young man who has seen your Marrigays.'

'Have you, then!' exclaimed Ives, in a deep voice.

'And Cotterell has been to see you about that poisoned dog, hasn't he?'

'That's true,' said Ives; he pleased Folly because he did not ask a foolish question about how Folly had learned that detail. 'Arsenic – '

'Yes, I know. Did *you* know that the Marrigays think their father was murdered – poisoned?'

After a long pause, Ives said: 'I did not.'

'Then that will explain a great deal which has puzzled you,' said Folly. 'This young man, the friend, came to tell me. He is anxious, for the sake of the family, that investigations should begin quietly. I think he's wise. First, of course, you will need an Exhumation Order, but that will cause little trouble. And if you find what you may find, then perhaps . . . '

Ives said quietly: 'If I find anything like that, I shouldn't care to handle the investigations on my own, Superintendent. I should ask the Chief Constable to get in touch with the Yard without delay.'

'That's exactly what I expected,' crowed Folly, 'and I should like to come down myself. You have no idea how wearisome London can be. Terribly so! Of course, the Marrigays *may* be wrong, but there are indications . . . '

He passed on to Ives all pertinent points which Dane had told him.

Cameron was in his office when Dane arrived just before five o'clock. At sight of the cricketer-journalist, he sent his secretary away, pushed cigarettes across his desk and said dryly:

'Nothing doing, eh?'

'You'd be surprised,' said Dane. 'A great deal of it is off

60

the record, but I've a story that can be printed.'

'Well, well!' exclaimed Cameron.

Half an hour later, Dane left the office feeling very well satisfied. Cameron had allowed him to write the 'official' story, which he already knew by heart. And Cameron had asked him to cover the investigation for the *Gazette*, on the understanding that Dane would use his own judgement about what news to send through.

Dane made arrangements with his partner, the editor of the local newspaper which covered a great area of West London, then went home and packed a bag ready for the morning.

He reached Marrigay House at half-past nine, and was received as if he were one of the family.

Marrigay's expression hardened at talk of exhumation, but he raised no objection. No one else at the house was told.

Dane went into Marston in the afternoon, and saw Ives. He liked the man, and was relieved to learn that the exhumation would take place after dark so as to attract as little attention as possible.

At half-past six he left the house with Peter, on the pretext that they were going to the *Arms* for a drink.

A new moon spread a soft glow over the churchyard. Men moved about – quiet, dark, shadowy figures, speaking in undertones, working by the dim light of the moon and, occasionally, the flash of a torch. The gravedigger and the verger had not been told what was afoot. The Vicar of Marrigay, an elderly cleric with a great store of worldly wisdom, had been helpful. He had promised to see that the verger had no reason to be at the church that evening, and to remain in the vestry himself. There he would try to make sure that any callers would be detained in the church, and thus be unlikely to see anything of what went on outside.

Ives and the Marston police-surgeon were in charge of the exhumation.

Spades struck the wet earth with soughing noises; moisture sucked at the steel. The piles of earth grew higher as the policemen dug more deeply. After a while, spades struck the hard wood of the lid of the coffin, the sharp, metallic sound travelling clearly across the night air. It reached Dane and Marrigay, who were standing in the shadow of a large yew hedge.

Marrigay stirred.

'This is the devil!'

'Rather go back?' asked Dane.

'No. Nearer. Come on.'

Dane thought it was foolish, but made no objection. They reached the fringe of the little group of men, who were digging more carefully now, scraping the earth away from the coffin and working round it. Soon, hooks at the end of long ropes were lowered, a man went down and secured them beneath the box.

'Ready!' he called.

Two men handled each of the four ropes; they heaved and strained, and earth gave way. A hook came loose. Marrigay stood motionless, staring down, tormenting himself – yet Dane could understand why he had thought it necessary to be here. The policemen began to heave again, this time without mishap. Soon the coffin had been carried to a small shed in a corner of the churchyard.

Ives and the police surgeon went inside.

CHAPTER VIII

EVIDENCE OF MURDER

The hut was small, and although the night was cold, Inspector Ives felt uncomfortably hot. Marchmant, the police-surgeon, was bending over the decomposing corpse. In spite of the chloride of lime which had been sprinkled

62

freely about the hut, the smell of putrefying flesh persisted. By the foot of the bench stood a young, sharp-featured man, and both he and Marchmant wore long white coats. Marchmant's broad, ruddy features showed up clearly in the light from a petrol-gas lamp which hung from a hook in the roof.

Marchmant looked up.

'You needn't stay if you don't feel like it.'

'I'll stay,' said Ives.

'All right. Keep by the door, will you, and give me room to move.'

His instruments were spread out on a shelf above the bench. He picked up a knife . . .

The assistant watched intently, but Ives looked resolutely away. He was never happy about post-mortems; a sense of duty compelled him to witness some of them, dogged determination kept him there now.

After a while, Marchmant began to talk.

'See that, Jimmy?'

'What about the liver?' asked Jimmy.

'Give me time,' said Marchmant.

He bent nearer . . .

All were silent while Marchmant continued to work with quick, decisive movements. He put some of the organs into porcelain dishes, then suddenly said:

'There's your liver!'

He glanced over his shoulder at Ives. 'You really needn't stay, old chap. We've found what you wanted, I don't think there's a shadow of doubt.'

'Arsenic?'

'Yes.'

'How sure are you?'

'Well, I shall hand over to Jimmy if I'm wrong! You'll have to have an inquest.'

'Yes,' said Ives, 'but I wasn't thinking of that.' He hesitated, looking at the police-surgeon but knowing that he had to make his own decision; whether to tell Marrigay yet? 'I'll see you later,' he said. 'How long will you be?'

'Another hour, before we've finished.'

'If I'm not in the churchyard and you want me,' Ives said, 'you'll probably find me at Marrigay House. I'll leave a message if I go, anyhow.'

'Right – good luck!'

Ives stayed outside the shed for a few minutes, glad of the clear air. He moved some yards away, so that the smell of chloride of lime did not reach him. A policeman materialised out of the darkness and asked:

'Anything I can do, sir?'

'Is Colonel Marrigay still about?'

'Yes, sir, back by the hedge.'

'Is the other man with him?'

'Yes, sir.'

'All right, thanks.'

Ives walked slowly along the paths of the churchyard, more difficult to discern now because the moon had almost gone and the stars were dimmed by clouds. He went to the gate by the side road, and was told that no one had shown any interest in the churchyard.

'Good,' grunted Ives.

He hesitated near the church. The Vicar would not object if he, Ives, asked for the use of the vestry for half-an-hour, in order to interview Marrigay. On the other hand, if a stray villager did come along –

He began to walk towards the hedge which hid Marrigay and Dane. He was not looking forward to another interview with the Colonel. He had seen him only once, and that after Dane had paved the way. Marrigay had been civil enough, but with a steely politeness; naturally, he hated the thought of this investigation. He was such an unpredictable customer, thought Ives.

But it was no use blinking at facts; there *was* evidence of murder. Inquiries had to be made at the house quickly. True, so much time had already elapsed that all vital evidence might already have been destroyed. A year-old crime was the devil to solve.

Of course, there was as yet no *proof* of murder; but

suicides by arsenic were rare, and this time the poison had undoubtedly been taken through the mouth. There was little doubt as to what the inquest verdict would be, in view of the evidence he and Marchmant could give.

Marrigay suddenly appeared in front of him.

'It's Ives, isn't it?' he asked abruptly, peering close into the Inspector's face. 'Well?'

'I'd rather like a quiet talk with you, Colonel Marrigay,' said Ives.

'Have you found anything?'

'Dr Marchmant thinks there is arsenic.'

'Oh, God!' groaned Marrigay.

Dane appeared, standing silently by the side of his friend. A car passed along the road, and for a second the head-lights cast their beam over Marrigay's pale face and bright eyes. His lips were set tightly, he looked hawklike, preda-tory; then the light passed him.

'You'd better come to the house,' he said abruptly.

'Thank you.' Ives kept the satisfaction out of his voice. 'Sergeant Owen!' he called, and a man appeared quickly. 'I want you to follow me to Marrigay House. Tell Armstrong to inform Dr Marchmant.'

'Right, sir.'

Sergeant Owen caught the trio up when they were near the open gates of Marrigay House. They walked across the lawns to a side entrance. Marrigay unlocked the door and stepped inside. Only a dim, reflected light lit up the inner hall.

'Take them into the study, Alec, will you?' asked Marrigay. 'I want to tell the others that I've brought some friends in.' He looked at Ives. 'No objection to my keeping it from my family yet, I hope.'

'None at all,' said Ives.

Marrigay walked off, and Dane led the way into the half-panelled study. The fire was dying, cheerless grey wood embers filled the grate.

'Better keep our coats on,' he advised.

Ives nodded.

Dane was able to study the two detectives more closely. Tall and bulky, with his blue jowl jutting forward, Ives was already known to him. Owen was a different type, a good-looking young fellow, probably in the early thirties.

Ives spoke quietly:

'Do you know Colonel Marrigay well?'

'Not really well,' said Dane.

'I hope he'll understand that the quicker we can get to work, the quicker we shall see the end of it.'

Dane said slowly:

'If I were you, I shouldn't make it too obvious that one of the family might be involved.'

Ives nodded his understanding.

Marrigay came in. He carried an armful of newly-split logs. Soon a pale flicker danced about the hearth; wood began to crackle.

Marrigay stood up, dusting his hands.

'Now let's have it,' he said.

'I think you have had the worst, Colonel Marrigay,' said Ives, quietly. 'This talk is quite informal, of course, and subject to confirmation later, but I'm afraid we shall have to assume that death was from arsenical poisoning, administered through the mouth. That means, it could have been self-administered or given to your father by accident *or* deliberately.'

'You mean you think he was murdered – that's hardly a surprise to me,' said Marrigay. 'How do you want to start the investigation?'

'I'd like to make a few inquiries,' Ives began.

'Does that mean you want to question everyone tonight?'

Ives gave a slow, reasoning smile.

'Not quite that, Colonel Marrigay. I must make my position clear. Until after the inquest, I can make no demands and am entirely in your hands. I think it will help if I am able to start right away. I know you're worried about the effect this might have on Mrs Marrigay – but it's just possible that we shall be able to find out a great deal without worrying her. If I can, I will. After the inquest, I'll have to question everyone, but now – you see the difference, don't you?'

'I see,' said Marrigay. 'What else do you want?'

'I'm told that about the time of his death, Mr Marrigay was on a bread-and-water diet,' said Ives, 'and that he took a certain powder, *Kaylene*, as prescribed by his doctor. Is that powder still in the house?'

'I don't know,' said Marrigay. 'We can't keep this from my sister any longer,' he said, 'I'd better fetch her.' He turned away abruptly and went to the door, flinging it open.

He stood in front of it, staring, aghast.

'What – ' he began, and the words were strangled in his throat.

Dane took a stride forward, to peer over his shoulder, and saw Mrs Marrigay standing in the hall.

Marrigay moved forward quickly, with his hands outstretched. His mother stood quite still, and did not flinch when he took her wrists.

'Now, Mother, it's cold out here,' Marrigay said gently, 'you mustn't – '

'I want to know who these men are,' said Mrs Marrigay.

Her voice was weak but firm and steady. This was the first time that Dane had seen her on her feet. She was taller than he had thought, nearly as tall as Joyce. She wore a grey dress, a diaphanous shawl clouding her shoulders. Her snow-white hair was worn high, with the regality of a crown. Though her features were set calmly, her burning eyes took immediate attention from the rest of her face.

'Now, Mother, some friends of mine have come to see me,' said Marrigay, 'you wouldn't be interested in what they have to say!' He tried to rally her. 'Let me take you along to the drawing-room.'

'I have come to find out what these strange men are doing in my house,' said Mrs Marrigay, 'and I am not going to let you take me anywhere until I find out.'

'But – '

'Don't be ridiculous, Peter!' Her voice and manner were imperious as she moved forward; Marrigay had to stand aside. She looked at Dane. 'I thought he *was* a friend,' she said, and there was biting sarcasm in her voice. 'But these others – who are they?'

'Mother! I –'

But it was obvious that Mrs Marrigay no longer needed telling. Her gaze fell on Ives, and she nodded icily.

'I *thought* so. You try to make mystery, Peter, but I know what is going on in my house. This is a policeman. I don't remember his name, but –'

'Inspector Ives, Ma'am,' said Ives, quietly.

'Thank you, Inspector. And what is your business?'

Marrigay said desperately: 'There have been some burglaries in the district, and –'

'I asked you not to be ridiculous,' said Mrs Marrigay tartly. 'They have not come about burglaries – unless there has been one at this house, and in view of all the precautions which we take, I hardly think that is likely. Have they come because they believe that your father was murdered?'

'What makes you ask that, Ma'am?' asked Ives.

She looked at him calmly.

'My brother informed me that he had heard the preposterous suggestion being made.' She glanced at Dane. 'Apparently my son has allowed himself to become a party to this absurd story. It does not surprise me that as a result he has brought the police here. I even believe that *I* am named as the original source of the story. I am hardly to be held accountable for anything I may say when I am gravely distressed in mind, Inspector.'

'Of course not, Ma'am,' said Ives.

'Then I will wish you good night,' said Mrs Marrigay.

She nodded to the detectives but not to Dane, passed Marrigay, and went into the hall. Marrigay looked as if he were about to follow her, but Ives stepped past him quickly and closed the door.

'Obviously she has no idea what we have been doing tonight,' he said. 'It will be wiser not to tell her, Colonel.'

'She'll have to know,' Marrigay muttered. 'I'd like to wring Uncle Nicholas's neck! I might have known I couldn't trust him.'

He broke off as the door was pushed open, and Joyce came in.

Her colour was high, and she was obviously distressed. She closed the door behind her and advanced into the room, looking from her brother to the detectives, but ignoring Dane; that stung him. All the men waited for her to speak.

'What was said to Mother?' she demanded.

'Why?' demanded Marrigay.

'She told me to tell her if your visitors weren't gone within twenty minutes. And – and she's closed and locked the door.'

To Ives and Owen, that information did not seem important. To Dane it was significant, and to the Marrigays astonishing. Dane remembered the open bedroom door, the nightlight burning dimly, and the fact that Mrs Marrigay had seldom closed her door since the death of her husband. Coming on top of her calm denial that there were any grounds for thinking that her husband had been murdered, when it was she herself who had started the suspicion, it must have shaken Marrigay considerably.

'Mother guessed that there were police in the house,' Joyce said.

Ives spoke in a quiet, soothing voice.

'We had to take action quickly, Miss Marrigay, and I'm afraid we've bad news for you. We now know that your father was killed by arsenical poisoning. Your brother was about to ask you to come and help us,' he went on quickly, 'we want to know if the *Kaylene* which you bought for your father is still in the house?'

'I – I don't know.' Joyce sat down heavily on the arm of a chair, then said, slowly: 'But of course I know, it's in the medicine chest.'

'May I have it?' asked Ives.

'Shall I get it?'

'I'd like to come with you,' said Ives. 'Now that Mrs Marrigay knows we're here, It won't greatly matter if we move about the house, will it?'

'I suppose not,' Marrigay agreed grudgingly. 'I'll take you upstairs.'

'Come with me, Owen,' ordered Ives.

Left alone in the room, Dane and Joyce looked at each other without speaking. Joyce pushed a lock of hair back from her forehead. She looked tense and strained; the frightening atmosphere of the last few months had been revived by the arrival of the police and the behaviour of her mother. The silence lengthened . . .

Dane felt that he must break it.

'It's a good thing they've started,' he said, gruffly, 'it stops us from wondering and guessing. It's much better to know the truth, isn't it?'

'I – suppose – it – is.'

'Joyce, what's affecting you like this?' Dane asked. 'Matters are moving rather quickly, but you were warned. You knew that once the police had any idea of what was afoot, they would make inquiries, didn't you?'

'Yes, of course,' she said, and turned her direct gaze towards him. 'Don't think I'm blaming you for anything. I just can't understand how Mother knew there was something amiss.'

'Now, come! Uncle Nicholas told her pretty well everything.'

'He didn't know everything,' objected Joyce. 'I don't know why, but Mother's attitude seems uncanny.' She brushed her hand across her eyes. 'I suppose Ives meant that they've exhumed the body.' She spoke stiffly.

'Yes.'

'And there isn't any doubt?'

'Apparently not.'

'Well, we'll have to let it come,' said Joyce. 'You're right, whatever we find out now can't be worse than the uncertainty, the fear.'

'I know,' said Dane, gently.

'I really believe you do. How long can you stay?'

'As long as necessary.'

'Bless you!'

'I hope I'll make myself useful,' said Dane. 'I've been thinking that you ought to let your sister and her husband

70

know at once. They don't want to learn about it through the newspapers,' he added rather clumsily.

'I'll telephone them,' promised Joyce, 'but I'd better have a word with Peter first. Here they come, I think.'

The three men came in. Ives bore the bland and propitiatory expression of one prepared to smooth over a social upheaval. He carried the *Kaylene* bottle unobtrusively, but with triumph.

'Thanks very much, sir. Now I know that you've had a great upset, and I don't want to add to it, but there's one thing I'd like to do, in view of the fact that Mrs Marrigay has been so nervous, and you've removed some of the precautions against intruders.' Ives gave a comforting smile. 'For your own safety, I would like to leave a man at the gates and another at the stile. I'd like to be sure that the dog won't molest them, of course.'

Marrigay said slowly:

'We don't want police protection.'

'I think you ought to have it,' said Ives, and for the first time showed something of the steeliness in his character. 'They'll be stationed outside the grounds.'

'You mean you're going to watch us!'

Ives said slowly: 'Colonel Marrigay, if the household was so distressed – frightened – that such extreme precautions were taken to keep people out, there must have been a reason. Either the danger remains or you know that it had been removed.'

After a long pause, Marrigay said:

'I can't argue against such logic. The dog will be kept under control, Inspector.'

'Thank you, sir,' said Ives.

He left the house, leaving behind him even more tension than there had been when Dane had first arrived. Marrigay fell into a sullen, silent mood. Uncle Nicholas stayed in his room. Joyce spent much of the next hour with her mother, and came downstairs a little after eleven o'clock, looking as if she had been through something of an ordeal.

Mrs Marrigay's door remained locked all that night.

71

Dane slept well but woke just after half-past seven, feeling depressed. As he shaved, he looked at his reflection glumly. He was not given to analysing his features; now contrasting his looks with Marrigay's and Joyce's he felt rueful. Thinking of her he had worked himself into a much more cheerful frame of mind by the time he went downstairs.

He saw Joyce going into the breakfast-room. She did not notice him.

'Peter,' she said sharply, as she disappeared. 'Have you seen Uncle?'

'No. Is he up yet?'

'He's not in his room, and the bed hasn't been slept in.'

CHAPTER IX

SEARCH FOR UNCLE NICHOLAS

As Dane reached the last stair, Peter and Joyce came hurrying out of the breakfast-room.

'Did you hear that?' asked Peter.

'I tell you he's not in his room,' Joyce said.

'We'll have another look.'

Dane turned and bounded up the stairs in front of Peter, Joyce shrugged her shoulders and followed. All three of them reached the room, which was immediately opposite Mrs Marrigay's. The large, carved oak bed was made, the bedspread and eiderdown untouched.

'Well?' asked Joyce.

Peter strode to a wardrobe.

'Have you looked in here?' he asked.

He checked the suits, their attenuated forms hanging in meticulous rows.

'I don't think there are any missing, except that light grey

72

one he was wearing last night.'

'What about suitcases?' asked Dane.

'He doesn't keep them here,' said Joyce, 'they're all in the box-room. I'll go and see if any are missing.'

She hurried out, while Peter continued to rummage through the wardrobe. Uncle Nicholas had a remarkable amount of clothes, and Dane wondered whether anyone but the owner could be sure what was there and what had been taken out.

Peter thrust his hands deep into his pockets.

'Something like this *would* happen,' he growled.

'We don't really know what *has* happened yet,' reasoned Dane. 'Could he have made his own bed?'

'He could, but he wouldn't. He's the laziest creature on God's earth.' Peter looked towards the door as Joyce came hurrying in. 'Any luck?'

'All the cases are there,' said Joyce. 'Peter, what are you going to do?'

'The first thing we're *not* going to do is to raise an alarm,' declared Peter without hesitation. 'If we tell the police about this before we know what the old beggar's up to, they'll be imagining all kinds of nonsense.'

'Has he ever run out on you like this before?' Dane asked.

Peter shook his head. 'He may have gone for a walk,' he suggested, without conviction.

Dane forced himself to laugh.

'My dear chap, he would hardly have "gone for a walk" and stayed out twelve hours! We must face the fact that he's either gone off deliberately, or something has stopped him from returning. Any "walk" finished last night.'

Peter grunted, disagreeably.

Dane said: 'Let's try and look at this thing properly. When was Uncle Nicholas last seen?'

The others hesitated, and then began to speak together.

'Last night – ' said Peter.

'After the police – ' began Joyce.

'Now that's the point,' Dane said. 'Was he in the house before the police arrived or after?'

'After,' said Joyce, firmly.

'Yes, I saw him when Mother came to the study,' Peter said, 'he was peering out of the drawing-room door.'

'Are you sure?'

'He was certainly here before Ives went upstairs with me to get the *Kaylene*,' said Peter with a touch of the acer had already shown towards Dane. 'Come to think of it was going into his room when I came out of the bath I remember thinking that at all costs he had seen what was going on. He was peering round the door, as usual.'

'Did you see him after Ives had left?' asked Dane.

'No, he wasn't downstairs after that,' Joyce said thoughtfully. 'I called out "good night" as I passed his door, but he didn't answer. I thought he was asleep.'

'What made you go up to his room this morning?' asked Peter.

'I went to take his post up. I could hardly believe my eyes when I saw the bed was made.'

They all went downstairs, and Joyce hurried towards the kitchen. She was back in a few minutes, shaking her head. Neither Leah nor Pengelly had seen Uncle Nicholas. Peter flung open the window and called to Lem, who came hurrying across the lawn, with Thor on a strong leash just behind him.

'No, Mr Peter,' he said, 'I haven't seen him. I have seen something, though.'

'What's that?'

'There's a policeman at the gate and another at the stile,' said Lem, coming close to the window.

'They're looking after us,' said Peter briefly, 'and I've promised to make sure that Thor doesn't get at any of them.'

'I'll see to that,' promised Lem. 'Is there anything else known about poor Saturn, sir?'

'Nothing yet,' said Peter.

Lem went off, and the others turned back into the room. Rather absently, Joyce began to serve bacon and eggs from a hot-plate. They kept up a desultory conversation during the meal; the disappearance of Uncle Nicholas had helped to take their minds off the visit from Ives and the exhumation;

but that would not last long, reflected Dane.

It was ten o'clock when they finished breakfast.

'Well, what are we going to do?' asked Joyce.

'He might come back any time,' said Peter.

'We're going to tell the police,' Dane said firmly.

~~r~~ grumbled, but without much feeling. Joyce agreed ~~th~~at it was the only thing left to them. It was Dane who went ~~to the~~ telephone and put in a call to Inspector Ives.

Ives was in his office, talking to Sergeant Owen. In front of him was Marchmant's report; the police-surgeon had not only given his own opinion about the arsenic, but had taken the organs to the pathologist at the hospital, whose opinion concurred. There was no shred of doubt about it; and Ives was giving Owen instructions about arrangements for the inquest, which would take place the following morning.

The telephone bell rang.

Within two minutes Ives had replaced the receiver and was giving Owen urgent instructions about Nicholas Lee.

'It may be a straightforward job,' he said. 'Or there may be more devilry afoot. You don't need me to tell you how to go about it.'

'I'll get cracking!' declared Owen.

Ives smiled as the door closed on the sergeant.

It was his good fortune, and he often reflected on it, that he was blessed with a sergeant who was exceptionally able.

The set-up at the Marston Police Station was a simple one. The Superintendent, Henderson, held the reins lightly. On an affair like this, Ives's advice would be readily accepted by Henderson as well as the Chief Constalble. Owen and two detective officers were assigned to him; and, with help from the police branch whenever it was necessary, Ives handled all criminal investigations not only in Marston but throughout the county. He was not staffed or equipped, however, for major investigation.

He rose, now, from his desk, picked up the papers, and went along to see Henderson.

That tall, thin, rather saturnine man looked at him keenly.

'You're looking worried.'

'I'm not so much worried as thoughtful,' said Ives, sitting down. 'Apparently Nicholas Lee had disappeared from Marrigay House.'

'Disappeared?'

'That's the opinion of the people at the house. I've told Owen to put a general call out, it's just possible that he's the culprit and has been frightened away. But –'

'But he may have been bumped off! Bloodthirsty beggar, aren't you?'

Ives did not smile.

'You know what I think about this business,' he said. 'Have you had a word with the Chief Constable?'

'Yes. O.K. to consult the Yard.'

'Good! And the inquest?'

'It's all being left to you. "Don't worry me just now" is his theme song of the moment. Still, I suppose it's something that he gives us a free hand. But I'm glad you haven't lost any time asking the Yard to help. The Marrigays are an odd family –'

'I'm not worried about the family so much as the crime,' said Ives. 'And the general set-up, of course. I tried to catch Colonel Marrigay on the hop last night, but he wasn't having any.'

'How did you try?'

Ives smiled.

'I suggested that he'd removed the padlock from the gate because he now knew there was no further danger,' he said. 'That was after he showed some reluctance about having men stationed outside the house. He didn't rise to the bait. All the same, I do wonder if it's true that that fellow Dane just walked in, and persuaded them to remove the barricades. They must have been dead scared of *something* to make a fortress of the house. If they're no longer scared, I'd like to know why. I'll be glad when Folly comes,' he added. 'I hope he doesn't hang about in London too long.'

'He'll come the moment it suits him,' said Henderson. 'You're not going to sit back and wait for him, are you?'

'Don't be an ass,' said Ives. 'I've plenty to do. But you ought to know that I'll need half-a-dozen men to look for Nicholas Lee. I want that copse near the house searched. And I'm going to put the Marrigay constable on to it, making inquiries among the villagers. We can't keep it hush-hush much longer. We've done all we can to study Colonel Marrigay's feelings!'

'I agree,' said Henderson.

'Thanks,' said Ives. 'Now I'm going to the village – if Folly rings through, telephone a message to P.C. Adams in Marrigay, will you?'

'Right,' promised Henderson.

Three-quarters of an hour later, when Ives and Owen arrived at the village with a young detective officer, the copse was being searched. Six policeman, including P.C. Adams, were beating through the patch of trees, in a long line, each man about three yards from the next. They had instructions to look for anything at all unusual, as well as for Uncle Nicholas. Ives and Owen stood by Ives's car, watching them. They could see part of Marrigay House between the trees, and Ives wondered a little uneasily what would happen if the Alsatian got loose. He was by no means satisfied with Marrigay's reaction to his request – and by no means certain that Peter was all he appeared to be.

'They'll find him, if he's there,' Owen remarked.

'They'd better,' said Ives.

'If he's not, we might send them out to Dunkley Mound,' went on Owen, 'Lee was always pottering about those old earthworks, digging for bones or relics. If he killed old Marrigay, and has decided it's time he did away with himself – '

Ives glared at him.

'If you talk nonsense like that when Folly's about, he'll put you down as a witless fool, *and* he won't be far wrong,' he went on coldly. 'We're going to have a look at the tree with the bullet hole.'

They discovered the tree and examined it with pains-
taking care. Ives took a small magnifying glass from his
attaché case, and peered at the hole, then touched the newly
cut wood gently with his little finger. It was slightly tacky.
He told Owen to make a note to find out how long sap remained on the outer part of the trunk of an oak after an
injury. Next, he examined the marks of the chisel or knife.

'Anything?' asked Owen.

'Have a look,' said Ives.

After his examination, Owen said thoughtfully:

'I wouldn't say it *was* a chisel. There are one or two marks
which look as though they were made by the point of a knife.'

'Not bad,' said Ives. 'Take the glass again.' He waited
until Owen was peering at the hole. 'Now, look at some of
the pointed marks, then towards the outer edge of the cut.
The knife or whatever it was was moved in a circular fashion.
See?'

'Yes.'

'And there are some tiny ridges, about an inch from the
outer edge,' continued Ives. 'You wouldn't notice them with
the naked eye, but – '

'I've got 'em,' said Owen, quickly.

'Well?'

'You mean, that whoever turned the knife made the ridges
and therefore there was a tiny break in the blade – that right?'

'Yes – it was a slightly broken blade,' said Ives. 'See
anything else?'

Owen's eyes widened.

'A few bits of metal – lead, probably, from the bullet.'

'Now I think you've got the lot,' said Ives. 'What's the
next step?'

'I know that one! Find the knife – and first, find out from
an expert what kind of knife it was.'

'Good,' said Ives. 'I'm going to get old Whittaker to come
and have a look at it, no one in Marston knows more about
knives than he does.'

'We've a pretty good idea what the knife looks like,' said
Owen. 'But what about the end of the hole, where the bullet

was – can we pick up anything from that?'

'We *might* get traces of marks on the bullet,' Ives agreed.

'We'll cut a piece out of the trunk of the tree and take it back to town. Then anyone else can play about with it. The tools are in the car – there's a job for you.'

Soon, the harsh noise of the saw on the green wood broke the quiet of the copse.

The searching policemen were now out of sight. Owen and Ives had spent nearly half-an-hour by the tree, when P.C. Adams came walking through the copse with long deliberate strides.

'We've been through, sir. Nothing to report.'

'All right – move over to Dunkley Mound and have a good look there,' said Ives.

'Yes, sir.'

'You'd better go through the grounds of the house first,' Ives amended. 'See young Pengelly, and make sure that dog's tied up.'

'Yes, sir.' Adams moved off, and Ives drove down the hill to examine the place where the trench had been made in the road. This was a bigger problem than that of the bullet-hole, because it had been mended so long ago. But with luck, thought Ives, he might be able to prove the kind of tool which had been used to make it. The road was of tar and flint but there was clay beneath, and marks remained in clay for a long time. He went down on one knee and examined the line which ran right across the road.

'I'd better have part of it up,' he reflected, as he rose to his feet. 'No one will interfere with *that*, anyhow.'

As he drew within sight of Owen, Peter Marrigay and Dane appeared in the roadway. Hearing them, he stopped, and opened his window.

'We've discovered where my uncle is,' Peter burst out. 'He's with my sister, in London – she's just telephoned. He's been violently sick, she tells me.'

CHAPTER X

MARJORIE AND ROGER

Marjorie Hurst stood watching Uncle Nicholas and the sleek-haired doctor who was sitting on the side of the bed, listening to the older man's heart. The stethoscope moved about the plump, flaccid flesh. Uncle Nicholas lay with his eyes closed, breathing stertorously.

The doctor straightened up.

Uncle Nicholas opened his mouth.

'Water,' he muttered. 'Water.'

'You can moisten his lips,' said the doctor, 'but don't let him drink any.'

'What – what is wrong with him?'

'I wouldn't like to commit myself,' said the doctor. 'Cover him up and stay here while I fetch something from my car, will you?'

'Of course.'

The doctor hurried out.

'Water,' gasped Uncle Nicholas.

There was sweat on his forehead and his face was grey with pain. Marjorie moistened his lips, then wiped his forehead and cheeks. His eyes were bloodshot, and his breathing was still heavy. He retched again ...

Marjorie covered him with blankets.

Uncle Nicholas lay quiet for a while.

The doctor entered the house again; Marjorie could hear him hurrying up the stairs.

She had been alone in this house in Barnes when Uncle Nicholas had arrived. She had been horrified when he had staggered into the hall, gasping with pain. Immediately he had rushed to the cloakroom, and she had heard him retching. Without losing a moment, she had telephoned for her doctor, then helped the sick man upstairs. For nearly an hour, she had been alone with her uncle, who, between spasms of sickness and pain, kept calling for water. She had allowed him to have half a cup, which he had vomited almost at once.

During one of his quiet spells, she had telephoned to Marrigay House.

The doctor came in, carrying a large case.

'I'm going to use a stomach pump,' he said. 'You'll be able to stick it, I hope.'

'Of course.'

Marjorie obeyed his directions quickly.

It was unpleasant; but she felt frightened lest her uncle should die and knew that she must steel herself to give the doctor every help he needed.

Marjorie stood by the side of the bed, her face very pale. Her hair was fair and straight, only her eyes showed any resemblance to Peter or Joyce.

'Will he be all right?' she asked.

'I think we'll pull him through. I'm sorry you're on your own, Mrs Hurst. I need some things from a chemist. If I telephone for them, will you fetch them?'

'Of course.'

It was good to have something to do. She heard the doctor talking to the chemist in the High Street, and caught odd words and phrases. 'ferric hydroxide, yes – the usual arsenic antidote . . . '

She covered Uncle Nicholas to his chin, and hurried downstairs to put on a kettle. This would happen on the one morning in the week when she had no help.

What had the doctor said on the telephone?

'Arsenic!' she breathed.

She let the kettle overfill, and water splashed into the sink. She emptied a little, lit the gas, put a hot-water bottle on the stove, and hurried upstairs for a second bottle. *Arsenic.* What on earth did it mean? Peter had telephoned her the previous night and said that there was some bother at Marrigay, and he thought she and Roger ought to go down there for the week-end. There was always some kind of

81

trouble at that house and she had little patience with it – nor had Roger. Neither of them had the heart to tell Peter and Joyce that they thought they were making a lot of fuss about nothing – Mother's absurd suggestion shouldn't have worried them, the trouble with both was that they were so highly strung. Undoubtedly, Peter had been neurasthenic since he had returned, there was little surprising about that, but what they ought to do was to make Mother see sense.

Roger had laughed when she had told him of the compulsive invitation.

'Well, we haven't been down there for some time, and we're free this week-end.'

'Then we'll go?'

'Oh, we'd better play it their way,' Roger had said.

He was always prepared to humour his eccentric relatives, even though he would not stay at Marrigay often or for long periods.

But – *arsenic*!

The doctor appeared in the doorway. She decided that he was too sleek, too dapper – yet he had been very quick once he had arrived, and appeared to know what he was talking about.

Arsenic!

'The chemist will have everything ready when you get there,' said the doctor, 'and I've telephoned to a nurse. If she isn't along in half-an-hour we'll have to get your uncle to hospital.'

'I see,' said Marjorie.

She was back in twenty minutes. The doctor was on the landing, talking to a dumpy little woman in a blue uniform.

Her every other phrase seemed to be: 'Yes, doctor.' But it was a relief for Marjorie to feel that she could now leave Uncle Nicholas in experienced hands.

And it was time she telephoned Roger.

She did that first, using the telephone downstairs. Roger was a comparatively insignificant red-tab at the War Office. It was never easy to get through to him, and she waited impatiently.

The Hurst's house was larger than they required – yet! Marjorie rested a hand against her thick waist, and in spite of all that had happened, she smiled. Yet! But it was almost impossible to run the house and keep it as she liked it to be kept with daily help only. It was a worry, but –

Arsenic!

'Hallo, Jorrie!' Roger's deep voice sounded in her ear.

'Roger! I've only got a moment, but *can* you come home? Uncle Nicholas is here, he – '

'Don't say that *he's* been visited upon us.'

'Darling, he's ill.'

'He always is.'

'Darling. This is serious. He's *gravely* ill – they may have to take him to hospital, and I'm so worried, the doctor asked the chemist for arsenic.'

'*What?*'

'I mean, anti-arsenic, or whatever you call it,' cried Marjorie distractedly, 'don't be dense, darling.'

'I'll be home before lunch,' Roger promised, suddenly authoritative.

'Bless you!' exclaimed Marjorie.

She replaced the receiver, and went along to the kitchen. She was making tea when the doctor appeared again.

'How is he?'

'I think we were in time,' said the doctor. 'And, if so, you can take the credit – if you'd delayed, I don't think he would have stood much chance.'

Marjorie dashed a lock of hair out of her eyes. 'I've just made a cup of tea, I thought you might like one.'

'Thanks very much,' said the doctor. 'May I wash my hands down here?'

'I'll get you a towel,' said Marjorie.

The doctor washed his hands at the kitchen sink and took a long time drying them. They were white, with long fingers and perfectly shaped nails, and he dried each finger with a meticulous care. When he had finished he accepted his tea and stood sipping it thoughtfully. 'Do you know whether Mr Lee has been taken ill like this before, Mrs Hurst?'

'Not to my knowledge,' said Marjorie. 'I – doctor, *didn't* you ask for anti-arsenic, or something?'

He nodded gravely.

'Yes – all the symptoms are of arsenical poisoning,' he said, 'but I may be wrong – although I don't think it's very likely. Does Mr Lee live here?'

'Gracious, no! He – '

A bell rang, and Marjorie went towards the front door, not knowing whom to expect. A large and bulky man stood looking down at her, with a controlled smile which told her nothing.

Behind him was a man of more normal size.

'Good morning,' said the caller. 'Have I the pleasure of addressing Mrs Hurst – Mrs Roger Hurst?'

'I am Mrs Roger Hurst,' said Marjorie.

'I am so sorry to trouble you, but I have been told by your brother that Mr Nicholas Lee is here. Is that so?'

'Yes, he is here,' said Marjorie. Why on earth had Peter told this man so quickly?

The caller produced a card.

'I would very much like to talk to you for a few minutes,' he said.

Marjorie took the card, and read: *Superintendent A. K. Folly, New Scotland Yard, S.W.I. Criminal Investigation Department.*

'You'd better come in.'

Folly ducked to enter the hall, and the other man followed. 'This is Detective Sergeant Jeans,' said Folly, as Marjorie led him into the drawing-room. 'How *is* Mr Lee?'

'He's seriously ill. The doctor's here now,' said Marjorie.

'*Is* he then! What a fortunate coincidence,' Folly boomed. 'I would very much like a word with him before he goes.'

'That's up to him,' said Marjorie. The man disquieted her; she could still picture the words 'Criminal Investigation Department' on his card.

'When did you last see your uncle?' Folly asked suddenly.

'I – I don't know, he – '

'Recently?' suggested Folly.

'A week or two ago – I think it was the day the Bells came.'

'The Bells?'

'Some friends,' explained Marjorie. 'He'd been to his Club dinner, so it was Thursday.'

'And he was quite well then?'

'Of course he was!' Marjorie said. 'This is a sudden illness.'

'Did he tell you he was coming today?'

'No, he just came. I'd no idea he was in London,' said Marjorie.

'Did he speak to you about his illness?'

'No – oh, why ask me all these questions? What is it you want?'

Folly placed the tips of his fingers together.

'To tell you the truth, Mrs Hurst, Mr Lee left Marrigay in somewhat unusual circumstances, and we are anxious to interview him, to find out what happened and why he went away. Have you heard from your brother during the last few hours?'

'He telephoned last night and asked us to go there for the week-end,' said Marjorie, 'but what's that got to do with Uncle Nicholas? You can't possibly see him, he's much too ill,' she added definitely.

'I shall do nothing which might cause a relapse,' said Folly. 'I'm sorry that you haven't heard anything more from Marrigay, because the news is *not* very good, I'm afraid.'

Marjorie said in a startled voice:

'What do you mean?'

'Last night the body of your father was exhumed,' said Folly, 'and traces of arsenic were found, it – '

'Arsenic!' cried Marjorie. 'No, no, it can't be! Arsenic!'

'My dear lady – '

'But it can't be! It can't be!'

Marjorie caught her breath, and then began to scream. She knew that she was behaving crazily, but could not stop herself. Both detectives stood staring at her helplessly.

The door burst open, and the doctor appeared.

'Now, Mrs Hurst!' He crossed to her, took her arm, and

led her to an easy chair. 'Sit down, you'll be all right in a moment or two.' He shot a quick, antagonistic glance at Folly. 'Sit down,' he repeated, and Marjorie relaxed in her chair, trembling now, and glad of the cool touch of the doctor's fingers.

Folly moved forward in some agitation.

'I am extremely distressed to have caused you such agitation, Mrs Hurst – '

'I think Mrs Hurst had better sit here quietly for a little while,' said the doctor. His crisp voice was authoritative. 'I'll bring you another cup of tea and a couple of aspirins, Mrs Hurst – and please don't worry, I'll take care of these gentlemen.'

Folly said: 'Oh,' in an outraged voice.

'If you'll come into the hall, please,' the doctor said to him.

Folly followed meekly, and the sergeant brought up the rear.

'Wait here a moment,' said the doctor.

Folly swayed to and fro on his small feet, frowning, and Sergeant Jeans, who knew that the great man was annoyed, did not make the mistake of speaking.

The doctor appeared with a cup of tea on a tray, went into the front room, stayed only for a few minutes, and then came out and closed the door quietly.

'I am Folly, of New Scotland Yard,' announced Folly.

'I am Dr Acland,' said the doctor. 'I don't know what you said to Mrs Hurst, but you chose a bad moment. She is already worried by the sudden illness of her uncle, and her own condition – '

'Condition?' squeaked Folly.

'She's pregnant,' said Acland.

'Oh, dear me,' said Folly, sitting down on a hall seat which was much too small for him. 'I didn't realise that. I am not an expert in such matters. However, it explains a great deal – or it may.' The last sentence appeared to be addressed to himself, and he half-closed his eyes. 'Well, well! I will apologise to the lady at the first opportunity. However – I have much to ask you, doctor.'

86

Acland said: 'About what?'

'Your patient.'

'What interest have you in my patient?'

Folly gave a brief and official explanation which, while ensuring the doctor's co-operation, did little to remove the barrier of hostility which remained between them.

'Lee's probably suffering from acute arsenical poisoning,' he said.

'And you told Mrs Hurst?'

'She overheard me on the telephone,' said Acland.

'I see. Can you tell me anything else?'

'There may be something else I can tell you, but not until I've had a chance to consult a colleague,' said Acland.

'Hmm.' Folly swayed to and fro. 'You may, perhaps, be able to answer a few simple questions. Have you any idea how long before you saw the patient the dose had been administered?'

'It might have been an hour or two, it could have been longer. As an opinion, purely tentative, I would say that it was probably administered sometime during the night or early this morning.'

'What makes you think so?'

'Other symptoms.'

'My dear fellow,' said Folly, in a peevish voice, 'I don't want to be insistent, but please don't imagine that I know nothing about the symptoms of arsenical poisoning. If the severe dose were administered last night, that is an indication that the patient had been taking arsenic over a period and had become inured to it. Is it chronic poisoning, made acute by an extra large dose?'

'It might be,' conceded Acland, 'but I'd much rather make a more thorough examination before I say anything further. That isn't unreasonable.'

'No, no,' agreed Folly. 'But I am impatient – I need to know as quickly as possible. In the circumstances,' he added, 'I'm sure that you won't object to consulting a police-surgeon.'

'Not at all.'

'I will arrange for one to call on you,' said Folly, and then suddenly he widened his eyes. 'No, I won't do that. The patient will be much better off in hospital. Don't you agree? Excellent! Now, I – '

Folly broke off as a car drew up, and turned to look out of the window. All three men stared at the man who entered the house. They had reason to stare, for Roger Hurst was a remarkably fine physical specimen. Nearly as tall as Folly, he was lean and powerful looking.

'My name's Hurst,' he said aggressively. 'And you?'

Acland smiled politely.

'I'm afraid this is rather unexpected, Mr Hurst, but – '

Before he could go on, the door of the front room opened and Marjorie appeared. She had been crying, and the tears were still wet on her cheeks. Roger cast one angry glance at the trio, then turned as she flung herself into his arms.

CHAPTER XI

UNCLE NICHOLAS 'EXPLAINS'

'Now I am fully aware,' said Folly to his sergeant, 'that I have not given you a good lesson in the ways and means of interrogating witnesses this morning. On the other hand, you may find some hints which will be useful. In the first place three people, two of whom are important in the case, are poorly impressed by me. Roger Hurst, whom we saw only for a few minutes, thinks that I am a pompous and bombastic *poseur*. His wife, who took an instant dislike to me, thinks that I am too garrulous, and the doctor is hostile.'

The sergeant hid a smile; or thought he did; Folly quickly disillusioned him.

'There is no need to overdo the humour, sergeant! I am

telling you for your own good.'

'Yes, sir, of course,' said the sergeant.

Folly, who was sitting at the back of his own car, folded his hands across his chest and stared straight ahead of him. The sergeant, at the wheel, knew that he could not expect a great deal of talk during the rest of the journey. And he was sorry, because although he was one of the many who liked to laugh at Folly, he had a tremendous respect for that remarkable man's ability. He, the sergeant, was pretty sure that Folly had not been discomposed by anything that had happened at Barnes. He had gone to the house to obtain certain information and impressions, and had obtained them.

At the Yard, Folly squeezed himself into the lift and was carried to the second floor. From there he immediately telephoned the resident pathologist, and held him in earnest conversation for ten minutes. Finally, he said:

'And this Dr Acland will be here at two o'clock. If you can go with him to the hospital, to which the patient is being moved at half-past one, I should be grateful.'

At four o'clock, when the pathologist and Dr Acland entered his office, there followed three-quarters of an hour of intensely technical discussion. The sum total of their deliberation was that, as traces of arsenic were found in the hair and skin, Uncle Nicholas had either taken arsenic previously, without it doing him serious harm, or the dose had been administered much earlier than Acland had first suggested. The pathologist and Acland ruled this second possibility out; so it became obvious that Uncle Nicholas had survived not only because Mrs Hurst had acted so promptly, but because his body had absorbed sufficient arsenic in the past to slow down the effect of this last dose.

'And but for that, he would be dead,' mused Folly. 'Yes – thank you, gentlemen, I am deeply appreciative. Tell me, Dr Acland, do you look after Mrs Hurst regularly?'

'No, I was the only doctor she could get hold of,' said Acland. 'You want Summers – I can give you his telephone number, if you like.'

'I should like it,' said Folly.

He telephoned Marjorie's regular doctor asking whether there was any indication that Marjorie had ever taken arsenic. The answer was an emphatic negative.

Next, he telephoned Ives. He asked the Marston Inspector to get in touch with the Marrigay family doctor and find out whether, as far as the doctor knew, any of the family had ever suffered from arsenical poisoning. That done, he said cheerfully:

'And I think this is going to be most interesting, Ives, I really do. I'm looking forward to meeting your queer family very much indeed. Oh, I *knew* there was one thing I wanted to ask you – that *Kaylene*. Is there any arsenic in it?'

'No, it's quite pure.'

'Oh, a pity. And the search for arsenic in the house is going on apace, I hope.'

'I'm doing what I can,' said Ives.

'I'm sure you are. Don't let the tantrums of the family affect you in any way. Oh, another thing – I am persuading the Hursts to come to Marrigay tomorrow morning. They wanted to stay near Uncle Nicholas, but I have assured them that he will be well cared for in the London hospital, and that they will be of much more use down there. The woman is liable to get hysterical – '

'What, *another* of 'em!' exclaimed Ives.

'She can hardly be blamed,' said Folly, 'and I should imagine that normally she is a fairly placid individual. When they're all together, find out how they get on, with a view to seeing whether there is any suspicion among them.'

'When are you coming?' demanded Ives, quickly.

'Just as soon as I can,' promised Folly, 'but there are one or two things I have to attend to here first. If I were you, I shouldn't worry about me just yet. One thing you might remember – you will, of course! – is to find out whether any of the family could have access to arsenic.'

'I've been at that one,' said Ives. 'They've a friend who was down here about the time of the father's death, a man named Bell. He's an industrial chemist – research, mostly, with his own small laboratory.'

'Ah! Where does he live?'

'In London. Number 11, Mayhew Road, Golders Green. I got the information from Joyce Marrigay. She's easily the most amenable.'

'Good, keep at her,' said Folly. 'When is the inquest?'

'Tomorrow morning.'

'What verdict do you expect?'

'I fancy we shall get "Death by Arsenical Poisoning, with no evidence as to how the Arsenic was Administered",' said Ives, somewhat heavily.

'Well, that will be enough to be getting on with,' Folly said. 'I'll be seeing you soon, then – good-bye for the present.'

He rang off.

At the Marston office, Ives ran his hand over his forehead, and opined that Folly was being mysterious, which was always a good sign.

On the Saturday morning, Dane prepared for a trying spell with Peter and possibly with Mrs Marrigay, who had announced her intention of getting up for lunch. She was the only one of the family who did not know that the inquest was to be held at ten o'clock. Peter was glum; his mood had not been improved by the sketchy story which he had heard over the telephone from Roger. None of them really knew what had happened to Uncle Nicholas, and it seemed as if the police were deliberately keeping back the information.

Peter was to go into Marston for the inquest, and Dane was going with him. Only medical and police evidence would be taken.

At half-past nine, Dane left to walk to the *Marrigay Arms*, where his car was now garaged. He passed the policeman on duty by the gate and another by the stile. He glanced curiously at the oak tree out of which a piece had been cut – Ives was being very thorough. He and the young sergeant had been in the house for a long time on the previous day, prying here and probing there, without saying what they were looking for. Owen had shown a great deal of interest in several old knives which were in Peter's room.

Obviously the thing they were most anxious to find was arsenic.

Abel Buller greeted Dane with quiet friendliness; the innkeeper had already voiced his astonishment that Dane had succeeded where others had failed. He seemed genuinely glad. 'It does a woman like Miss Joyce no good to stick in one place all the time,' he said, and Dane had agreed. As he took out the car and drove up the hill, Dane thought a lot about Joyce. He had known her for so short a time, and yet she had come to matter to him enormously. In the house, he was always alert for the sound of her voice or her footsteps, he enjoyed the few occasions when they sat alone together; he believed he was helping her simply by *being* about. He was not doing much else, he thought ruefully; he had started the ball rolling, but it was out of his reach now.

Peter was not at the gate where Dane had arranged to pick him up, but Joyce was there, her hair blowing in the fresh southerly wind, a basket on her arm.

'Hallo,' she called out. 'No Peter?'

'We've plenty of time,' Dane said.

'You remind me of Marjorie when you say that,' Joyce said, 'she always had the patience of Job, too, but Marjorie – '

'Go on,' encouraged Dane.

'I really shouldn't,' said Joyce, 'although I suppose you ought to be warned about Marjorie and Roger. They're – dears.' She hesitated.

'I'm beginning to see,' remarked Dane, dryly.

She laughed. 'The truth is that Peter always finds Roger desperately boring. That's partly Peter's fault, of course. He could never stand amateur baritones.'

'Oh, ho! A songster!'

'And Marjorie plays,' added Joyce, in a rather gloomy voice. She leaned against the side of the car, looking thoughtfully down the hill. 'You might like Roger enormously.'

'I shall probably like Marjorie,' said Dane.

'Oh? Why?'

'I've become very fond of the rest of the family,' said Dane, and added quickly: 'Here's Peter.'

There was a faint flush on Joyce's cheeks. Then, waving to Peter, she turned and strode down the hill. Dane was watching her when Peter drew up.

'Nice girl, my sister,' Peter remarked dryly.

'There has to be one winner in every family,' said Dane. 'Ready?'

'That's why I'm here,' said Peter. 'Alec – '

'Yes.'

'Mind if I drive?'

'Not a bit,' said Dane.

As they approached Marston, it occurred to Dane to wonder why the inquest was being held in the town and not in the village. Was that another move by the police to ease the feelings of the family?

Peter turned off the main road, and pulled up outside a small wood and corrugated iron shed.

'Here's the place,' he said. 'That's Ive's car, isn't it? I suppose the newspapers will be represented in strength,' he added, slowly. 'You know, Alec, it's an odd show, but I'm becoming almost used to the idea!'

＊

The inquest took an hour and three quarters. The small 'courtroom' was crowded, and there were several reporters from London whom Dane recognised. The coroner, benign and benevolent-looking, conducted the proceedings with admirable restraint, and the verdict was as Ives had prophesied.

The only evidence called had been that of the police, of Marchmant, and of Dr, Livesey. This last was the doctor who had attended the dead man for 'influenza'. He had agreed that he might have been mistaken about the first symptoms, but pointed out that, if he had been, the patient would not have been likely to make a partial recovery after treatment for gastric influenza.

No evidence of vital importance was given and the whole

thing was over sooner than Dane expected.

Avoiding the few reporters who were waiting, Peter took the wheel as if Dane's car belonged to him. As he drove towards the High Street, he asked abruptly:

'Care to have some lunch in town?'

'Aren't Marjorie and Roger likely to have arrived?' asked Dane, surprised.

'Yes. I'd like a little while to adjust myself,' Peter said.

'It's a bit hard on Joyce.'

'Oh, have it your own way,' growled Peter. He changed gear as he turned into the High Street, crashed them badly, and only just missed a cyclist. Long before they reached the unrestricted area, the speedometer needle was showing fifty miles an hour. He sat staring ahead of him, chin thrust forward and mouth shut tightly. Hedges, trees, and telegraph poles flashed by. He took a sharp corner too fast, and the car skidded. Dane clutched the handle of his door in sudden alarm.

'Sorry,' grunted Peter. 'Haven't driven a car for six and a half years!'

'And you had to practise on me!'

'Your nerve's as good as anyone's,' said Peter. 'Do you know what right the police have to barge in and out of the house?'

'None, I should say,' said Dane, 'but if I were you I'd let them do whatever they liked.'

'Otherwise, what?'

'They'll wonder if you have an ulterior motive.'

'Nonsense! They can't suspect *me*,' said Peter sharply. 'I was still on the other side of the world when my father died.'

'They might think you've a good reason to want to help one of the other members of the family,' Dane pointed out. 'If you start being awkward with the police after the consideration they've shown you, you'll deserve all you get.'

Peter said nothing, and Dane hoped that his reasonable advice – sharpened by the speed of the car – would have some effect.

They reached the top of the first of the series of hills which led into Marrigay. At the foot was a large, old-fashioned, yellow car, with a square top and high chassis. The sight of it amused Dane.

To his surprise, Peter suddenly trod heavily on the accelerator, sending the Singer shooting forward.

'What's the hurry?' demanded Dane.

'There can't be *two* antiquated Austins on this road,' commented Peter, obscurely. 'Can you read the number?'

'AJ 34561 – might be 81.'

'So it *is* them,' breathed Peter. He began to smile, put his finger on the horn and kept it there, its strident note blaring out. He caught up with the yellow car and squeezed past it. The driver turned his head, in some alarm.

'*Da-da-da-daa*!' Peter brayed on the horn.

The driver and his companion suddenly relaxed, smiling broadly. The woman waved. Peter slowed down and both cars came to a standstill.

'Who is it?' demanded Dane, sharply.

'Eh? Oh, sorry. It's the Bells.' Peter got out of the car; the others were also getting out of the yellow monster. They met in the middle of the road, shaking hands warmly, and Paula suddenly pulled Peter towards her and kissed him roundly. She was a big, plump woman with something in her face of an amiable horse. Bell, much slimmer but as tall, had a melancholy expression relieved only a little by his smile.

'Alec!' called Peter, at last.

Dane climbed out of the car and approached.

'Paula and Arthur Bell – Alec Dane, who's come to the rescue of the benighted Marrigays,' said Peter, and there was a much brighter note in his voice. The encounter had undoubtedly cheered him up greatly, dispersing much of the depression brought on by the inquest. 'You've heard of the Bells, Alec, haven't you?'

'Of course,' said Dane, and reflected that they had been at Marrigay when the old man had first been taken ill.

'Isn't it *Great* Dane?' asked Bell, in a deep voice.

'You've got him,' said Peter.

Paula said in a husky, rather masculine voice: 'How are you, Mr Dane? And if you've done anything to make Peter see a glimmer of sense, congratulations.'

Peter said, laughing: 'Well what's brought you this time?'

'Roger telephoned us late last night and told us that something was the matter,' said Paula.

'We immediately rushed down,' continued Bell. 'A Marrigay in need, you know.' He paused. 'We'd better get on, hadn't we?'

'I'll go on, you three stay together,' suggested Dane. He got back into his car and drove ahead thoughtfully. He did not go above thirty-five miles an hour, but left the Austin a long way behind. He was glad the Bells had arrived; Joyce had given him some indication of their effect on Peter, but he had not thought it would be so marked.

Two policemen were digging in the road at the bottom of the hill, as he passed, he saw that they were digging part of the trench which had been refilled.

He wondered why that was considered necessary. Thinking of Marjorie and Roger, he drove his car courageously through the gates of Marrigay House. Now everyone who had been present on that first fateful week-end was gathered together. The sight of Lem, coming from the garage reminded him that only Marrigay, Lem and himself had not been there.

'Hallo, Lem,' said Dane, 'how are you this morning?'

'Well enough, sir,' said Lem, 'how is Mr Peter?'

'Bearing up,' said Dane, 'he met Mr and Mrs Bell on the road, and – '

'The *Bells*!' exclaimed Lem, 'are *they* here?'

And his face blanched.

CHAPTER XII

OLD PENGELLY

Lem made no attempt to explain why the mention of the Bells affected him so remarkably; and Dane did not think it the right moment to ask questions. He changed the subject quickly.

'I'd better put my car away, hadn't I?'

'I'll go and open the doors.'

Lem hurried off, and Dane knew that he was still troubled. He waited for a few minutes, then drove past the house towards the garage. He had been right when he had thought them to be converted stables. They were large and roomy, with space for four cars, in different stalls.

Having opened the door, Lem had gone off.

Dane heard the sound of voices.

Not far away, standing at the corner of the vegetable garden, Lem was talking to his father. Old Pengelly leaned heavily on a fork, and his bent back seemed weighed down by years. He looked, now, towards Dane, his wrinkled face brown as stained wood.

Dane strolled towards the two men.

Pengelly touched his forehead.

'Mornin', sir.'

'Good morning,' said Dane, cheerfully. 'Getting ready for spring planting?'

'That's so, sir,' said Pengelly. His eyes were dark and beady. 'Always plenty to do in a garden this size.'

'And you keep it wonderfully well,' said Dane.

'I keep it tidy,' said Pengelly, 'now Lem's here, happen I'll be able to do more, eh, Lem?'

'I daresay,' said Lem. He avoided Dane's eyes, and at that moment there came the sound of a car changing gear. The yellow car flashed between the trees.

Pengelly's eyes hardened.

'Is the dog fastened up safely?' asked Dane.

'It is, sir,' said Lem. 'I'm taking no chances now Mr Roger's come.'

'Oh?'

'That dog nearly got him down last time he was here,' said Lem. 'Maybe you've heard. Just went for Mr Roger – dogs do take a dislike, times.'

As he talked, Dane was thinking: 'He's talking for the sake of talking. I'd better get the other business off my chest now.' 'Lem,' he said aloud, 'what worried you when I told you that Mr and Mrs Bell were coming?'

'Why – why, nothing, sir.'

'Lem, how often have I told ye not to lie?' asked Pengelly, in his curiously rough voice. 'There was reason for him being strange, sir. Good reason.'

'Oh,' said Dane.

'Father – ' began Lem desperately.

''Tis my belief that if the Bells had not been here that week-end, the Master would be alive this day,' said old Pengelly flatly. 'That's the truth, sir.'

'It's a remarkable thing to say,' said Dane.

'Maybe it is.' Pengelly rubbed the back of his hand across his nose. 'Aye, maybe it is – but I believe it, *and* I'm not the only one as does.' He sniffed.

Lem said: 'Father, you shouldn't – '

Then he broke off at the sound of a falling spade, and stared towards the end of the garage.

Dane looked in the same direction. Detective Sergeant Owen stood there. Realising he had been seen, he came forward openly. He made no sign, however, that he had heard their conversation, but walked towards the door and disappeared into one of the stalls. Pengelly began to dig, as if nothing unusual had happened, and Lem turned scared eyes towards Dane.

'He shouldn't have said that, sir. He – he's only guessing.'

'Perhaps it's as well that we know what he thinks,' said

Dane, reassuringly. 'I shouldn't worry too much, Lem.'

He nodded and smiled, and walked towards the house, glancing into the stall where Owen was handling the tools which Uncle Nicholas had used when he went out on his 'excavations'. Owen appeared to be immersed in his thoughts, and Dane, much worried, continued on his way towards the house.

Pengelly must have some reason for thinking as he did.

Well, the police would soon be asking questions. And he suspected that very soon they would virtually take possession of the house. It was the right thing, they *had* to get rid of this shadow which was hanging over them.

All the others, except Mrs Marrigay, were in the drawing-room. Dane heard the sound of voices as he entered the porch. A voice which he did not recognise came clearly, followed by a sharp question from Peter.

'Why the blazes didn't you tell us before? If he's suffering from arsenical poisoning, it might – ' he broke off.

'End of Chapter One,' came Bell's deep voice. 'Dry up, Peter. You don't know what it might mean. Guessing's no good. Tell the police all you know, and let them work it out.'

'But if someone poisoned Uncle Nicholas – '

'Could have been an accident,' said Roger.

Dane could imagine the withering glance which Peter sent him.

'Oh, yes – an accident. People do go about shovelling arsenic into their mouths instead of caster sugar!'

'Now, old chap, I'm *not* going to get annoyed,' declared Roger, 'I've come down to try and help out, you know, and Marjorie was anxious to be here. I'm not going to start quarrelling. How's luncheon, Joyce? We're starving.'

Dane allowed a moment or two to pass before he went into the room. Roger and Marjorie were duly introduced by Joyce, and the atmosphere became much more normal. Even Peter, who told him what had happened to Uncle Nicholas, kept calm during the narration.

'Now we know that the murderer is still around and about,' Peter said. 'Nice thought, isn't it?'

'Don't!' said Marjorie, sharply.

'My dear sis, we've got to be practical – ask Dane.'

'A spot of common sense never did anyone any harm,' remarked Bell.

'Let us, then, face up to the worst. And the worst is that my father was murdered, that someone has now had a crack at Uncle Nicholas, and we don't know who will be the next.'

'I can't – I can't believe it!' muttered Marjorie.

'Now, Jorrie!' Roger rested a huge hand on his wife's shoulder. 'You mustn't let it upset you, it will all work out.'

'But *why* should it happen?' cried Marjorie.

Peter looked at her, and Roger, catching the exasperation in the glance, turned dark with anger.

'*Why*? That's the turning point of the whole business. Why should anyone kill anyone? Who stands to gain?' Peter went on wildly, but no one answered, and Bell looked a little reproving. 'Now that I've really faced up to it, none of you like the idea. But the question's got to be asked, hasn't it, Alec?'

'Obviously,' said Dane. 'Now that Uncle Nicholas has been given this stuff, the police will have every right to come and make as much of a nuisance as they want. And if a spot of advice will help – keep *nothing* back.'

'Hear, hear,' said Bell.

'Maybe we've nothing to keep back,' said Peter. 'Maybe we've a lot.' He laughed. 'The police aren't here, the door can be locked – supposing we now take our hair down.'

'Peter!' exclaimed Joyce.

'Well, why not?' asked Peter.

The atmosphere grew tense again. Peter knew something, and – with the possible exception of Marjorie – so did the others. Bell looked uncomfortable, and Paula smiled rather tautly.

'Is this the right moment?' asked Bell.

'It's as good as any,' said Peter shortly. 'It's time we faced it – your own words. Joyce and I had a jolly good reason for murder, we inherited a large sum. Tinker Bell, you owed the old man ten thousand quid. He was pressing for it, wasn't he? My informant is old Pengelly, who heard you quarrelling with him the day before you left. And Marjorie inherited a packet, while Roger was greatly in debt to the old man, who was also hoping for a little on account. He didn't like to think Marjorie had married a wastrel.'

Joyce said tensely: 'I think you ought to be kicked, Peter.'

'Oh, not I,' said Peter, 'but whoever killed Father ought to be hanged. I don't take a very good view of it, you know.' His voice was silky, but it was obvious that he was restraining himself with a great effort from bursting out in great fury. 'Here you are, all nice and smug, all rushing down to find out what the trouble's about – as if you didn't know! – all anxious that we should tell the police about everything, except any little skeletons lurking in your own personal cupboards!' He swung round on Dane. 'Well? Have I done the right thing?'

Everyone stared at Dane.

It was not easy to keep calm and to make his voice sound casual, but he said quietly:

'You know, Peter, you're making mountains out of molehills. Take any family you like, and you'll find just as many *possible* motives for murder. You're right about one thing, though, real trouble always comes when the skeletons are kept hidden. The police have a way of digging such things up. They'll probably find a lot of other motives, too.'

Peter stared at him arrogantly.

'And I think you've forgotten some other things,' Dane went on. 'The attack on Joyce, and the attack on you. What's the motive for them?' He smiled at Marjorie. 'If your reasoning's right, that leaves only Mr and Mrs Hurst, who presumably will inherit from you. Not that I know much about that situation,' he added, 'and we're rather talking without the book – but you see how absurd it is to take anything for granted or to assume that the obvious is the right solution, don't you? And – *why* should anyone try to murder Uncle Nicholas?'

No one attempted to answer that.

'Is he rich?' asked Dane.

'He – he had only a small income,' said Joyce in a low voice.

'I can tell you why he was probably poisoned,' said Peter. 'He knew who –'

'Oh, dry up,' said Bell, sharply. 'You've been turning these things over in your mind until they've become obsessions. Tell everything to the police and leave it to them.'

'Even about your debt?'

'Everything.'

'And your quarrel with my father?'

'*Everything*,' repeated Bell. 'It may interest you to know that before I left I'd made amicable arrangements with your father. He was on edge when we quarrelled – sickening for the flu – and if it hadn't been for that, there would have been no quarrel at all.'

'So you do admit a quarrel,' said Peter.

'It was no secret. You knew, Joyce, didn't you?' asked Bell.

'I – I heard a little of it,' said Joyce.

There was a lull in the discussion, and Dane said:

'Just one other thing.' The luncheon gong began to boom out as he began to speak. 'You were fired at, Peter – can you guess why anyone had a pot-shot at you?'

Peter said: 'Yes, I can.'

'Well, why?'

'Peter!' cried Joyce.

Peter said in a quiet and deadly voice: 'You know, I've been against bringing anything up before. I thought it best to let things slide. I didn't want to face up to it – how right you were, Dane! But I can see the error of my ways, now. Yes, I can tell you why I was shot at. Because most of the money went to Mother. Because if Joyce and I die, everything she has will be left to –'

Roger took two great strides across the room. Peter stood up to him, but a terrific blow across the face knocked him down. Before he could recover, Roger took him by the coat lapels and shook him with increasing anger. The big man's face was dark with rage and his eyes were glittering. He shook Peter until his teeth chattered and his head bobbed to and fro, oblivious of Dane and Bell, who tried to drag him away.

'Roger!' roared Bell.

'And if I hear another squeak like that out of you, you swine, I'll smash you to bits!' said Roger in a tense, even voice.

He flung Peter into a chair.

During the silence which followed, no one moved. Then a voice came from the window:

'Really, gentlemen!'

Folly stood there, looking, in calm ambiguity, at the scene.

CHAPTER XIII

FOLLY'S DELIGHT

'Really, gentlemen,' repeated Folly.

Now he was in the room, with the door open behind him.

'Why this violence?' he demanded.

'Who the hell are you?' growled Peter.

'My name is Folly, Folly of New Scotland Yard, and I came to speak to you – you *are* Colonel Marrigay, I believe. I did not expect – '

'You'll get a lot of things you don't expect here,' said Peter.

'That I can understand,' said Folly, his glance sweeping over Roger. 'And I may even suggest that you may find that some things are not quite what *you* expect.'

Roger jerked his head up.

'Before you utter the heavy speech of denunciation which I see you are preparing to give me,' said Folly smoothly, 'may

I remind you that you have just committed common assault and, in my hearing, threatened to murder Colonel Marrigay.'

Roger gasped.

'Oh, no!' gasped Marjorie, 'no, he – '

'He lost his temper, Mrs Hurst, and I hope that he will realise that it is unwise for a man of his great physical strength to lose his self-control also.'

Peter shot a quick, cold glance at Roger.

'What do you want to ask me, Folly?'

'I should like a few words with you in private.'

'You've chosen a bad time for it.'

'Why is that?'

'Luncheon's just ready,' said Peter. 'Won't it do afterwards?'

Folly swayed to and fro on his feet, and then inclined his massive head.

'Very well. It is now one forty-five. May I see you at two-thirty?'

He went into the hall. The others moved after him, filled with a single determination to restore some semblance of normality. Shaken by the exhibition of violence, Dane, looking speculatively at Roger, realised that his calm manner and general good nature covered a fierce and uncontrollable temper.

It was going to be a pretty grim luncheon, reflected Dane, as he followed the hostile group, but before they reached the dining-room, Dane heard his name called. Looking round, he saw Owen standing in the doorway.

'Can you spare a moment, Mr Dane?' asked Owen.

'Yes.' Dane, glad that he could leave the others if only for a few minutes, hurried towards him.

'Superintendent Folly would like a word with you,' said Owen.

Folly and Ives were standing just outside the drawing-room window. Folly had one hand in his pocket, and was listening earnestly to what Ives was saying.

As Dane drew nearer, Folly looked round, and his face brightened.

'Why, Dane, how good of you to neglect your lunch for me! I rather wanted a word with you – I heard much of what was said, of course. The question I want to ask is this: is *every* person who was at the house that fateful week-end here now?'

'As far as I know, yes,' said Dane.

'Oh, there's one other thing,' Folly added, casually. 'That man from the *Sunday World*. Have you seen him again?'

'No.'

'Curious,' said Folly, 'very curious. The description you've given me is fairly accurate, isn't it?'

'As accurate as I can make it,' Dane said. 'But remember I only saw him in a poor light.'

'Of course,' said Folly, 'of course. Many thanks!'

Dane returned to the dining-room. Joyce and Paula were doing their best to behave naturally, but between Peter and Roger there was obvious enmity.

Dane found himself wondering whether a guilty conscience had made Roger lose his temper.

Folly stood and watched Dane enter the house, then beamed at Ives. Ives could see little to be so delighted about, and said so.

'Oh, my dear fellow, *think*!' exhorted Folly. 'We couldn't have arrived at a more opportune moment, and that young sergeant of yours was very wise to warn us that there was a quarrel. But for him we should have driven up the drive, and they would have stopped. As it is, we've heard a great deal that *might* be helpful.'

'We heard Peter Marrigay make a wild accusation and get what was coming to him,' said Ives.

'Yes, that's one construction. And you won't miss the obvious possibility that Roger Hurst had some powerful reason for going berserk. What *is* the financial set-up here, do you know?'

'I think Peter Marrigay was right when he said that Mrs Marrigay inherited the bulk of the money, although the others came off pretty well.'

'Was old Marrigay wealthy?'

'According to popular opinion, yes.'

'Oh,' Folly blinked. 'We aren't very concerned with popular opinion, are we? Wasn't his will published?'

'I didn't see it.'

'We'll have to check at Somerset House,' said Folly. He rounded his voice. 'Well, here's an interesting situation. Young Owen told us what Pengelly said to Dane, the conversation in the room confirmed it, and now we know that Roger Hurst is hard up, and inclined to be a spendthrift. What is more, to have Roger and Peter at daggers drawn, and everyone nicely worked up – I think we ought to be very satisfied, Ives.'

'Being worked up is their state of normality,' commented Ives sourly.

'Not quite like this,' said Folly. 'You know, old fellow, you're just a *little* annoyed because I told Dane that we overheard a great deal, aren't you?'

'Frankly, yes,' said Ives.

'But you shouldn't – '

'Surely it would have been better not to let them know.'

'Oh, my dear chap, certainly not. Dane will tell them – or tell some of them, and it will be common knowledge before the day is out. When it comes to questioning them, they will be very nervous.'

Ives said obstinately, 'I never trust nervous witnesses.'

'Ah, but I am inclined to ignore precepts when anything unusual occurs,' purred Folly. 'Frankly, I'm delighted.'

He paused when Owen came round the corner, smiling broadly.

'Exactly what are you so happy about?' inquired Folly.

Owen rubbed his hands together.

'Well, Roger Hurst went off the deep end; that means that there must have been something in – '

'Sergeant! Really! You mustn't jump to foolish conclusions. To form any opinion of the case at this early stage is not only unwise, it is ridiculous.' He glared at the crestfallen Owen. 'We are not yet in possession of the facts. We know some possible motives, but there may be others. And if, as you seem to, you mark Roger as the most likely suspect, how do you explain the poisoning of his Uncle Nicholas?'

Owen did not answer.

'Precisely – you can't,' said Folly. 'We have checked up on Nicholas Lee. He begged a lift to Marston and caught the eleven-twenty train to London. He spent the night at his club, left there at nine o'clock yesterday morning – apparently in good health – and went to the Hursts, and by the time he reached there he was ill. I've already told you – we have evidence of a ticket-collector that he looked so ill that the man asked him to stay in the waiting-room to rest, but Nicholas Lee insisted on going to the Hurst's house. Now – *why?* That is another question we have to ask ourselves. We can, if we like, imagine some of the circumstances which compelled the man to leave Marrigay House. The exhumation – the presence of the police – alarm – a hurried jaunt to see the Hursts. Interesting.'

'But that supports *my* theory!' exclaimed Owen.

'Indeed?' Folly stepped to the garden seat, and sat down. 'Explain,' he said, coldly.

'If Nicholas Lee knew that Hurst was involved, he would rush off to warn him *if* – '

'Ah. If. I am glad you admit that there is a matter for conjecture,' said Folly, acidly. 'You are now assuming that Nicholas Lee and Roger Hurst were dually involved. That Lee hurried to warn the arch-criminal, whose wife poisoned Lee as soon as he arrived, believing he would die and never be able to tell the truth. You ignore the ticket-collector's evidence.'

Owen hesitated. 'Well – '

'Oh, come,' said Folly, 'you disappoint me. If – I repeat *if* – anything like that were true, would Lee have stayed at his club? Would he not have gone straight to the Hursts' house, and not spent a night deliberating?'

'I suppose he might have done,' conceded Owen.

'Thank you,' said Folly, 'for that small grain of sagacity. I can see you coming a nasty cropper one of these days if you

107

jump to conclusions. Don't spoil good work. We are not at the stage of guessing, we are gathering information. A remarkable amount has been gathered, but we need more. Details of the will. The financial position of all the people concerned. The reason – which is probably the most important point – why the Marrigays shut themselves in this house until Dane arrived. Why they suddenly opened up the grounds. When we have that information together with all the other evidence, we shall be able to start making guesses. But while we have no justification yet for speculating on the identity of the murderer, we have every justification for speculating on the possibility of further victims. And for the time being we must assume that Mrs Marrigay is in some danger, since she inherited.'

'I've wondered about that,' said Ives.

'So we had better have a man outside her window by day and by night,' said Folly. 'I intend to warn Marrigay about the position and thus get his agreement to our stationing a man in the house. I thought that Owen might be the most likely man, but – '

Owen's expression was so dismayed that Folly laughed.

'All right,' he said. 'Go home and get some rest, sergeant, and be here for duty at six o'clock tonight. If that's all right with you, Inspector?'

Ives nodded.

Folly heaved himself up.

'Promising young man with an all but fatal tendency towards guessing,' he said, 'no doubt you're doing everything you can to eradicate it. You know, Ives, I'm beginning to feel distinctly chilly.'

Ives said: 'Do you think Marrigay will let us put a man in the house?'

'I do. And we won't worry about other eventualities until they are upon us,' said Folly. 'And now I'd very much like to have a look at the trench in the road. Where are Lee's tools?'

'The important ones are down at the gate. Shall we walk?'

'Walk? Good gracious me, no! I *never* walk,' said Folly, 'and I'm tired of standing out here in the cold.'

He squeezed into his car, took the wheel, crashing his gears noisily. Turning over-widely, he caught sight of someone at a first floor window. He looked up.

Mrs Marrigay did not appear to know that she was observed. She was standing absolutely still, staring stonily down at them.

As the car moved off, Folly said:

'I think *she* could tell us a thing or two, you know. She isn't going to be easy to interrogate, of course, she will pretend that she's *non compos mentis*, from what you tell me. However, we have tackled more recalcitrant witnesses than old ladies imbued with family pride and inborn stubbornness.'

They collected three digging tools from a policeman guarding them at the gate, and drove down the hill. One policeman was still by the trench, part of which was opened up. Folly squeezed himself out of the car with some difficulty, and turned over a little of the dry, sandy gravel. The actual cut in the road was very obvious – it had been filled in hurriedly and somewhat carelessly.

Ives selected a short-handled pick.

'I wonder why this has been so carefully cleaned, while the rest of the tools are caked with mud and clay,' he remarked as he drove it into the surface layer. It made a distinctive mark. Then he pointed to a similar mark on the side of the hole.

'These were the tools all right,' he said. 'And they are always kept in the garage. Anyone at the house could have got at them.'

'*Or* anyone from outside,' Folly remarked. 'Have you asked to be shown all the knives that there are about the place?' he added, 'and found out if any of the inmates keep revolvers?'

'Not yet, but Owen's had a good look round.'

'How about the bullet hole in the tree?' asked Folly.

'The piece of tree is being expertly examined, and I've photographed the hole,' said Ives. 'We haven't a really good ballistics man nearer than Salisbury,' he added, 'and I

109

thought you might get that examined at the Yard.'

'I will,' promised Folly.

'We'd better get back,' said Ives.

'I don't think it will matter if we keep them waiting for a little while,' mused Folly. 'I've been intending to have a word with the innkeeper – I think this is the moment. We *will* walk to the inn,' he added, with the air of a martyr.

'But why?' asked Ives.

'Eh? Well, I'm very interested in the man who broke into the grounds. *Very* interested,' remarked Folly airily. 'I've had report from the editor of the *Sunday World*. No official representative has been sent here recently.'

As they reached the inn, Abel Buller appeared in the doorway, smoothing down his green baize apron. Buller was quiet, slow and deliberate in his response to Folly's oblique approach, and it was soon made clear that he had, in fact, definitely seen the man with the hooked nose.

'Has he been here often?' asked Folly.

'Times, for a drink,' answered Buller.

'Did he tell you his business?'

'No, sir.'

'Do you know what he did while he was here?' asked Folly.

'No concern of mine,' Buller remarked, 'but I think he was here the day Miss Marrigay came off her bike.'

'I *see*,' said Folly. 'Did you mention that to the village constable?'

'I couldn't be sure,' Buller said evasively.

'Hmm. When did you last see the man, Mr Buller?'

'He was here in the morning – off just before the other gentleman – '

'I see. Was the stranger back that night?' asked Folly.

Buller shook his head.

'If you should see him again, please inform Inspector Ives at once,' said Folly. 'And thank you very much, Mr Buller!'

He was silent as they returned to the car, and sat at the wheel for some minutes, looking straight ahead. Now and again he sighed. At last he turned to Ives and gave a quick, puckish smile.

'That miscalled reporter is important, you know.'

'Well, you've put a call out for news of him, haven't you?'

'Oh, yes. But I wonder if he will be found. There are curious factors in connection with him,' Folly added. 'If he often comes here, the Marrigays probably knew he was a danger. I don't think Peter Marrigay was very frank with Dane over him. Now he's gone – and with his going, just *after* his last known appearance here, Marrigay opened up the house. It *is* curious, isn't it? One might imagine, perhaps, that he was paid off. Well, we must get on!'

It was nearly a quarter to three when they returned to the Marrigays. The family and their friends were just leaving the dining-room.

Peter raised no objection to Owen being stationed in the house that night; but even Folly could not tell whether he was seriously worried by the suggestion that there was danger for Mrs Marrigay.

Dane wished that Roger and Marjorie were anywhere but at the house.

Nothing anyone could do had even temporarily healed the breach between Peter and Roger.

Dane was puzzled because the police had not questioned any of them – he had expected questioning to start with Peter, and was surprised that Folly had merely informed him what he wanted done.

Early in the evening, Joyce telephoned the hospital to inquire about Uncle Nicholas, and was told he was 'fairly comfortable'.

No one showed any inclination to discuss the mystery of his illness; Peter had put paid to all reasonable discussion. In Dane's opinion, the Bells and the Hursts would return to London on Sunday evening.

Little was said about Mrs Marrigay, who remained in her room. She had not, after all, come down to a meal. According to Joyce, she was outwardly unaffected by the presence of the police.

Marjorie, complaining of a severe headache, went to bed

111

just after nine o'clock, and Roger soon followed. The Bells tried to persuade Peter to talk about his war experiences, without much success. They went to bed at ten, and Peter retired to his study alone. Joyce and Dane were left in the drawing-room, beside the dying embers of the fire.

Joyce said slowly:

'Things haven't really improved, Alec, have they?'

Dane sought vainly for something encouraging to say.

'It's all so puzzling,' Joyce went on. 'And the behaviour of the police doesn't seem to make sense. They've looked through the medicine chest and the kitchen cupboards, taken the tools out of the garage, but that's all. They seem to be waiting for something to happen.'

'Folly's a cagey bird,' said Dane. 'Joyce, do you wish I hadn't started all this?'

Impulsively, she put her hand on his.

'No, it had to come sooner or later. It's just that – I can't make anyone out. Peter's behaviour – Roger's – even Tinker Bell's. I did know about his quarrel with Father, but I didn't know what it was over. Now that we know that Father was murdered, it puts everything in a different, and rather horrible, light.'

When they went upstairs soon afterwards, there was a light in Peter's study.

Detective Sergeant Owen was quite determined that he would make no mistake that night. He had already suffered enough from the tongue of the great Folly, who had so unfairly lured Owen on to making a rash statement, and then demolished it in one brilliant exposition.

Owen was determined *that* would not happen again!

Peter Marrigay was the last to go to bed. He came up the stairs, looking, thought Owen, like an earthbound eagle – the phrase pleased the sergeant – and, ignoring Owen, he tapped on his mother's door and called 'good night'. There was no answer.

Owen watched him disappear into his room.

A clock struck twelve.

112

There was a bright light on the landing, but no lights on in the bedrooms. A man was snoring – Roger Hurst, he decided after a moment's reflection, and was angry with himself for having to pause, Folly would expect him to reel off the names of the people in each room.

He heard a man walking round outside the house; that would be P.C. Adams, who was on night duty, and none too pleased about it.

Owen sat down, and lit a cigarette.

He had smoked it half-way through, when he took it from his lips and looked at it. There was a smell of burning; if it came from the cigarette, he'd take the whole packet back tomorrow!

No, it was somewhere else.

He looked at his clothes and the carpet; they were all right; but there *was* burning, somewhere near. He jumped up. As he did so, he saw smoke curling from under the bottom of Mrs Marrigay's door.

CHAPTER XIV

IN THE MOONLIGHT

Through a mist of sleep, Dane heard a confusion of sounds. People were shouting, someone was banging on a door, there were heavy thuds. At first he thought it was a violent and confused dream, and then he recognised Peter's voice.

'What the devil!' Peter exclaimed.

Dane flung back the bedclothes and jumped out of bed. He pulled the door open, shivering in a draught which cut along the passage. On the landing Peter was struggling to put on a dressing-gown and talking in a loud voice to Owen, who was battering on Mrs Marrigay's door with a chair.

'Get an axe!' roared Owen, 'don't stand there doing

113

nothing, get an axe!'

A tall, slim pink-clad figure passed Dane.

'All right, I'll get it,' cried Joyce, and fled down the stairs in a headlong rush.

'What's up?'

This was Roger, who came striding along the passage; and by now the smell of burning was so strong that no one could mistake it.

'*Fire!*' shouted Adams, from outside. '*Fire!*'

Dane called to Roger.

'Come and put your shoulder to the door, will you? We must get it down.'

There was a sound now of crackling and hissing which could not be mistaken. But no cry, no indication that Mrs Marrigay was aware of the danger. Roger launched himself at the door, which creaked, but stood firm.

'You'll never get it down that way,' Peter muttered. 'Come on, Alec. Outside. The window.'

He rushed towards the stairs.

Dane stayed behind.

'Let's all have a try together,' he suggested.

His calmness and Roger's helped to steady Owen. But there was no room for the three of them to assault the door at once, and Owen, the heavier of the two, pushed Dane aside. With Roger, he hurled himself again and again at the wood, but though it seemed to give a little, it did not yield.

The smoke was becoming thicker, and the smell was strong. Grey eddies curled from the bottom of the door. Dane wondered if he should go after Peter. But it would take some time to get a ladder to the window, and Joyce would soon be back with the axe. Odd thoughts flashed through his mind. Why was the door still locked? Why didn't Mrs Marrigay call out? How had this thing happened, with Owen inside and the policeman outside? What had gone wrong?

He saw Paula and Bell coming along the passage.

'Where's Joyce?' Paula demanded.

'Gone downstairs, for – '

There was no need to finish the sentence, for Joyce came

running up the stairs, her hair flying, a wood-chopper in her hand. Roger, moving swiftly, took it from her, then swung round and began to belabour the panel nearest the lock.

'I'll go to Marjorie,' Paula said. She turned round, and Dane heard her say: 'Oh, Pengelly.'

The old gardener, Lem, and his wife, were standing behind her. Pengelly was muttering to himself, and between the bangs on the door Dane caught the words: 'I knew it, I knew it.'

'Now we won't be long,' Roger said.

The panel gave suddenly, and he pushed his hand through, fumbling for the lock. Smoke eddied through the hole. He backed away, coughing helplessly, and Dane jumped forward. He could feel the knob under his fingers – it was no ordinary fixture, and even then he wondered at the old lady having such a lock fixed to her door.

The door opened at last.

He pushed forward, and thick smoke billowed into the passage. It caught his throat but he rushed into the room. Coughing painfully, he reached the bed. Someone pushed him aside, someone else dragged him out of the room.

Out of the murk Roger came staggering, with Mrs Marrigay in his arms. Her hair had caught fire and her night-dress was smouldering. She was unconscious. Owen rushed forward with a blanket, wrapping it round her head and shoulders. Through all the turmoil, like an insistent and undying obbligato, ran old Pengelly's repetitive muttering. He was looking at Tinker Bell with a hard and accusing stare.

Folly's car, with Ives at the wheel, raced along the road to Marrigay, its headlights carving a great beam of white light in the darkness. Telegraph poles and wires, hedges and trees, stood out in sharp relief and then fell behind, only to be replaced by others. Now and again a rabbit crossed the road, and once a fox slunk swiftly in front of them. They roared up hill and down, and Folly, sitting at the back, held grimly on to the arm-rests and stared at Ives's rigid head and shoulders.

'Where's the nearest fire station?' Folly asked.

'Marston,' said Ives. 'An engine started out before we did.'

'Hmm.'

Down the hill and then up again – and as they neared the gates of the house, a policeman appeared in the head-lights. He jumped to one side. Ives swung the wheel over, then turned into the drive. Now they could see the yellow flames coming from a window and through the gaps in the trees people gathered outside the house. A stream of water was being played on the roof, steel-helmeted firemen directing it.

Ives brought the car to a screaming standstill, and Folly got out, caught his coat on the handle, cursed, and pulled himself free. Ives was out seconds before him.

Now that he was here, calm descended upon Folly. He stood watching, assessing the situation. The fire seemed to be confined to one room on the first floor. Water from two hoses was pouring into a window above the room where the flames seemed to have the firmest hold.

'I think we will go inside,' said Folly quietly.

As they entered the hall, Owen was coming downstairs, with Peter Marrigay. Owen's hair was singed and his face was blacked with smoke; Marrigay looked more like a ruffled bird of prey than ever.

'Well?' breathed Folly.

'My mother is dead,' said Marrigay, abruptly; and went towards the kitchen.

'Is Marchmant here?' Ives asked, heavily.

'He is with her now, sir,' said Owen.

He looked on the verge of despair. Ives felt sorry for him, and looked at Folly; Folly would have no time for sentiment, for softness.

'My dear fellow,' said Folly in his gentlest voice, 'you really mustn't let it get you down like this. No one in the world will blame you.'

'I blame myself,' muttered Owen.

'Now come along – let's go in here.' Folly pushed open the drawing-room door, but paused on the threshold. 'You say that the doctor is with Mrs Marrigay – *is* she dead?'

'Yes.'

'And there's nothing we can do for the moment?'

'I – I don't think so.'

'Then come along in here,' said Folly.

Ives looked at him with new respect and greater understanding; something of the burden seemed to have been
lifted from Owen's shoulders.

'We needn't keep you long, and you must have those
burns attended to,' said Folly. 'just tell us briefly what
happened.'

Owen obeyed.

He had smelt the burning only a moment before he had
seen the smoke. It had been a shocking half-hour. After the
big fellow, Hurst, had taken Mrs Marrigay into the next
room, they had realised that the old lady was dead. It
wouldn't have been so bad, Owen said, if Mrs Hurst hadn't
come on the scene. All the others seemed to control themselves, but she went absolutely berserk.

'Berserk?' echoed Folly.

'Well, sir, it made her violent. Hurst had to carry her
forcibly to her room. I suppose it was the shock.'

'Possibly,' said Folly. 'Please go on.'

'There isn't much more to say, sir,' said Owen. 'I telephoned you the moment the old lady was safely out of her
room, and then I helped to subdue the fire. It's done a lot of
damage, but the room isn't destroyed – not gutted, I mean.
Dane, Marrigay – *all* of them – helped me. There were a
couple of fire-extinguishers, and we ran a hose-pipe from
the bathroom. I wanted to try to preserve something – to help
us find the cause of it.'

'In the circumstances, that was admirable presence of
mind,' said Folly. 'Just one other matter – of great importance. What was the general behaviour of the men like when
the discovery was first made?'

'First-rate,' said Owen, ungrudgingly.

'*All* of them?'

'Yes, they all kept their heads. Marrigay went outside,
and was getting in through the window when Dane went in

117

through the door. Hurst broke the door down – oh, they did very well.'

'What about Bell?'

'There wasn't much he could do, until they'd got her out,' said Owen. 'Then he kind of took over, sir.'

As he spoke, Peter appeared in the doorway, carrying logs and kindling wood – just as he had once done in his study. He nodded, without speaking, and went down on his knees and lit the fire.

Folly said quietly:

'That is burning up very quickly, Colonel Marrigay.'

'You object?' asked Peter, with exaggerated courtesy.

'Not at all. My interest is due to curiosity as to the method,' said Folly. 'I am particularly concerned, at the moment, with conflagration.'

Peter said in a voice completely devoid of expression:

'We keep kindling wood soaking in paraffin and logs drying out in the boiler house. Both for the purpose of lighting fires.'

'Of course,' said Folly. 'Have you any idea how the one upstairs started?'

'I *thought* – forgive me if I am wrong – that that was one of the problems you were here to solve.'

Folly said quietly:

'Colonel Marrigay, we are all extremely sorry about your loss. But there is no reason why you should be vindictive. You understand, I am sure, that we have to find out quickly whether this fire was accidental or whether it was started deliberately.'

'*What's* that?' gasped Joyce.

She stood in the doorway, Hurst and Bell and Dane, tired, unhappy and dishevelled, grouped round her.

'What's what?' asked Bell.

Joyce closed her eyes; Roger took the tea-tray she was holding, and Dane put his arm about her, as she swayed.

'Folly's just made the suggestion, that this might have been arson,' said Peter, who was the only one who appeared not to be burned at all. 'I don't think that need shock us – we

118

know it's possible. Now we're all together, I'd like to get one thing clear.' He looked at Folly.

'Please proceed,' murmured Folly.

'The house is at your disposal,' Peter said, in harsh, clipped tones. 'Go where you like, take what you like, ask any one of us anything you like – but for God's sake get this solved!'

'We will,' Folly said, in exactly the right tone of heartiness, 'indeed we will, and I'm very glad indeed to hear you make that statement, Colonel Marrigay. For a start, the inspector and I will go upstairs to the bedroom. You may be sure we shall endeavour to ease this terrible situation as much as we can for all of you.'

He swept from the room, Ives and Owen closing in behind him. Upstairs, they found Mrs Marrigay, lying on the bed, covered with a sheet. Marchmant, the police-surgeon, was sitting beside her. He glanced up with a grim smile as they entered.

'You've taken your time,' he remarked.

'We came as quickly as we could,' said Folly, testily. 'How did she die?'

'Probably suffocation, possibly shock,' said Marchmant.

Folly said: 'How quickly can you do the post-mortem? I want to make sure that she did die of one of these two causes, and that she wasn't poisoned.'

Marchmant said: 'What makes you think she might have been?'

'Oh, my dear fellow – poison has been used so often in this case, and it is just possible that she was murdered and that the murderer tried to hide his method by starting the fire. Alternatively, of course, the fire *may* have been the means of murder.' He was swaying to and fro, pressing the tips of his plump, pale hands together.

'I'll look at her first thing in the morning,' promised Marchmant.

'Thanks. Meanwhile, we'll have to get her away from here,' said Folly. 'Any impressions of the family to give us?'

'They've all taken it well,' said Marchmant, 'except

119

Marjorie Hurst, and I suppose it isn't surprising in the circumstances.'

'I wish I could be sure that woman isn't taking advantage of her condition,' said Folly, in a piping voice. 'However, we shall find out in due course. Please arrange for the ambulance, Ives, and then join me in the room next door.'

The smell of burning, which was everywhere in the house, was much stronger in Mrs Marrigay's room. The windows were broken, gaping holes appeared at every pane. The bed and bedclothes were soaked with water, and the head of the bed was only a charred, wet mess. Oddly enough a table which lay on its side close by with a broken saucer near it was hardly burned at all.

Trinkets and oddments on the dressing-table, which was in a corner near the window, had not been touched, although they were blackened with soot.

As Folly and Ives stood looking round, Owen came hurrying into the room.

'There's one thing perhaps I ought to mention, sir,' said Owen. 'Pengelly seemed to nourish heavy suspicions against Bell.'

'Hmm, yes,' commented Folly. 'He has shown some animosity towards Bell before. We must try to discover the reason for that. All right, thank you, sergeant.'

As Owen went out, Folly stood by the end of the bed, looking round, and suddenly something in the corner caught his attention. He went towards it, bent down, and picked it up. Ives saw a nearly shapeless lump of wax in his hand – with a tiny, blackened wick.

Folly smiled at the wax.

'Well, well,' he said, 'now we *can* be fairly sure that it was arson – unless Mrs Marrigay smoked. Did she?' he added, sharply.

CHAPTER XV

ARSON

It was discovered by Ives that Mrs Marrigay did not smoke.

'On the whole, I think I'm glad,' said Folly, still holding the night-light in his fingers. 'And that tells us a lot, Ives, doesn't it? Here is a used night-light – see the blackened wick – which was on that table by the side of the bed. When the table fell, the night-light rolled across the floor and finished up in the corner. The heat made it soft and it began to melt slowly. If Mrs Marrigay had dropped off to sleep and the bedclothes had caught in this, the wax would almost certainly have melted entirely. The table it was standing on isn't touched by fire, except a little at the feet. The saucer isn't scorched at all, and the electric lights are all in order, there's no question of a fuse. The fire started near the head of the bed, that's quite obvious, and there are no electric points or cable near it. I'm right, aren't I?'

'Yes,' said Ives, his eyes showing his admiration for that quick assessment of the situation, 'but all you've shown is what *didn't* start it. It's possible that she lit a match and dropped it on the bed – '

'If she dropped a match like that she would have cried out in sudden alarm, and Owen would have heard her,' said Folly.

'Ah – yes,' said Ives.

'So there is no obvious way in which the fire started,' said Folly. He was talking as much to himself as to Ives, and suddenly turned and looked at the door. Round it was nailed a rubber draught excluder. '*That's* why the smell and the smoke were such a long time making themselves obvious,' remarked Folly, happy in his flow of explanation. 'Owen would have noticed it a long while before but for that. You

121

know, Ives, I think we can say that this was arson, that it was spontaneous combustion, that it started when she was asleep, and we may well find that she died of suffocation. I wonder if she took sleeping tablets?'

'She did,' said Ives, 'but not regularly.'

'That doesn't matter! Her friends and family knew she took them,' Folly declared. 'It would be fairly easy to make sure that she had some tonight. Then when the smoke came from the fire, she would breathe it in and perhaps die of suffocation without waking up. We shall be able to check all these things, of course, but you'll grant me that's possible.'

Ives nodded.

'So now we want to find out how the fire was started,' said Folly. 'There are several ways of starting a fire and being a long way away from the scene when it starts. Move a little to one side, will you?'

Ives obeyed, and Folly went on to his hands and knees and peered beneath the bed.

'Ah!' he exclaimed. 'Ives, we're lucky!'

He lifted with infinite care a minute piece of broken glass.

'Have a look underneath,' he invited.

They knelt down together.

In spite of the mess of sagging springs and burnt wool, it was possible to see other fragments of broken glass, including one or two large pieces.

Folly straightened up, holding the glass in his sooty hand, and frowning at the dirt. 'We want that bed moved and we must be on the scene and very much alert when the floor's searched,' he added. 'Can we have some men in now?'

'What are we going to look for?' asked Ives.

'Haven't you come across much arson?' countered Folly.

'Very little.'

'Pity. Still everything adds to one's experience! I think we shall look for pieces of glass as well as for a piece of burnt cork. And after that, for a piece of wire or something which could fasten a container under the bed.'

'Container of what?'

Folly's voice hushed to a trance-like invocation. 'I envisage something like this: a small glass or acid-proof container fastened under the bed in such a way that the acid which it held dropped on to the cork of a bottle below. The bottle would contain a certain chemical compound – there are several – which would ignite when it came in contact with the acid. The timing would be judged approximately, you see – the acid would have to eat through the cork before the damage was done. The longer and thicker and tougher the cork, and the weaker the acid, the longer that process would take. But as soon as the first drop of acid fell *into* the bottle beneath – instantaneous combustion would follow.'

Almost lulled to a doze, Ives said politely, 'Thank you for explaining it.' He hesitated. 'I wonder why they should want to kill the old lady?'

Folly shrugged.

'Inheritance, possibly. Or the fact that she knew too much. The motives in this case aren't going to be easy to find, however.'

'What makes you say that?' asked Ives.

'My dear fellow! Think! What is the one *almost* inexplicable thing that happened? The Marrigays barricading themselves in this house. First, the two women, the servants and Nicholas Lee. Then, the Colonel. All were persuaded it was necessary. Yet they admitted their friends to the house – the people who are now here. Presumably, they saw danger from without – beyond this close circle of relatives and friends. Yet all the evidence so far available is that someone within the circle is responsible. We even have Marrigay himself practically accusing both his brother-in-law and his friend – of whom, I gather, he is very fond. Isn't that puzzling? And doesn't it suggest that a motive we don't yet even suspect is lying about?'

Ives said slowly: 'I can't see it.'

'Perhaps I am seeing what doesn't exist,' conceded Folly, making a tactical concession. 'But I am asking myself whether the Colonel didn't *deliberately* throw out these suggestions believing that one of our men would hear him. You see, Ives, there must be a reason for these things; the shutting themselves in; the sudden decision to remove the barricades; and if the Colonel *knew* there was no longer any need to worry, *knew* the source of the danger and for some reason or other wishes to conceal it, wouldn't he be inclined to trail a red-herring?'

'Maybe,' said Ives. 'It's a bit tortuous, but – '

'Marrigay's a tortuous individual,' remarked Folly.

'Granted. I've always thought that if we could find out why he really decided to let Dane come to see you, and opened the grounds, we should be well on the way to discovering the truth.'

'And I fully agree,' said Folly warmly. 'Of course, we may be wrong. On the other hand – ' he smiled cherubically. 'Well, we shall see! For the moment, we can congratulate ourselves – professionally, of course – that through tonight's unfortunate occurrence, we have won ready access to the house. There's another good thing – we can be reasonably firm about keeping everyone under our eye. The only person whom I think we can rule out from suspicion is young Pengelly.'

'And Dane,' said Ives, absently.

'Dane? What on earth makes you think that?'

Ives stared.

'Surely *you* feel happy about him? He wasn't there a year ago. You yourself recommended him, and – ' he broke off, but when Folly continued to stare, continued a little awkwardly. 'I wondered about him at first, but you seemed so sure of him.'

'Did I really give *you* that impression?' asked Folly wonderingly. 'I do apologise. It was the one I intended him to have. For ourselves, we mustn't forget that the transformation came immediately after his visit. I think we ought to watch him just as carefully as the others.'

'I *have* wondered,' repeated Ives.

'Of course you have. And there is another indication of his unusual interest,' Folly went on. 'He jumped at my suggestion that he should come down here and help with the investigations. And – unless my eyes deceive me – he is *very* interested in Joyce Marrigay. Did that interest arise suddenly? Or has he known the sister for some time?'

'We'll find out,' said Ives, heavily.

Downstairs the N.F.S. officer in charge of the fire-fighting reported that there was no longer any danger of another outbreak. Did the police need him?

He was grateful when Folly said 'No'.

The damage was not extensive and had been mainly confined to Mrs Marrigay's room.

Four men searched the rubble underneath the bed, and by four o'clock enough pieces of thick glass had been found to make the shape of a bottle. There was also some thinner glass – only a few slivers of it, but enough to suggest that there had been two containers under the bed. On a piece of the burned and broken wire mattress was a strip of metal. It was easy to imagine that this had held the glass tube from which acid had dripped. A long piece of charred cork was found which Folly preserved with great care, and sent by special messenger to Scotland Yard. An analyst would examine it and telephone a report.

A tired Folly said piously that they had done a good night's work. A weary Ives agreed.

Marjorie was asleep; she had been given one of Mrs Marrigay's sleeping tablets. Paula was lying down, and Roger was also resting. Peter, who seemed as bright and alert as if he had been asleep all night, was in the drawing-room with Joyce, Dane and Bell.

They had talked almost incessantly, covering the same ground over and over again. Towards four o'clock, Joyce's eyes were so heavy that she closed them.

'Supposing we put some rugs over her and let her sleep there,' said Bell.

After covering Joyce carefully the three men went into the hall.

'I know one thing,' Peter said in a surprised voice, 'I'm hungry!'

'And I can well understand that, gentlemen,' piped Folly, who with Ives closely following, was coming out of Mrs Marrigay's room. 'You will forgive me, I know – but I was going to ask you if you could find *me* a snack. I have a large – some might call it an overlarge – body to sustain!' He smiled amiably.

'Oh, we can find something,' said Peter, 'but you'll have to come into the kitchen.'

'Gladly,' said Folly.

Ives looked a little uncomfortable, but followed them nevertheless.

It soon became apparent that Folly was genuinely hungry; sandwiches disappeared as soon as they were put in front of him, but adroitly he led the conversation into just those channels which were most important. Ives was astonished at the amount of information which was forthcoming during that half-hour.

The fact that Uncle Nicholas always carried a small bottle of saccharine tablets with him seemed to afford Folly a great deal of interest. Mrs Marrigay's sleeping pills, the number she took, whether she always got them herself or whether one of the family gave them to her was discussed. It came out that Uncle Nicholas looked after her as much, if not more, than Joyce did. The fact that she had a great influence over him was made only too apparent. Folly asked about the lock on the bedroom door, and Peter explained to him that it had been fixed soon after his father's death, but had seldom been used.

Both Uncle Nicholas and Joyce could handle guns and revolvers. There had been revolvers and ammunition in the house ever since Peter could remember. The police had been shown the locked cupboard where they were kept.

Pengelly and Lem were also useful shots; and Roger and Bell, who had been in the army, could certainly handle revolvers.

No, Peter had not known that the bullet had been cut out

of the oak tree until the police had drawn his attention to it. He didn't think a knife was missing and he had not seen a revolver since his return. Yes, he had examined Joyce's bicycle following the accident, and knew that the brake cables had been cut – no, they hadn't been repaired.

It was nearly five o'clock before they finished. As Folly left them, Ives remarked;

'You didn't ask the very questions I most wanted answered.'

'What were they?'

'About the fire – the acid, the combustible mixture, the bottle the stuff was contained in,' said Ives.

Folly smiled.

'We have told them we suspect arson; I don't think we want them to know that we've discovered the method. Besides, Bell was there.'

'And he's the man who has access to the chemicals,' Ives commented.

'Exactly. Let us watch Bell – whom Pengelly suspects, and who undoubtedly quarrelled with old Marrigay,' said Folly. 'We know that Bell is in a position to get these chemicals, as an industrial chemist he would have access to arsenic, too, but – as a suspect he sticks out so clearly. I am always distrustful of the obvious. Still, that doesn't mean that we won't find out all we can about him,' Folly went on. 'Before I start questioning them about arson, however, I'm going to send a man to his laboratory.' He smiled broadly. 'As a matter of fact, I think it would be a very good idea if we were to go to London ourselves.'

'Before you question them here?'

'It won't do them any harm to be kept in suspense for a few hours,' said Folly. 'We will get one of your men to drive us up, and have our breakfast on the way. Sleep I *can* do without, if it's necessary, but food, no.'

They were in London by ten o'clock.

A detective officer remained on duty at Marrigay House, in charge of the police who seemed to be everywhere. They did not leave until after dark.

Monday was a depressing day.

There was only one good thing, as far as Dane could see; the quarrel between Roger and Peter appeared to have been patched up, and the two men talked reasonably about the situation. There were other things to think about, however. Several newspapermen arrived about ten o'clock. Dane made a brief statement, asking that no one should be quoted; he knew his men, and knew also that there was no fear that they would fail him. He also telephoned the *Gazette*.

Neither Folly nor Ives put in an appearance.

Paula and Bell tried to behave naturally, but there was nothing natural about the situation. Every movement they made seemed to be spied upon. Old Pengelly had one encounter with Bell, and passed him, muttering darkly.

It was a little after four o'clock in the afternoon when the telephone bell rang, and a man asked for Bell. Bell hurried from the kitchen.

'Hallo, who is it? Oh, yes, Armitage. What's the trouble?' He listened . . .

'*What*?' he exclaimed suddenly, with a different note in his voice. Dane bent forward, and saw him leaning against the wall absolutely still; a vein was standing out on his forehead and his eyes were blazing.

'What did you tell them?' Bell barked. 'What's that . . . what?'

It was not surprising, perhaps, that everyone seemed to be drawn to the hall, as by a magnet.

At last Bell said:

'I see. All right, thanks . . . Yes, of course you did the right thing.'

He replaced the receiver; no one moved or spoke.

He fumbled for cigarettes.

'Sorry,' he said, wearily. 'A bit of a shock. Folly and Ives have been to the lab. Dragged my assistant out of his rooms and pestered him with questions.' He gave a short laugh. 'Some of my stock has been removed.'

'Stock?' asked Paula, in a high-pitched voice.

'Arsenic. Some acids. It – '

He broke off, as a car turned into the drive. Those in the hall could see it through the open front door. Dane caught a glimpse of Owen at the wheel.

'Tinker – ' Paula said slowly.

'Looks bad, doesn't it?' asked Bell, mirthlessly.

Owen came in quickly. Behind him was a detective officer from Marston, a man whom none of the others had seen before.

Owen lost no time.

'I wonder if you can spare a moment, Mr Bell?'

'Why?' Bell demanded, harshly.

'I think it would be better if we can have a private talk,' Owen said.

'Damn that,' growled Peter. 'Let's have it in the open.'

'Go on,' agreed Bell.

'Very well, sir,' said Owen, formally. 'I wish to ask you whether you will be good enough to come to Marston with me. There are one or two questions we would like you to answer.'

'Tinker!' Paula's voice was high-pitched.

Bell looked at her, and forced a smile.

'I shouldn't worry too much about this, old girl. Yes, I'll come,' he said to Owen. 'Get my coat, Peter, will you?'

CHAPTER XVI

THE MAKER OF KNIVES

Folly and Ives reached Marston just after eight o'clock, looked in at the police station, and left almost immediately after learning that Bell was in the waiting-room, under guard, and that Mrs Bell, Roger Hurst and Joyce were at hand – they had all followed the car in which Bell had been taken to the town.

129

Ives was driving Folly's car, and they turned off the High Street and into a narrow, ill-lit road.

They parked the car at the far end of the street and walked back to a shop with small glass windows, behind which, on a faded cloth, reposed small knives, daggers and swords. Over the window, on the broad fascia board, were the words: Maker of Knives, illuminated by an oil-lamp. But the maker of knives did not declare his name.

Ives pushed the door open. The bell was still echoing when a gnome-like old man appeared from an inner room.

'Good evening, Mr Whittaker,' greeted Ives. 'This is Mr Folly, from London.'

'Aye,' said Whittaker.

He turned bright eyes towards Folly. The contrast between the two was astonishing; there could be few smaller and wizened men than the maker of knives, few larger than Folly.

'You'd better come to the back,' Whittaker said.

He opened a flap in the counter. Folly edged himself through, into a larger room.

A great beam stretched across the ceiling, which was blackened with smoke, and in one corner was a lighted forge. The walls were adorned with knives and swords, all of excellent workmanship.

'Well, now,' Whittaker said.

Without looking round, he stretched out a veined hand, and took one of two blocks of wood from a shelf behind him; it was a piece of the oak tree in the grounds of Marrigay House.

'Have you had time to examine the knives as well?' asked Ives.

'Aye. It wasn't carved wi' one of them.' Whittaker nodded towards several knives on another shelf – all taken from Marrigay House on Owen's first search.

'Sure?' piped Folly.

'I wouldn't say a thing 'less I were,' said the old man, the broad vowels of his words slurred like old Pengelly's.

'What about this one?' Ives asked, and held out a knife

130

he had been holding in his hand – a knife with two nicks out of the blade.

The old man took it, examined it calmly, stood up and carried both knife and wood nearer to the light. He peered at them intently. Next, he placed the blade of the knife on one of the marks made by whoever had cut the bullet out; and pressed. He took the knife away.

He showed no sign of excitement, but repeated the action; this time he pressed harder, cutting into the wood.

'Aye,' he said. 'That's the one.'

A knuckly finger pointed to two marks, running parallel, in the piece of wood.

''Tis identical,' he said. 'Same scratch – same shape where the blade's chipped – no doubt at all.'

'You'd swear to it?'

The old man looked up.

'I'd give the opinion under oath, and rest happy,' he said.

The knife had been found at Bell's laboratory.

Folly and Ives got out of the car in front of the police station, but before they were at the top of the steps, three people came hurrying towards them along the pavement – Joyce, Paula and Roger. Folly heard them and looked round, Ives wished they had not been caught just then.

'Folly,' called Roger.

Folly stopped.

'Good evening,' he said, mildly.

'Look here – ' began Roger.

'Are you detaining my husband any longer?' demanded Paula breathlessly.

Folly pursed his lips, hesitated, and said:

'I wonder if you will all come in for a few minutes – we can't talk out here.'

Ives led the way into the charge-room, which was empty.

'Now, Mrs Bell,' said Folly, in his most unctuous voice, 'we have a number of questions we must ask your husband, and it depends entirely on how he answers them whether we

131

detain him overnight.'

'Just because some poison was stolen from his lab – '

'Stolen?' barked Folly. 'Who said it was stolen?'

'There was a burglary.'

'When?'

'He doesn't know when.'

'Nor did his assistant know,' breathed Folly, without letting her finish.

'He's a new assistant!' snapped Paula, 'the previous one was dismissed for being unreliable. I suppose Armitage found the stocks didn't tally with the records.'

'I *see*. Thank you, Mrs Bell.' Folly looked at Ives and patted his pocket. 'That is most interesting. Tell me, have you seen – '

He paused.

'Seen what?' demanded Paula.

'I was just wondering,' said Folly, staring pointedly at Ives and tapping his pocket, 'whether you have seen – thank you, Inspector – that knife, Mrs Bell.'

Ives tumbled to it, and was holding the knife in his hand. Joyce exclaimed: '*That* one!'

'I've never seen it before,' Paula said sharply.

Folly switched from her to Joyce with remarkable smoothness.

'Is that so, Miss Marrigay. And where have you seen it before?'

'It's been in Peter's study for – years.'

'Whereabouts in the study?'

'He usually had it on his desk,' said Joyce, 'he used it as a paper-knife.'

'And you are sure it's the same knife?' Folly held it out to her, but added sharply: 'Please don't touch it!'

'I'm quite sure,' she said. 'But – '

'If you are sure, how can there be any but?' demanded Folly.

'It's been sharpened,' Joyce said, 'it was never as sharp as that.'

'I see. When did you last see it?'

132

Joyce hesitated.

'Surely you remember that, as you recollect the knife so well,' said Folly, blandly.

'No, I don't,' said Joyce, 'it's one of those things one sees so often one takes for granted. I could have sworn it was still on his desk. He might know when it was lost.'

'*Lost*,' echoed Folly. His voice boomed hollowly about the small, barely furnished room.

Until that moment the pace had been so swift that none of the three visitors had looked round, but now Joyce glanced about her, and the dreary hopelessness of the room was reflected in her expression.

Paula Bell had lost much of her vivacity. She was breathing heavily with her lips tightly compressed.

She broke the silence with a question, although it was obvious that she knew the answer.

'Did you find that at – at the lab?'

'Mrs Bell,' said Folly, in an unexpectedly gentle voice, 'circumstances have arisen which make it *quite* imperative that we should detain your husband. But I should say this, for at such a time it is only too easily forgotten. No one who is not responsible for these crimes will suffer. My friend Inspector Ives and I will certainly jump to no conclusions and we will take drastic action only when it becomes unavoidable. It is now unavoidable that we should make a charge against your husband, who will be quite at liberty, of course, to call on legal aid. If you would care to see him for a few minutes, that will be all right – although a police officer will have to be present. Would you care to see him?'

Paula nodded.

'Then I will not keep you waiting long,' promised Folly.

Bell decided not to ask for legal aid. He was charged next morning with 'complicity in an attempt to cause Colonel Peter Marrigay serious bodily harm by shooting', pleaded Not Guilty, and was remanded for eight days, after evidence of arrest had been given by the police.

The Bells each made a statement to the police, which tallied in all material details. A fortnight or so before, Bell had discovered a window in his laboratory had been forced. Assuming that the burglar had been disturbed before he had opened the safe – in which several hundred pounds were kept – Bell had done nothing. Pressed as to why he had not reported the incident to the police, he said that as nothing appeared to be missing, he had not considered it worth worrying about.

Bell maintained that he had not been near Marrigay for three weeks; and the bullet had certainly been removed within the past ten days. But he admitted that he had made several trips to Salisbury on business; and it would have been easy for him to get to Marrigay and back from there. He had been in Salisbury on the day that Peter had been fired at, *and* on the day of Joyce's accident.

He was in serious financial difficulties.

Years ago old Marrigay had lent him the money on which to start his business; but neither of the Bells had any financial sense. They lived in a house which they could not really afford, Bell's running expenses at the laboratory were too high, and he was being pressed by his creditors.

'And there,' said Folly, two days after the arrest, 'I see a great weakness, Ives. Don't you?'

Ives was sitting back in an armchair in Folly's hotel bedroom, and Folly was sitting on the edge of the bed, eating biscuits.

'I suppose you're right,' Ives conceded.

'Could one deduce a certain lack of enthusiasm?' suggested Folly coyly.

'One certainly could,' said Ives heavily, the rightness of his own theory blossoming within him. 'Bell was here when old Marrigay was poisoned, he had the quarrel about money, he knew that Marrigay could have sent him to Carey Street – for all we know, Marrigay threatened to do so. And for all we know, Mrs Marrigay was aware of it. He has everything needed for the crimes – arsenic, the acid, all the chemicals necessary for that fire-raising contraption. He could have

134

taken the knife when he was here for a week-end a few weeks ago.'

'Oh, come!' protested Folly, in a shrill voice.

'And Bell was in the vicinity when Peter Marrigay was shot at,' continued Ives imperturbably. 'Of course, there are weaknesses in the case, but I think we could make it stand up. Don't you?'

'Suppose you propound the weaknesses,' suggested Folly.

'If Bell stood to inherit anything from the older Marrigays, the case would be open and shut,' recited Ives, happy that Folly was listening to him. 'But his only known motive – and that isn't absolutely conclusive – is that by killing the old man he would keep himself out of the bankruptcy courts for a bit longer. It was a private loan, I've discovered, the executors wouldn't have known about it. His motive against the old woman is even more problematical, too.'

'I *never* like problematical motives,' murmured Folly.

'Bell's a bit odd,' said Ives, slowly. 'Typical brainy man. You can never be quite sure what they'll do next. Oh, I'd be happier if we could get a clear-cut motive, and I think we ought to go all out to find one.'

Folly gave a shrill little laugh.

'Without feeling very optimistic! It's peculiar, Ives, but here we have an extremely complex case. You'll admit that. At one time, there seemed little or no chance of finding out anything *quickly*. But suddenly, things appeared to fall into place. That's partly due to your thorough work, and yet – it's almost too easy. From the moment that Peter Marrigay was heard to suggest that Bell had a motive, the evidence accumulated. Old Pengelly and his mutterings made us even more suspicious, and then – missing arsenic, the knife, everything! And yet the very fact that arsenic *is* missing from Bell's laboratory makes me wonder. *Would* he take a bottle away? Wouldn't he be more likely to take a little of the stuff out of a bottle, and keep it in a screw of paper?'

'Possibly,' said Ives, 'but –'

'Ah! If he didn't, who did?' Folly sat back on the bed, and

the springs creaked. He brushed off a few crumbs from his waistcoat with fastidious care.

'If Bell didn't do it, he's being framed,' said Ives slowly.

'Exactly,' breathed Folly. 'And that is what worries me. We have a peculiar household. We have an atmosphere of tension, anxiety, suspicion, *fear*. Evil personalities inspire such an atmosphere. There is evil in that house, perhaps in the family. Of all the crimes which are most despicable, that of trying to cast on an innocent person the blame for a crime is the worst. I am afraid that might be the explanation, my friend. I think we shall find out,' said Folly, 'although my greatest anxiety is lest the weight of circumstantial evidence should become so strong that the case *must* be brought against a possibly innocent man. If I am right, someone is fiendishly clever.'

Ives grunted.

'Well, let us try to stop brooding like this,' said Folly, rather testily. 'What are things like at the house?'

'Owen says they're all going about pretending that nothing is the matter,' said Ives. 'There's one thing – Hurst is agitating to get back to London. His wife wants to go with him.'

'Our excitable mother-to-be,' mused Folly. 'I keep wondering whether her tantrums *are* due to her condition. However,' he stood up, and the springs creaked again. 'We can't keep them here. I don't know that we want to. I will make sure they are watched, of course. You know, Ives, I think I ought to return to London for a few days. Until the next hearing of the charge against Bell, at all events. All the obvious things have been done down here. Yes,' he added pensively, 'all the obvious things . . . '

Between them, they had checked everything that needed checking.

'All the obvious things!' Folly repeated, explosively, 'and yet we both shy from one fact.'

Ives did not speak.

'Yes, we shy from this – we have a theory to explain the murder of the older Marrigays, the attacks on Joyce and Peter, but we have none which explains the attempt to poison

136

Uncle Nicholas. Isn't that so?'

Ives stirred.

'We know that there were several tablets made of the commercial arsenic, mixed with his saccharine,' he said dryly. 'And if Bell killed Mrs Marrigay because she knew too much, and mixed the tablets, it would have been easy enough for him to slip them into the little bottle which Uncle Nicholas always kept in his pocket.'

'Ah – *always* kept in his pocket,' echoed Folly.

'There were several hundred tablets in the bottle, only a few of them containing arsenic,' Ives argued. 'The last time Bell was at the house, he could have gone into Lee's bedroom, popped them in, and slipped out again without anyone knowing. Your people in London think that he had the dose above twelve hours before the symptoms developed – that means, when he was in the Archaeologists Club – and it squares up with everything else. They also say that Lee had been taking arsenic over a long period in small amounts – '

'Another weakness in the case against Bell,' said Folly, 'you see that, of course – of course – of *course*,' he went on, waving his hand in the air. 'Bell could have arranged for the arsenic among the saccharine tablets but not for small doses before that – '

'He might have known that Lee took arsenic regularly.'

'There aren't *many* deliberate arsenic-eaters,' Folly pointed out. 'Now, Ives, I think that's a flaw, too. Oh, I believe we could make a jury believe that Bell was responsible, but we don't want to, unless we're sure. I know you think I'm being foolish, but I'm anxious in case we make a grave mistake.'

'All right,' said Ives. 'You base the mistake theory on the possibility that someone broke into Bell's laboratory, stole what he needed and planted the knife. Yet Bell isn't even sure of the day of the alleged burglary! And who could have done it?'

'*Any* of them, except Mrs Marrigay,' said Folly. 'Joyce and Peter spent that day in London, remember – and the Hursts could have done it at any time. Oh, it's possible! Still, we have several days to play with, and there are some things I want

137

to do in London. You won't feel that I'm letting you down if I go back for a day or two?'

Dane sat in the drawing-room, with his legs stretched out and one of Uncle Nicholas's books on mythology in his hands. It was one of the Scandinavian sagas, and as he read of the giant Ymir, he thought uneasily of Roger.

That huge man had been incredibly 'cheerful' since Tinker Bell's arrest. The armistice between him and Peter was often at breaking point; it was easy to understand why Joyce had warned him against Roger. In such a mood of deliberate *bonhomie* he was almost unbearable.

Roger, the giant Ymir, vague, fragmentary thoughts passed through Dane's mind, and all the time there was a sound in the background – the whining of a dog.

He put the book down, thinking about the poisoning of Saturn.

The whining stopped. Dane picked up the book again, but this time it completely failed to hold his interest. He heard Joyce walk along the passage.

'All right, Peter,' he heard her say, and the study door closed. Joyce's footsteps sounded clearly.

She opened the door.

'Hallo, how's the invalid?'

'Improving fast.'

'Don't try it too soon,' Joyce advised. She looked at his bandaged foot. 'Roger and Marjorie are going back in the morning,' she said. 'Marjorie's just told me.'

'Is that a good thing or a bad one?'

Joyce laughed.

'I'll leave you to judge! Peter's glad – I've been afraid of a real outbreak of trouble between them, but surely we'll get safely through tonight.'

'Oh, yes,' said Dane. 'I – '

He broke off abruptly, for someone shouted outside; the shout was followed by a fierce barking which seemed to grow louder. Next came Roger's voice – and to the couple in the drawing-room it seemed to be filled with alarm.

Peter's door opened, and Marjorie came hurrying down the stairs.

CHAPTER XVII

THE BITE OF A DOG

Roger Hurst had been talking to Lem, in the garage. Nearby, Thor had been whining and scratching at the door of the stable where he was shut in, but neither of the men had taken much notice.

'Well, I must get in,' Roger said. He lowered his voice. 'I want to say just one thing to you, Lem.'

'Yes, sir.'

'Keep cheerful – behave as if nothing is the matter,' exhorted Roger earnestly. 'It won't help any of them to brood, you know. It's a most unhappy business – *most* unhappy – but it can't be undone. I'm relying on you, Lem.'

'I'll do all I can, sir, I'm sure,' said Lem.

Roger turned away from the garage. He whistled to himself as he approached the side entrance to the house. In the west, a great storm-cloud was covering the sky, casting a strange, eerie light on Marrigay House.

He was near the door when he heard a shout behind him.

He half-turned as the long, lean shape of Thor came hurtling through the air. He struck out blindly, catching the dog in the chest. The great teeth snapped viciously, the dog fell back.

Roger turned to face it squarely, bellowing:

'Keep down! Keep down!'

'*Be careful!*' cried Lem. 'Don't move!'

Roger stood with his feet firmly planted, staring at the dog, which was crouching only a yard in front of him. He could

139

see the white teeth and lolling tongue. Thor was growling deep in his throat; the hair was stiff along his back.

'Thor!' shouted Lem in a shrill voice. 'Quiet, Thor!'

The dog's growling sounded more ferocious.

The side door opened and Peter called out:

'What's this?'

'Keep away!' said Roger in a tense voice, 'don't interfere, I –'

Thor leapt again.

His attention being diverted for a split second, Roger did not see the start of the spring. One moment the dog was growling, next it was at him. The heavy body thudded into Roger's chest, the front paws clawed his face. The teeth snapped, but missed, although Roger staggered under the onslaught. The dog dropped to the ground and, before Roger could recover his balance, was on him again. This time the big man crashed down.

'*Thor!*' bellowed Peter, running up.

Roger just heard the call, but could feel the dog's hot breath on his face. The fangs closed over his arm, causing agonising pain. He tried to swing his free arm round as the dog released him and snapped again; a fang tore through his cheek. Next moment Peter was beside him.

Lem came up, gasping, as the dog backed away, gulping for breath.

'Careful, Mr Peter, careful.'

'Get a gun,' growled Peter. 'Get –'

Thor leapt at Roger again.

Peter shot out his foot, catching it in the chest, sending it staggering backwards. Others were coming out of the house, now – Dane, Joyce, and Marjorie, who was calling out in alarm.

'Roger, oh, Roger!'

The dog got up, turned as if to make off, and then came back, leaping at Roger as he tried to get up. Marjorie screamed.

Roger shot out his hands.

He caught Thor's throat in his great fingers, and held tight. Holding the brute at arm's length, he made a fantastic picture. The blood was coming from the gash in his cheek and over his sleeves. Thor was gasping for breath, now, twisting and turning his lithe, sinewy body. But the writhing grew less violent and Peter said in a taut voice:

'Get that gun, Lem.'

'Won't need a gun,' growled Roger.

He twisted his hands round the thick throat. Thor was making odd, gasping noises.

There was a crack.

'No, you won't need a gun,' Roger said. 'Damned brute.'

He flung the dog away. He was dead.

Peter was on the way to Marston, with Roger in the back of his own car. Roger's cheek and arms had been bathed with antiseptic, but the gash in the cheek was serious and needed stitching. He sat silently, holding his hands up to his chest. Peter drove at breakneck speed . . .

In the house, Paula was upstairs with Marjorie.

Dane and Joyce were in the drawing-room and Lem was standing in front of them, cap in hand, his broad face set in lines of distress.

'Are you sure you don't know who released the dog?' Dane demanded.

'I'm *quite* sure, sir. T'was getting dark, ye'll remember. I didn't even *hear* a sound, except that Thor stopped whining. First I noticed, he was after Mr Roger.'

'Where were you?'

'Still by the door of the garage, sir.'

'Who else was in the garden?'

'My father, sir.'

'Did he go near Thor?'

'He says he didn't go anywhere near that stable, sir, he dassn't. Thor never liked him, sir, only Mr Peter and I could handle Thor.'

'Didn't you see *anyone* else?' asked Joyce.

'I – I can't say that I did,' said Lem, awkwardly. 'Mr Roger came out to talk to me about the garden, that's all I saw.'

'All right,' said Dane.

Lem nodded, touched his forehead and backed out of the room, greatly embarrassed and troubled. Joyce passed her hand across her forehead.

'It must have been an accident.'

'Of course it was an accident,' Dane said vehemently, 'but someone let the dog out. I doubt if they'll ever admit it. Hallo, this sounds like Owen.'

The sergeant's quick, light footsteps had become familiar, and he came into the room as Dane opened the door. His expression was grim as he nodded to Joyce.

'Well?' asked Dane.

'The door fastens with a hook into a staple,' said Owen shortly. 'Have *you* been out this afternoon, Mr Dane?'

'No,' said Dane.

'Have you, Miss?' asked Owen.

'Not since lunch-time,' said Joyce.

'Look here – ' began Dane.

'I'm trying to find out if anyone *saw* anyone,' said Owen tersely. 'One of my men says that he thought he saw someone moving about the grounds a little while before it happened. Neither of you have seen a stranger?'

Dane said 'No,' and Joyce shook her head.

'Do you know where the others were?' asked Owen.

'Mrs Hurst was upstairs,' said Dane. 'Colonel Marrigay was in his study, Mrs Bell – ' he hesitated.

'She's been in the kitchen with me most of the afternoon,' Joyce said. She spoke almost too quickly, and Owen looked at her thoughtfully.

'I see, Miss,' he said. 'Thank you.'

As the door closed behind him, Joyce exclaimed:

'He *can't* think it was deliberate!'

'Oh, he can,' corrected Dane. 'I'm surprised, though. I can't imagine why anyone should want to set the dog loose.'

'He didn't ask us where Peter was,' said Joyce thoughtfully.

It was easy to understand what she was thinking; her

thoughts had flown to crime, and would do, until this mystery was solved. Everyone knew about the dog's ferocity, yet the door had been opened. It was even possible that it had been done in the hope that the dog would attack Roger.

Joyce said: 'Thor always hated him.'

'You've said that before,' said Dane. 'Sit down, darling, and don't look so worried.'

Afterwards, he remembered how easily that 'darling' had slipped out, and that neither of them had seemed to take any notice of it. They sat staring into the fire.

Dane wondered what the police would think of this latest development; he knew that Joyce was wondering whether Peter would be suspected of letting the dog out. The animosity between Peter and Roger was well known to everyone in the household.

Peter had been in his study; but he could have slipped out through the side door, gone to the stables and returned, without anyone hearing him.

Paula *might* have slipped out, but there was no reason as far as he knew why Paula should bear any animosity towards Roger.

Oh, he was a fool! It was so much saner to believe that someone had accidentally opened the stable door, it could be done easily enough with a careless movement of the arm or shoulder. Thor had then slipped out and attacked the man he had always disliked. That was the only sensible explanation, and –

Joyce said:

'Alec.'

'Yes.'

'Peter had just come in when I saw him.'

'Oh,' said Dane, lamely.

'And –'

'Go on,' Dane urged, quietly.

'Paula had been out.'

'Are you sure?'

'She said she must have a breath of air. She was out there

143

when it happened – she came along from the side of the house. Remember?'

'Look here,' said Dane. 'You mustn't start imagining that there was any malice behind this business.'

'I'm so afraid that there was,' said Joyce. 'I can't help it, Alec. It's with me all the time, it's with *us*, this dreadful sense of evil. Father – Mother – Uncle Nicholas – now Roger.' She broke off.

'He *loved* those dogs,' she added, in a strangled voice. 'Alec, where is it going to end?'

'I don't think you need to assume that this has anything to do with the crimes,' Dane said, with more assurance than he felt.

'No, of course not. Only I wish Peter and Paula hadn't been out.' Joyce jumped up. 'But I must go and see how Marjorie is.'

Dane was angry with himself for feeling helpless and futile.

At the back of his mind was the same fear that lurked in Joyce's mind; that it *had* been deliberate, that someone had wanted Roger to be attacked. If the police once suspected that, they would almost certainly suspect Peter. Why *had* he been out?

Peter returned just after six o'clock. All of them heard his car coming up the drive. Marjorie jumped up and flew to the front door. Joyce and Paula hurried after her. They heard her ask in a sharp voice:

'Where's Roger?'

'He's all right, old girl,' said Peter reassuringly. 'He's staying at the hospital overnight.'

'But they wouldn't keep him –' Marjorie began with a note in her voice which suggested hysteria.

Peter said quietly:

'Now look here, Jorrie, you've got to take a grip on yourself.'

'That's all very well,' Marjorie said, 'but it's you who have

144

made life unbearable, almost from the first moment you saw Roger.'

'Yes, I know,' Peter said, his voice rather crestfallen. 'It hasn't been easy for me, you know. The thing is, Jorrie, we can't talk to you about the situation because we don't know what might send you off into a tantrum. Try to take it easier.' He patted her arm. 'Hallo, Dane! Evolved any theories as to how the beast got loose?'

'I'm leaving theories to the police.'

'Wise fellow. What about you, Joyce?'

Joyce's smile was unusually bright.

'Oh, yes, darling! I've deduced that you crept round to the stables and set Thor free, just to put the finishing touch to your rows with Roger. Oh, Peter, if this – '

Peter said sharply:

'Don't be silly, Joyce. I didn't go out this afternoon.' He gave a hard, brittle laugh. 'You'll be putting ideas into Jorrie's head. Nothing has been happening while I've been out, I suppose?'

Dane found himself thinking that the change of subject had been too slick. *Had* Peter been out? And if so, why had he lied?

CHAPTER XVIII

UNCLE NICHOLAS IMPROVES

On the Wednesday morning, Nicholas Lee woke up feeling very much better. Neither the doctors nor the nurses had mentioned the word arsenic, no one had suggested that the police were interested in what had happened to him.

After a very light breakfast, he sat up in bed and asked for a newspaper. The nurse hurried along to the Sister's office.

'Number 37 wants a newspaper,' she said, as the Sister, looking almost forbiddingly competent, glanced up. 'Didn't you say he wasn't to have one?'

'I did.'

'Shall I just forget it?'

'Most certainly.'

When the nurse had gone, however, the Sister reached out for the telephone and asked for Whitehall 1212. Soon, she was telling Superintendent Folly that Mr Lee was asking for a newspaper.

'Now that's a most encouraging sign, most encouraging,' said Folly. 'He's showing great improvement, then?'

'I don't think there is very much the matter with him now,' said Sister. 'He mustn't have a paper yet, I suppose?'

'I think I'd better come along and break the news to him,' said Folly. 'I'll be over quite soon. Tell me, has he been at all talkative?'

'He's said very little.'

'I see, thank you,' said Folly.

At half-past nine, he entered the hospital, with a sergeant to whom he gave explicit instructions. The sergeant was to stand outside the door, which would not be properly closed, and make a note of all that was said. A detective-officer was to remain in the passage afterwards; from now on, Uncle Nicholas was to be closely watched.

Twenty minutes later, Folly went into the small private ward. Uncle Nicholas looked up in some surprise at his huge figure.

'*Another* doctor,' commented Uncle Nicholas. 'I do wish that you would tell me what is the matter with me.'

'You're well on the mend now, you know,' said Folly. He pulled up a chair. 'No, Mr Lee, I am not a doctor. I am a policeman.'

'A – *policeman*!'

'That is so,' said Folly. 'Mr Lee, when you realised that Inspector Ives of Marston had visited Marrigay House, *why* did you leave so suddenly?'

There was a long, tense pause.

146

'Well?' asked Folly, at last.

Uncle Nicholas drew in his breath.

'I – I was so frightened,' he said in a quivering voice. His words were barely audible, and now he closed his eyes. 'So – frightened.'

'That the Inspector might learn the truth?' asked Folly.

'Yes – yes, that was it,' said Uncle Nicholas, without opening his eyes. 'But – I have been frightened for so long. That house – that *terrible* house –' he shivered. '*Must* I go back there?'

'I think that is a matter for you to decide,' said Folly, gently. 'Your relations –'

'I don't want to see them again! The only one who ever showed me any real consideration was Marjorie, the others all thought that I was mad. Sometimes I thought they were trying to *drive* me mad!'

'But that would be a very evil thing!' exclaimed Folly.

'Evil – that is the word, evil!' cried Uncle Nicholas, pouncing on the word as if Folly had given him a heart-warming gift he was loath to let go. 'The house and the people in it were evil, and I was afraid, desperately afraid. And when I knew that the truth – *part* of the truth – had been discovered, I knew that they wanted to get rid of me, and so – so I flew to Marjorie.'

'And you went straight to her,' murmured Folly.

'No, no! I went –' Uncle Nicholas paused, and ran his hand over his forehead. 'I feel so weak, can I – can I have a little drink?'

Folly poured out a glass of water from a jug by the invalid's side. Uncle Nicholas sipped slowly, and then put it back on the table.

'No, I didn't go straight to Marjorie,' he muttered. 'She is *enceinte*, perhaps you know that. I knew a late visit would give her a shock. So I stayed at my club. Next morning, just before I left, I felt ill. I thought it was a passing trouble, a nervous disorder, but it became so bad that – I collapsed when I reached her house. How I managed to get so far I really don't remember.'

147

'It was remarkably brave of you,' murmured Folly.

'I – I had to get there,' muttered Uncle Nicholas. He leaned forward, touching Folly's arm. 'Tell me the truth, was I poisoned?'

'I am afraid so,' said Folly.

'So – so she went to *those* lengths!' gasped Uncle Nicholas. He lay back and closed his eyes.

Folly made no comment, and waited with exemplary patience. The sounds of the hospital continued about them; but none of these things affected Uncle Nicholas, whose last words seemed to echo about the room. 'So she went to those lengths.' When nine men out of ten would have urged the invalid to go on, Folly sat without moving.

'I was – always – so frightened,' said Uncle Nicholas in a husky voice. 'I have tried to protect her – I have to tell you, my own sister – oh, dear God, it is too terrible to contemplate!'

'Ah,' murmured Folly.

'First – her poor husband. Then – her brother. Poor George – he had no idea – no idea at all. But – she killed him. She knew that I believed that. From the time he died I was afraid, and yet I prayed that I was wrong.'

'Yes,' breathed Folly.

'I always knew that George's death wasn't natural, once in a fit of rage she told me how she hated him,' said Uncle Nicholas. 'He wasn't faithful to her, and she was so terribly, passionately possessive. It wasn't until a little while before he died that she discovered the truth. She told no one, she would not have told me, except that something he had said angered her and she could not keep it to herself.'

'How did she kill her husband?' asked Folly.

'Just as she must have tried to kill me!' cried Uncle Nicholas. 'I did not want to believe it, I fought against admitting it, even to myself, but I recognised the symptoms of my illness. Arsenic! Oh, what a terrible thing! It – it was in with my saccharine tablets. That last cup of coffee I had for breakfast at the club – so bitter –'

'I see,' breathed Folly. 'How soon after you had drunk the

coffee did you begin to feel ill?'

'Not very long. Not half-an-hour. But I was halfway to Barnes before I began to *fear*,' said Uncle Nicholas.

Folly said: 'You must tell me where she got the arsenic, Mr Lee, it might – '

'She might use it again!' cried Uncle Nicholas. 'Yes, I will tell you, she stole it from Bell – a friend of the family – soon after he started up in business, he is a chemist. We all visited the laboratory nearly two years ago, she stole it then. And on that night when she was in such a *terrible* fury she told me that she had enough poison to kill everyone. I protested, I tried to reason with her, but she has such a powerful personality, there was little I could do. But she mustn't do any further harm! There is no telling how far she might go!'

'You needn't worry any more, Mr Lee,' said Folly. 'She is dead.'

'*Dead!*' sighed Uncle Nicholas.

There was another pause, long and tense, At last Uncle Nicholas's lips began to move.

'So – she killed herself.'

'What makes you think that?' asked Folly.

'It is so obvious! She realised that when the police discovered the truth, after the exhumation – '

'So you knew about that,' murmured Folly.

'Of course, of course,' cried Uncle Nicholas, 'It is entirely useless trying to keep anything from *anyone* at Marrigay House! Old Pengelly sometimes helps the grave-digger in the village, he knew from the beginning what was happening and he told me – and he told her,' went on Uncle Nicholas. 'Once she realised the police would find out, she couldn't face investigation, she – ' he broke off. 'Oh, perhaps I am wrong, perhaps she died naturally, but – '

'No, she died by fire,' said Folly.

'*Fire!*' breathed Uncle Nicholas. 'I can hardly believe such a thing could happen. And years ago it was such a happy family. To end like this! *Fire*,' he repeated in a hushed voice. Uncle Nicholas closed his eyes again; he seemed easier now, as if he had thrown a great burden off his shoulders

149

'And the children are all safe?'

'Yes.'

'Then – then we have something to be thankful for,' said Uncle Nicholas.

'A great deal, perhaps,' said Folly. 'I am sorry that I had to bring you such news, Mr Lee – '

'I quite understand,' said Uncle Nicholas. 'I quite understand. But – but I am tired now, sir, very tired. Perhaps I can rest.'

'Of course,' said Folly. He stood up immediately, and tip-toed out of the room. He touched the sergeant's shoulder, put a finger to his lips, and they walked quietly along the passage until they were beyond the chance of being over-heard.

'Did you get all that?'

'Nearly everything, sir.'

'Transcribe it as quickly as you can, and let me have it at my office,' said Folly. He smiled down at his companion. 'And what did you make of it?'

'If he knew of Mr Marrigay's unfaithfulness, the others probably did,' said the sergeant.

'Yes – yes, that's one way of looking at it. A deep, buried motive – marital disloyalty, the oldest cause of crime in the world – yes, possibly.'

'Possibly?' echoed the sergeant.

'I mean possibly the children as he called them, may have known about it,' said Folly, 'but – *can* you explain why they shut themselves up in that house?'

'Well, no, but – '

'Let us say this,' said Folly. 'We have been told another story. We must test it for facts. Some of them are undoubtedly true, some of them may be the figments of his imagination, and – you know, sergeant, he protested a *little* too much about some things, didn't he? And the shooting incident – the cycle accident – the poisoned dog – *they're* not explained either. Was the old woman responsible for a campaign against her own flesh and blood? Did love turn sour and become

150

hatred so deep that she became homicidal towards *all* of them?'

Folly got into his car and sat at the wheel for some time, looking thoughtfully in front of him. Then he let in the clutch and started off, narrowly missed the wing of an ambulance which was standing near the gates. He drove without further mishap as far as Barnes, and drew up outside a house on the wall of which was a brass plate bearing the letters: *'Dr A. P. Acland, M.D., M.R.C.S.'*

At his ring, a maid opened the door.

'If you will come with me, sir.'

Acland was sitting at a desk in his surgery. He smiled somewhat warily.

'Good morning, Superintendent.'

'My dear fellow, how *are* you?' asked Folly, genially.

The maid came in, carrying a tea-tray and a plate of biscuits.

Folly beamed.

'How welcome – thank you, doctor!'

'Now, what can I do for you?' asked Acland, when the tea was poured out and Folly had selected a couple of biscuits with the utmost care.

'I've one or two little anxieties, you know,' said Folly. 'About Nicholas Lee's mishap. You've seen the newspapers – '

'Yes.'

'Now, you'll remember that Mrs Hurst became rather excited, and you pointed out that it wasn't unnatural in the circumstances.'

'That is so.'

'How had she behaved before I arrived?'

'Very well,' said Acland.

'No panic?'

'She impressed me as an extremely capable and level-headed woman,' said Acland. He smiled. 'I'm only giving you an opinion, you know.'

'Oh, my dear fellow, I'm not looking for *evidence*, I just want to get everything in its right perspective,' said Folly

151

innocently. 'You did mention arsenic on the telephone, didn't you?'

'Oh, yes,' said Acland. 'My actual words, as far as I remember, were that I wanted ferric oxide and the usual arsenic antidote.'

'I see. And you can assure me that the shock which Mrs Hurst had when she heard the word "arsenic" would account for her change from the capable level-headed woman to –'

'There wasn't any change then, as far as I know,' said Acland. 'She went to get the stuff from the chemist for me, and she continued to behave admirably until you arrived.'

'So the change in her manner came later, when she was called upon by a policeman,' murmured Folly.

'I think anyone might have brought it on.'

'Might?' echoed Folly.

'You know as well as I do that it's quite impossible to be sure about a woman's reaction,' said Acland. 'Just what do you want to know, Superintendent?'

Folly smiled blandly.

'Actually,' the doctor went on, 'you want to know whether she gave me the impression that she expected to learn that it was arsenic, and whether I think you, as a policeman, frightened her,' said Acland, dryly. 'Well, obviously, it's possible. I can't say more.'

'You're very shrewd,' said Folly, 'I should have expected it, of course, the way you handled the patient was remarkable. But for you, he might have died.'

'Personally, I doubt it,' said Acland. 'I've thought about it a good deal since I conferred with your expert, and I think Lee stood at least an even chance of getting over it.'

'I *see*,' said Folly, heavily.

Absently, he picked up another biscuit, ate it, then stood up briskly.

'You've been very helpful, very helpful indeed. And you still believe that the arsenic was taken by the patient some hours before you saw him?'

'Oh, yes.'

'Thank you,' said Folly. 'Now, you can help me with one

152

more thing – the address of Mrs Hurst's regular doctor.'

'Dr Summers,' said Acland, promptly. 'He goes to Putney Hospital every Wednesday morning, to give anaesthetics.'

Half-an-hour later, a burly, grey-haired man, smelling faintly of ether, entered the Secretary's office at the Putney Hospital. He looked at Folly with obvious interest.

'This is to do with Mrs Hurst and her uncle, I suppose.'

'You're absolutely right,' said Folly, 'and I would very much appreciate a little information about Mrs Hurst. She's had a series of nasty shocks, you know. You've doubtless read of her mother's death at Marrigay.' He paused, and Summers nodded curtly. 'And her husband was injured yesterday. Now I'm wondering whether, in her condition, that kind of thing is bad for Mrs Hurst.'

Summers smiled, sardonically.

'There's a lot of nonsense talked about the fragility of a woman when she's pregnant. They're tough, how tough you don't know!' He smiled again. 'It isn't likely to do her any harm, provided she takes reasonable precautions, and gets plenty of sleep.'

'Is Mrs Hurst a highly-strung woman?'

'No, quite the reverse.'

'But in her present condition – '

'Oh, she'll probably have a few outbursts of hysteria,' said Summers. 'That's nothing to worry about. What have you got in mind – putting her in the witness box?'

'Could she stand that?'

'If she had to. Though I shouldn't make her do it if you can avoid it. Now and again I've had to attend a woman whom it *might* have upset badly enough to bring on a miscarriage, but I haven't any fear about Marjorie Hurst.'

'You know her well?'

'Fairly well.'

'She's always had a placid nature?'

'Yes.'

'She hasn't given you the impression that she had anything on her mind?' said Folly, tentatively.

'She has not,' declared Summers, brusquely.

153

'Have you treated her husband?'

'He's never been ill,' said Summers, 'but when the kid comes Hurst will give us more trouble than his wife!' He gave a short laugh. 'I've got to go up to the theatre again, if there's nothing else – '

'No, nothing else at all, thank you, you've been most helpful,' said Folly.

He was at his office just after one o'clock, and the first thing he saw on his desk was a typewritten message, headed: *Telegram received from Marston, 12.04: Dane hurt advise your return, Ives.*

'Well, well!' breathed Folly, 'and on a Wednesday, too!'

With that apparently fatuous remark, he lifted the telephone, dictated a telegram advising Ives that he would return that evening, then went out to a nearby chop-house, where the appetite of Superintendent Folly was marvelled at, carefully studied, and invariably satisfied.

After lunch, he called on the senior partner of Green, Medley and Green, the firm of solicitors which had handled the Marrigay's family business for many years.

To the white-haired solicitor, Folly told the tale which Uncle Nicholas had told him. The old man made no comment, beyond:

'Mr Lee has always been somewhat eccentric, you know. And, possibly, subject to delusions.'

'I might get a specialist's opinion,' mused Folly. 'But – and I ask you to be frank, sir – *was* he right about Mr Marrigay's liaison with another woman?'

'Can you expect me to answer that?' asked the old man.

Folly beamed.

'I understand you, sir. One other thing. Were there any children of the liaison?'

The old man did not speak; but he gave a brief and worldly smile.

Folly stood up, thanked him warmly, and drove with greater recklessness than usual to Scotland Yard. He studied some reports which were on his desk. The truth about that

154

liaison had been discovered; the woman's name was there.

He telephoned Ives.

'I wanted to ask you one thing, Ives. No unidentified bodies have been found in Limshire recently, I suppose?'

Ives laughed.

'I am quite serious,' rebuked Folly.

'Oh, of course.'

'Put Owen on to enquiries about such a body, will you?' said Folly, frostily.

CHAPTER XIX

OLD PENGELLY'S HOBBY

Alec Dane, sipping his early morning tea, was vaguely puzzled by his lightness of spirit. There had been no good news on the previous day, yet he could think of the dog's attack on Roger and of the whole unhappy business, without that feeling of acute distress which, lately, had been so often upon him.

Why?

He smiled suddenly.

For half-an-hour the previous evening, he and Joyce had been alone in the drawing-room.

Joyce had said very little, but in her company the stresses and strains of the past few days had seemed to become lighter.

She was in the breakfast-room when he went downstairs. Suddenly, at her smile, he leaned over her.

'Oh, my dear!' he exclaimed, and kissed her.

'Good morning!' said Peter, from the door.

Dane started and released Joyce. Peter, smiling crookedly, came into the breakfast-room.

'Don't mind me,' he said, dryly. 'I bow to the inevitable.'

Both Joyce and Dane coloured furiously.

'Now don't act like children,' said Peter, briskly. 'The Lord knows we can do with a bit of cheer in this accursed household. I woke up with a feeling of astonishment – no alarms during the night. If you need it, you've my blessing,' he added, flippantly, 'but I would go easy on that foot if I were you, Alec.'

'It's much better,' said Dane.

'Due, I take it, to a general lightening of oppression. Anyone seen Marjorie or Paula this morning?'

'Paula's coming down in a few minutes, Marjorie's having breakfast in bed,' said Joyce.

'Anyone thought to telephone the hospital about Roger?'

'Paula has,' said Joyce. 'He'll be home some time today.'

'Splendid,' said Peter, with a show of heartiness. 'No news of Tinker Bell, I suppose?'

'Nothing,' said Joyce.

'I can't believe the Folly merchant's got the right man in Tinker,' said Peter. 'It would be a relief in one way, if he were guilty, we should all feel easier, but – '

'What a good friend you are,' said Paula from the door.

'Oh, Lord!' exclaimed Peter. 'I've put my foot in it again.' He jumped up. 'Don't take any notice of my witticisms, old girl. I was being dispassionate. And I did say I thought Folly – '

'*You* brought up the subject of that damned loan,' Paula said, but although her colour was high, she patted Peter's arm. 'Sit down and eat your breakfast. Of course, it's nonsense to think that Tinker had anything to do with this. It does mean one ugly thing, though.'

'Hmm-hmm?' asked Peter, sitting down and beginning to serve her with scrambled eggs.

'*Someone* has tried to throw the blame on him,' said Paula.

'You take it calmly,' remarked Peter.

'I've been thinking a lot about it,' said Paula. 'Getting worked up won't help. Tinker's in trouble, and I've got to help to get him out of it.'

156

'So from now on, you're about to impose on us a rigorous dissection in order to judge which one would do the dirty on Tinker Bell.'

'That's it.'

Peter began to eat.

'What's happened this morning?' asked Joyce, wonderingly 'Everyone seems – '

'Cool, calm and collected,' mumbled Peter. 'Yes a remarkable change. Personally, I doubt whether it will last when Roger's back. You know, he's a worthy soul and there are moments when I like him, but – I just *can't* live in the same house with him and his camaraderie. Any idea who the villain is, Paula?'

'Not yet,' said Paula.

'Have you confided in the police?'

'You may think it funny,' said Paula, 'but I've a lot of respect for the police. Ives is a thoroughly good fellow, and that man Folly – '

'He's a man with a single purpose,' said Dane, 'and he'll behave like anything from a nincompoop to a Seventh Day Adventist in order to get results.'

'The police always get their man,' quoted Peter. 'I wonder which one of us it is?'

'It *could* be someone from outside,' Joyce said.

'Oh, yes? In spite of the watching policemen and the locked door, you really think it possible that someone from outside got into Mother's room and set fire to her bed?' said Peter. 'I've been having a chat with one of the Roberts. He let slip that the fire was started by a fiendishly ingenious gadget, which took some time to fix. I don't believe that anyone outside could have done it.'

'That's what I think,' said Paula.

'I don't know why you're assuming that it must be one of the family,' said Dane, slowly.

All eyes turned towards him.

'Speak,' ordered Peter.

'There *are* the servants,' said Dane.

'Don't speak,' amended Peter hastily.

'I don't see why we should rule out the Pengellys,' said Paula evenly. 'After all, old Pengelly hasn't missed a chance of trying to blame Tinker.'

'Now, take it easy,' protested Peter. 'I don't mind suspecting Joyce, but when it comes to wondering whether the cook is hiding a load of arsenic, I boggle.'

'But let's suppose that old Pengelly is involved,' said Dane, reasoningly. 'He's always in the grounds. He could have cut those bike cables, fired at Peter, introduced poison into your father's medicine, fixed up the contraption in the bedroom, and – *he* could have let Thor out. Someone did, you know – we may as well say the obvious.'

'Telling list of evidence,' commented Peter, 'but one thing knocks the whole build-up into smithereens.'

'And that?'

'What is the motive?'

'Equally, what motive has Tinker?' demanded Paula. 'Oh, I know there's the obvious one, but anyone who knows him also knows that he doesn't give a damn about money. If he were to go broke, it wouldn't really worry him. He's first and last a chemist, and he's brilliant enough to get a research job anywhere!'

'Talking of motives,' said Peter cussedly, unwilling to admit the brilliance, unable to deny it, 'the police haven't worried us much about them. If we face facts again, only Joyce, Marjorie and Roger who count as one, and I have good ones. We all inherit. Substantially, too.'

'I wonder if Mother made a will,' said Joyce.

'Oh, yes,' said Peter. 'I looked in on old Middleton after I'd taken Roger into hospital. I gathered that the police had asked about it, too. Middleton is going to ring up and suggest a time to come out and read it to us. It is strange how apathetic we all *appear* to be, as to the disposition of the family fortune.'

'Father left us enough,' remarked Joyce.

'Nearly seventy thousand.'

'Let's see, was that before or after death duties?'

'After,' said Joyce.

'Hmm,' said Peter. 'Nearly twenty-four thousand for each of us. The police would undoubtedly consider that a sufficient motive for murder, and – '

He broke off, and Paula and Joyce stared at him in amazement. His air of deliberate calm had gone, he stared at Joyce as if a great light had dawned upon him. They waited for him to speak, and at last Joyce exclaimed:

'Peter, what is it?'

'Just a thought. Of no consequence.' He took some toast from the rack, and refused to say another word. Conversation withered as if he had pulled it up by the roots.

Joyce and Paula went into the village after breakfast. Dane, his injured foot still keeping him inactive, was the last to leave the breakfast-room. He was speculating on Peter's sudden change of manner when he heard his name being called from the study.

Peter stood with his back to the fire.

'Well?' asked Dane.

'I had a nasty thought at breakfast,' Peter declared. 'Idle speculation's one thing, cold logic's another. Incidentally, your talk of Pengelly was nicely done, it'll make Joyce and Paula wonder if it could be someone outside the family.'

'Possibly, but what was your unpleasant thought?' asked Dane.

'Obvious enough, when you come to think of it. The only member of the family who hasn't been attacked is Marjorie. Fact, isn't it?'

'I suppose it is,' conceded Dane slowly.

Soon after this conversation, the telephone bell rang. It was the solicitor, asking for Peter, who decided to go into Marston to see him. Borrowing Roger's car, he drove off a little after ten o'clock.

Marjorie being still in her room, Dane was left to his own devices.

There were two policemen and a detective-officer in the house, but by now everyone had become so used to them. So

159

used, that neither Peter nor Dane knew that the conversation at breakfast had been overheard, and that Peter's confidence had also been jotted down by a detective-officer.

Pondering over Peter's new slant, Dane realised that he liked Marjorie.

Peter was right, of course; but the Pengellys also had been free from any form of attack. Dane could not quite make out what the police were doing, and was surprised that Folly had returned to London. It did not greatly matter, he decided; and while he was here, he might as well try to work the thing out himself. He did not want to think that anyone of the family was implicated, therefore the Pengelly family were worthy of attention.

For the first time, he went up to the second floor.

There was a box-room and a lumber-room, and a room which Pengelly used for his wood-carving. The lumber-room had been damaged by water during the fire, and traces of this were plain enough. Dane found himself speculating about that fire. It may have been started simply to kill the old lady; but it might also have been intended to destroy something in the house. He wondered if the police had thought of that.

He opened the door nearest him, and entered a large double bedroom filled with comfortable and outmoded furniture. On the mantelpiece were several carved figures; feeling a little guilty, Dane went to look at them.

They were grotesque – twisted, warped and sinister. They were, however, beautifully carved; and he was reminded of the bullet which had been carved out of the tree.

Were these Pengelly's work?

He remembered the talk of the old gardener's hobby.

In all, there were a dozen such figures in the room. After inspecting each one of them, he went out.

He thought he heard a movement on the stairs.

He went towards the head of the staircase, but saw no one. Although there was no reason why he should not be up here, he was, undoubtedly, prying in a place which was private to the Pengellys. Now that he was here, however, he decided to make the most of it. He glanced into Lem's bedroom. Nothing unusual.

He looked into the box-room, and remembered that it was here that Joyce had come to see whether any of Uncle Nicholas's suitcases were missing. How long ago that seemed!

There was only one other room, apart from the one that had been damaged. He opened the door, and saw a bench along one wall, a row of tools, and several small blocks of wood. One of the blocks was, in fact, a carved figure in its early stages. So this was where old Pengelly worked.

He saw several books on a revolving book-case near his hand; all of them heavy, leather-bound, not the kind of literature that one would expect old Pengelly to read.

He picked up one of them and opened it –

The name *Nicholas Lee* was written on the flyleaf in Uncle Nicholas's small, neat handwriting; it was another of Nicholas's books on mythology. Did *Pengelly* read such stuff as this?

Dane found himself brooding over what he knew of mythology. It was essentially primitive; as such, it might appeal to the primitive in old Pengelly. He put the book down and picked up another.

At the first page he opened, he stared transfixed; for on it was a picture, identical with one of the carvings he had seen in old Pengelly's bedroom.

There were several similar drawings; Pengelly appeared to have taken them as his models.

His interest thoroughly aroused, Dane picked up yet another book, and found it so light in weight that he dropped it in surprise. All of the others had been heavy, this one was like an empty box. It *was* a box. The outer edges had been carved to look like uncut leaves, it was a beautiful piece of work, but not a book. Yet there was the leather binding, and it had a title in a language he did not understand.

He picked at the top cover with his nails, and prised it open.

It wasn't empty; it contained a paper bag, of the kind in which small quantities of sweets were sold, and the bag had

161

broken open. A white powder, fine as flour, was spread about the box.

He thought: *Arsenic*!

He stood absolutely still, then he put the book-box down slowly, staring at the bag. The other books might be false, too. He picked up half-a-dozen, putting them down because of their weight. Then he picked up one unevenly balanced.

He shook it up and down.

Yes, something very heavy was inside.

He prised the lid open, and found himself staring at a short-barrelled revolver.

Dane replaced everything exactly as he had found it. The discovery was of the first importance. Bearing the significant vision of the gun and the white powder in his mind's eye, he left the little room, closing the door behind him.

He thought he heard a whisper of sound on the stairs again, but no one was there.

Half-way down, he tripped over something he did not see. He could do nothing to save himself, but pitched down into the passage, hitting his head against the wall.

CHAPTER XX

THE ARREST OF PENGELLY

Owen, who had just arrived and was talking to one of the policemen, heard the crash. Without saying a word, he dashed up the stairs. As he reached the landing, Paula and Marjorie appeared outside Marjorie's door.

At the same time, old Pengelly came out of Uncle Nicholas's bedroom.

Owen noticed all of these things as he rushed towards

Dane, who was lying with one leg stretched out, the other bent under him.

Owen went down on his knees beside Dane. His eyes were closed, and there was a mark on his forehead.

'Is he *dead*?' whispered Marjorie.

'No deader than I am,' growled Owen.

'Let me help you with him,' Paula strode forward.

Between them they lifted Dane and took him into his bedroom. A policeman, standing on the spot where Dane had fallen, stooped down and picked up a piece of string. Then he glanced towards the next landing. 'Well, I'm – ' he broke off. Only old Pengelly seemed to notice him.

There were tacks in the stairs, and the severed ends of a piece of string lay there.

Pengelly moved towards the policeman, who blocked his way.

'You can't come past here.'

'Can't I go to my own room now?' Pengelly's voice was plaintive.

'Not for the next few minutes.'

'But – '

'Not *just* yet,' said the policeman.

Old Pengelly looked at him, his eyelids drooping. Then he shrugged his narrow shoulders and moved slowly down the stairs.

The policeman, delighted with his own astuteness, slipped the piece of string into his pocket and looked downwards intently. The tacks were clearly visible. He took one out and put it in his pocket, leaving the other where it was.

Footsteps sounded below.

Joyce's voice called: 'What's the matter?'

'It's all right, dear,' answered Paula.

Joyce brushed by the policeman, and went towards Dane's room.

Dane was on the bed, his eyes closed. Paula and Marjorie were piling blankets on to him, Owen was holding Dane's wrist.

'Not *Alec*!' breathed Joyce.

163

She gripped Dane's hand. It felt cold. 'Not *you*, darling,' she said in a low-pitched voice.

'He's only knocked out, Miss Marrigay. Just keep him warm, and he'll be all right,' said Owen, authoritatively.

'What happened?'

'He seems to have fallen down the stairs,' said Paula.

'But – what was he doing upstairs?'

'That's what I'm wondering,' said Owen. 'Excuse me a minute, please.'

He hurried outside, beckoned by the excited constable.

Five minutes later, he was on the telephone pouring out the story to Ives; and because of the tacks and string, Ives immediately sent a telegram to Folly.

It seemed to Dane that he was lying at the bottom of a deep, dark pit. He thought he could hear voices coming out of the darkness, but they were vague and indistinct.

He lay still.

Gradually, the gloom lifted, pierced by a faint grey light. The voices became louder. He tried to open his eyes, but that brought such pain that he gave up the attempt.

'*He's coming round!*'

That was Joyce's voice. Joyce, of course. He tried to open his eyes again, but pain defeated him. He felt something cool on his forehead. Misty figures bent over him. The light was so bright that he turned his head away from the window, and heard Paula say:

'I'll draw the curtains.'

'Hallo, Alec,' said Joyce.

She was leaning over him, smiling. He reached out and touched her hand.

'I'm all right,' he muttered.

Someone else came into the room – Marjorie. A hot-water bottle was pushed beneath the bedclothes.

Presently, Joyce and Paula helped him to sit up, and Marjorie arranged the pillow behind him. One of them poured out coffee, and Joyce held the cup and saucer in front of him. He sipped.

'Ah!' he exclaimed. 'I – '

'What is it?'

'Is – is Owen here?' His voice was weak and desperate.

'He *was*,' said Paula.

'Get him,' insisted Dane.

'Look, Alec,' said Paula, 'you mustn't jump to the conclusion that this has anything to do with what's been happening. You slipped.'

'Your foot – ' began Joyce.

Dane said: 'I must see Owen.'

'Someone calling for me?' Owen demanded. He stood on the threshold, smiling, keen, eager. 'Hallo, Mr Dane – are you feeling better?'

'Come in. Joyce, do you mind – '

As the door closed on the three women, Dane said insistently:

'Owen, don't let anyone go upstairs.'

'That's all right,' said Owen, 'I've a man by the staircase.'

'Have Pengelly's rooms been searched?'

'Oh, yes,' said Owen, frowning.

'Well, you didn't make much of a job of it,' said Dane, his faint voice fiercely urgent. 'There are two imitation books in the bookcase – the gun and some white powder, arsenic I think, are hidden inside them.'

'Up – there?' gasped Owen, his voice rising.

'Yes,' said Dane. 'Hurry!'

Owen telephoned Ives again from Peter's study, with a note of suppressed excitement in his voice.

Ives arrived a little after half-past twelve. Peter Marrigay had not yet returned, no one was about in the front of the house except Owen, who had been waiting on the porch. His voice still held a tone of suppressed excitement. 'Now it *does* look as if we've found something, doesn't it?'

'We've found *something*,' Ives said dryly. 'Where have you put the things?'

'I've put them upstairs – and stationed a man in the bathroom. I thought someone *might* attempt to get the stuff away.'

'Good.'

'Miss Marrigay says we can use the breakfast-room,' Owen said. 'It's the best room in the house for talking, we can't be overheard easily.'

'Good!' repeated Ives.

They entered the room, and Owen closed the door.

'I haven't let the grass grow under my feet,' he rattled on, exuberantly. 'I've made a written report, but – '

'Tell me what you've found,' said Ives, heavily stemming the flow.

'It seems plenty,' declared Owen. 'I've reconstructed it on the basis of what Dane told me. He'd reasoned that old Pengelly had an opportunity to do practically everything that's been done, and he went upstairs to look through his rooms.'

'Why?' asked Ives.

'On the spur of the moment, he says,' said Owen. 'All the others were out, and he was bitten by this idea, so up he went. He saw those carvings which the old boy's got up there, and found out that they were figures of the Norse gods. He picked up one of Nicholas Lee's books and found that it was a fake, holding arsenic. The revolver was in another. I've left both things just where I found them.'

Ives nodded.

'He started to come downstairs to tell me what he'd discovered,' said Owen, 'and didn't notice that the string had been put across the stairs. Astonishing business, that string – I wouldn't have thought anyone would have the nerve to get to work on it so quickly, but Pengelly – '

'Yes.'

'He was upstairs,' Owen said.

'Sure?' demanded Ives.

'Well, I found some garden mud on the top stair and some traces on the upper landing,' said Owen. 'There was quite a lot of mud in Nicholas Lee's room, and Pengelly had obviously been in there – apparently he had permission to borrow any books he wanted.'

'I see,' said Ives. 'You say you haven't said a word to the old man yet?'

'No.'

'Let's go upstairs,' suggested Ives.

He put his case on the desk in the gardener's work-room, and took out a small jar of fingerprint powder, a small brush and a blower. Owen spread powder over the different articles, including the fake books, then blew the surplus powder away. Fingerprints showed up clearly.

Ives examined them through a magnifying glass.

'Two different sets, with a possible third,' he said. 'Give me that large envelope, will you – the one with the specimen prints in it.'

Owen took the envelope out of the case.

He and Ives had collected fingerprints from all the members of the household, using various tricks to get them.

'Well?' Owen squeaked.

'Pengelly handled the hammer, but that's reasonable enough,' said Ives. 'We'd better try the bannisters.'

'What about the gun?'

'Wiped clean. Dane's prints are on the books.'

'Aren't Pengelly's there?'

'I'll want to check,' said Ives.

They checked to good purpose. Recent prints of the old gardener were on the bannister rail, on one of the books – that which had contained the revolver – and on the handle of the hammer. The tacks were compared under a magnifying glass; there were traces of fingerprints on one.

Ives sent for Pengelly.

The old man looked at him out of narrowed eyes.

Yes, he had been upstairs – that was where he slept. He had been into Mr Lee's room to replace a book. He had found the hammer and tacks in the kitchen, and put them away in the tool cupboard. No, he had not known that anyone was in his work-room. He had entered Lee's room only a few minutes before Mr Dane had fallen. Why had he wanted to go upstairs? It *was* his room, he had wanted to get some tobacco. Yes, he had made the imitation books some

167

years ago – he couldn't say why.

He answered each question with seeming reluctance, drawing at his old, charred pipe.

He did not seem surprised when Ives charged him with being in possession of a firearm without a licence and with the possession of arsenic. And when he was taken off, his wife and son stood staring after the police car, sullenly unemotional.

CHAPTER XXI

FOLLY RETURNS

Folly came bustling into the police station a little after seven o'clock, and found Ives sitting at his desk, with a pile of reports in front of him.

'Well, how are things going?'

'I've detained old Pengelly,' said Ives.

'Really!'

'I couldn't do anything else,' said Ives. 'Just where he comes into it, I don't know, but he had . . . '

He told Folly the story in great detail.

'Not bad,' said Folly, 'not bad at all. One obvious gap, however.'

'Oh, yes,' agreed Ives, a little too quickly, prepared to name the gap himself – now that it had been seen – rather than allow Folly to do so. 'Pengelly couldn't have thought this business up alone.'

'Most unlikely,' said Folly, 'you would see that at once, of course. There are other gaps. Pengelly's never been to London, has he?'

'So he and his family say.'

'Has he been away from the house for a day recently?'

'Joyce Marrigay says no, quite definitely.'

'So, he couldn't have hidden the knife in Bell's laboratory,' said Folly. 'A point we mustn't forget. Beginning to wonder if you might be wrong about Bell, now?'

Ives smiled wryly.

'I'll grant you that,' he conceded.

'Splendid! But we aren't going to be deceived by appearances,' said Folly, virtuously. 'Look here, old chap, I am desperately hungry. I had practically no tea, and it's nearly half-past seven. *Could* we talk over a meal?'

'I've booked a table at the *Lion*,' said Ives, waiting for commendation.

'How thoughtful!' cried Folly, 'how exceedingly thoughtful! The *Lion*, now is it far? I hate walking, and – '

'It's just round the corner.'

'Splendid!' said Folly.

Settled in a corner in the dining-room of the *Lion*, they talked freely of Pengelly's opportunity for committing practically all the recent crimes at Marrigay, his lack of motive, and the fact that, if he were responsible, he had been working with, or for, someone else.

'What I can't understand is Pengelly being foolish enough to put the string across the stairs, knowing it would almost certainly be spotted,' Folly said thoughtfully.

Ives shook his head.

'I think you've missed something there.'

'Have I?' Folly smiled. 'Tell me.'

'It was a bit of bad luck, I think, that so many of the others were upstairs at the time,' said Ives. 'If he'd had five minutes in which to work, Pengelly could have taken away the tacks, and made it look normal. Dane's gammy foot would have easily accounted for the fall.'

'Hmm.' Folly allowed a look of extreme admiration to play over his plump features before continuing, at some length, along his own line.

'It looks pretty formidable,' said Ives, at last.

'Now, how about the others in the case. First, Marjorie, whose tantrums have puzzled me. I am assured that she was not much upset when Uncle Nicholas was first taken ill at her house, but she was considerably so after the doctor diagnosed arsenic, and my own arrival. So, poison and a policeman affected her! And since then she has definitely not behaved in character. But there are other things which I have discovered, this time about Nicholas Lee.'

Ives looked at him thoughtfully.

'Let me make it clear,' said Folly, 'that I *am* speculating. If I draw conclusions, they are tentative only. That's understood, isn't it?'

'Yes.'

'Now I have been wondering about Uncle Nicholas and his surprising decision to leave Marrigay House and go to London – the action of a very frightened man. And he to d me a remarkable story. He practically took oath that Mrs Marrigay was responsible.'

'*What?*'

'Remarkable, isn't it?' asked Folly. 'He talked about the unfaithfulness of her husband, of her love turning to hate, he said that she admitted she had arsenic, he even told me where and when she obtained it! Oh, it was a most convincing story! And one, of course, which cannot be checked, because the old lady is dead. Now although he was supposed to know nothing about her death, he did not seem as surprised as I thought he might have been. And it occurred to me –'

'Lee himself was poisoned!' Ives reminded him.

'Oh, yes, we'll come to that in a moment,' said Folly. 'Let us first think about Lee. He is a somewhat eccentric man, with a passion for the barbaric mythology of the very early days of man, a man whose mind *might* be warped. Don't you agree?'

Ives nodded.

'Then you yourself have pointed out a connection between Uncle Nicholas and Pengelly,' went on Folly, dreamily. 'The old man reads the same books. He carves models from drawings in some of the books. He had access to Lee's room whenever he likes. Moreover, Pengelly is an old family servant, and might well be regarded as a friend. All

170

three of the Pengellys are accepted in such a way by the family, aren't they?'

'Yes,' said Ives.

'Then we have a connection which is stronger than it might at first appear,' said Folly. 'Supposing the two men are conspiring together in this, would it not be reasonable for Pengelly to try to distract attention from Lee by directing it towards the Bells?'

'I suppose so,' Ives said, 'but – '

'I will stand all the ridicule you like to pour on my theorising soon,' said Folly, 'but do let me finish, there's a good chap. We must accept that Pengelly, under Lee's influence, might try to divert suspicion. And while I do not for one moment believe that Pengelly was responsible for *thinking* out these crimes, he might well have committed them, or some of them, under Lee's direction.'

'But Lee – '

'Please! Lee *was* poisoned, yes, we will come to that in a moment. Let us forget it while we deal with the other possibilities. Motive. Now imagine this strange fellow, buried in the past yet living in the present, looked upon as a rather simple-minded eccentric strongly influenced and domineered by his sister, tolerated by her children - can't you imagine such a man conceiving an idea of *revenge*. Can't you imagine that he would develop first dislike, then intolerant hatred, and, with his warped mind, so steeped in the crude myths, and harsh retaliations of the gods, can't you imagine him planning some horrible thing?'

'I suppose so,' said Ives, reluctantly.

'And then, think of some of the things with which we have to deal,' said Folly. 'Ives, I ask you to pay the closest attention. We have two Alsatian dogs, Thor and Saturn. Thor was the god of war, Saturn the god of agriculture and of good living.'

Ives said quickly:

'Lee would naturally give them names like that.'

'Oh, yes. But follow me closely. Old Marrigay died on a Sunday – remember? His wife died also on a Sunday – a

171

moonlit night. Roger Hurst – a soldier – was attacked by the dog on a Tuesday. Dane, a newspaperman, was hurt on a Wednesday. I am, perhaps, being even more foolish than usual, and I should hate Owen to know what I am thinking,' Folly murmured, 'but the days of the week are named after the mythological gods. Sunday – the Sun God, the Fire God. Monday, the day of Diana, Goddess of the Moon. Tuesday, *Thor's* day, and Wednesday, Woden's day, after the god Woden, who sent his ravens round the world in a quest for news.'

Ives said slowly: 'Now, Folly!'

'Oh, I'll grant you that it sounds absurd and that I may be wrong,' said Folly, quickly; 'but I ask you to think about it. Here are two men, steeped in mythology. Here are elementary facts in mythology. Here are a series of crimes, which, in their different ways, have some association with those elementary facts. It's worth thinking about.'

Ives, unable to help himself, began to laugh.

'I *must* tell Owen!' he chuckled.

'Ives, you wouldn't be so unkind! I have been doing what I am always advising him not to do – thinking aloud. But – it's remarkable. I insist that it's remarkable!'

'It's wonderful!' gurgled Ives.

'You are amused,' said Folly, sharply. 'Yet I advise you to think along the lines of my suggestion. Waiter! Coffee, please. And while you are thinking you might care to bear these facts in mind,' went on Folly. 'Nicholas Lee has taken arsenic before. The arsenic *appears* to have been taken in his coffee, disguised as saccharine tablets. He himself *could* have taken a dose, however, before going to the Hursts, knowing full well that he would get prompt medical attention and also knowing that he would not die. Moreover, he would be away from Marrigay House at the time of the fire. Now he may possibly have fixed that contraption to Mrs Marrigay's bed, regulating the dripping of the acid on to the cork so that it would take a certain time to reach the combustible in the thicker glass bottle beneath, although Pengelly may have done that. Another thing. He declares that he began to

172

feel ill very soon after drinking his coffee at breakfast, and says further that it was so bitter that he did not finish it. Yet he likes his coffee black and sweet – a remarkable concoction! – and would surely put in plenty of saccharine if there were not enough sugar. Do these facts impress you more?' he demanded.

'*Now* you're talking,' said Ives.

'Thank you. I suggest to you that it is at least *possible* that Nicholas Lee poisoned himself, and, working with Pengelly, did the other things. It is also possible that he was able to exert such an influence over Pengelly that the old man would let Thor loose on the Tuesday and attack Dane on the Wednesday. Well?'

Ives said slowly: 'You've shaken me, you know, although Dane only happened to be upstairs.'

'Yes, and therefore vulnerable. I have tied the facts together, and formed a theory,' went on Folly, 'a theory I think well worth following up. There are, of course, other possibilities arising from it.'

'Such as?'

'I think you ought to puzzle them out for yourself,' said Folly, severely. 'Have you finished?'

'Yes, I'm ready.'

'Then I think we will go to Marrigay House, and see how things are there,' said Folly. 'Thank you for an excellent dinner.'

Peter had been in Marston most of the day, and returned a little after five o'clock, with Roger sitting beside him. They seemed to be on good terms. Roger's face and arm were heavily bandaged, but he was cheerful, and carried Marjorie off to their room soon after his return.

Peter, going in search of Dane, found him in the drawing-room with Joyce and Paula.

Peter stopped on the threshold.

'Hallo, what have you been up to?'

'Falling down stairs,' said Dane cheerfully.

'Have you heard?' asked Joyce sharply.

'Heard what?'

'About Pengelly?'

'Now, what's this?' demanded Peter.

Joyce told him.

He sat on the arm of a chair, frowning as he listened. He did not speak for a while after the story was told. Then he said explosively:

'Bloody fools!'

'I don't know about that,' said Dane.

'Oh, no – your bright idea,' said Peter. 'I can believe the rest of us might do something like this, but Pengelly – it's fantastic! I'll see the police.'

'I don't see *why* it's so fantastic,' argued Paula. 'And they wouldn't have arrested him unless they had reasonable evidence.'

'No one knows what the police consider reasonable,' said Peter, sarcastically. He dropped heavily into a chair and lit a cigarette.

'Middleton is coming out here tomorrow to read the will. The funeral is on Friday. No music, just a quiet ceremony. All right?' He sounded aggressive.

'Yes,' said Joyce, quietly.

'I've also engaged Middleton to look after Tinker Bell,' Peter said, looking at Paula.

He broke off, for Roger's footsteps thudded on the stairs, and above them was Marjorie's voice.

'But we can't be *sure*, darling,'

'Never mind about that,' growled Roger, and pushed open the door.

CHAPTER XXII

MARJORIE REMEMBERS

'Well, what is it now?' asked Peter, with an edge to his voice.

'Roger, it's not fair,' said Marjorie. 'I might be quite wrong.'

'We'll have to find out about that,' said Roger, ignoring the tartness in Peter's voice. 'Marjorie's been keeping something to herself all the time,' he declared, 'she thought it was the best thing to do – but no wonder she's been worried.'

'Well, *what*?' demanded Peter.

'Roger, *no*!' Marjorie came into the room behind her husband, looking distraught. 'It isn't fair.'

'Anything's fair if it helps to get at the truth,' said Roger.

He spoke with difficulty because of his injured cheek, but there was a hard glint in his eyes, and Dane saw that nothing would put him off.

'Yes – all's fair in this show,' Peter said. 'Out with it.'

'It's about that knife that was found at the lab,' Roger said.

Paula jumped up.

'Marjorie's remembered that when Uncle Nicholas came to see us, last time, he *had* the knife,' said Roger.

'I only think he had,' said Marjorie. 'Uncle Nicholas took some things out of his pocket, you know they are always filled with a hopeless tangle of oddments, and the knife was among them. He put it back quickly, but – '

'Well, *well*,' breathed Paula.

'And there's something else,' said Roger.

'Go on,' Peter growled.

175

'Uncle mentioned that he'd been to Tinker Bell's lab, but it was still locked up.'

'Are you suggesting that Uncle Nick went back and planted that knife?' demanded Peter, in a harsh voice.

'At the moment I'm dealing in facts, not suggestions,' said Roger, heavily.

'Peter, you must see what it means,' said Paula, swinging round, 'It might clear Tinker – '

'At Uncle Nick's expense.'

'You can hardly expect me to worry too much about that,' said Paula. 'Tinker is my first consideration.'

'But Uncle Nick's a victim of poisoning,' Joyce exclaimed.

'I don't profess to understand it, but I think we ought to tell the police,' said Roger. 'I can't make out what Nicholas was up to, but the fact that the knife was found at the lab is the chief reason for Tinker Bell being in jail, and it's up to us to throw doubt on whether he knew it was there. That's only fair.'

'Of course,' said Peter, dryly. 'Have you remembered anything else, sister dear?'

'No, I don't remember anything else,' Marjorie said in a wounded voice, 'and I don't believe that Uncle, any more than Tinker, would have had anything to do with it.'

'I see,' said Peter. 'Well, I suppose, as usual, Roger's right, and we'll have to tell the police. Ives said that he would be here some time this evening – mind if we wait until then?'

'I suppose we'd better,' agreed Roger.

Folly and Ives arrived together. Folly looked definitely smug when the story was told to him, while Ives hid astonishment. Dane studied the two policemen closely, and came to the conclusion that they had something up their sleeve.

Peter was first to be questioned and afterwards, at Folly's request, went into his study to wait for the others – they were allowed to confer after the interrogation, but not before it. Dane went along to the study and the others waited for their turn in the drawing-room.

'Well, what do they want?' Dane asked.

Peter laughed.

'I wouldn't like to say. Folly's got some queer notion that there was trouble between my mother and father. The insolence of these beggars!'

'They have to do their job,' remarked Dane.

'Oh, of course,' said Peter, dryly. 'But I do know one thing. Folly's unbearably smug this evening.'

'I thought so, too,' said Dane, worriedly.

Joyce and Marjorie came in, and all had been asked whether they knew of any reason for jealousy or ill-feeling between their parents. Although innumerable questions had been put to each one of them, that particular question seemed the main purpose behind Folly's interrogation.

Joyce looked up suddenly and asked in a strained voice:

'Peter, did he ask you if Mother was different just *before* Father died?'

'He did, and I told him that I don't practise telepathy,' said Peter.

'But - she *did* change.'

'Afterwards,' Marjorie exclaimed.

'It had started before. You wouldn't notice it, not living here. Afterwards, she aged so much. *Does* Folly know - '

'Folly knows nothing, don't get that crazy idea into your head.'

Yet it was a disturbing suggestion.

Roger Hurst left the breakfast-room, where Folly and Ives were sitting, and closed the door behind him. Folly, at a small table, sat with the tips of his fingers pressed tightly together.

'Well,' said Folly, at last.

'Nothing to substantiate Lee's story about trouble between husband and wife,' said Ives.

'Nothing at all,' said Folly. 'We can't accept that as final, of course, Mrs Marrigay may not have told her children. On the other hand, you would think that there must have been something noticeable, yet none of them seemed to be hiding anything - don't you agree?'

'Yes.'

'So the appearances against Nicholas Lee and Pengelly look blacker,' said Folly. 'You know, Ives, we might have another go at Lee's room – and at Pengelly's, if it comes to that.'

'We shan't find much else in Pengelly's,' commented Ives.

'You never know – let's go up,' said Folly. 'There is one good thing, Marrigay is undoubtedly offering us all the help he can. In his position some men would have made it very difficult for us. In spite of his somewhat arrogant manner, I am inclined to like the Colonel. It would be civil to tell him what we're going to do,' he added.

'It might also be civil to tell me what you're going to look for,' suggested Ives.

'Corks,' said Folly, briefly.

Ives stared . . .

Peter raised no objection, and the two detectives went first to Pengelly's room. Owen and Ives had already searched it thoroughly, and Ives did not think it possible they they had missed anything.

Folly seemed to make only a cursory examination.

Two or three corks were lying in one of the drawers of the bench, but they were smaller than the burnt piece which had been found under the bed. Folly put them in his pocket, however, and examined the bench with much more interest than he gave to the rest of the room. There were a couple or more little round marks on it, which were rough to touch.

'See them?' asked Folly.

'He's been using some kind of drilling tool on there,' commented Ives.

'Possibly. They're discoloured.'

'He stains his images.'

'Hmm, yes,' said Folly and to Ives's surprise, he bent down and studied the wooden floorboards in front of the bench. There were similar round marks on the floor.

'I don't see why you're interested,' said Ives.

'I think you will,' said Folly, '*if* you'll only think about it.'

He had not been quite himself since dinner, and Ives

178

accepted that philosophically. Nevertheless, Ives was pre-occupied with the possible significance of the little round marks as they finished in the workroom. They went next to Lee's bedroom. Ives could believe that Lee was guilty except when he thought of the mythological basis which Folly had suggested; this still amused him.

Lee's bedroom door was locked; Ives unlocked it, and switched on the light.

Two or three of Pengelly's carved figures met their gaze; they saw nothing else of consequence. Folly and Ives opened every drawer and looked in every possible hiding place, but found no corks.

'It doesn't look as if you're going to be lucky.' Ives commented.

'There's time yet,' said Folly, 'we haven't looked through his pockets. You might make a start, there's a good chap.' He himself was studying the carpet. Ives obediently turned to the suits and overcoats. Now and again he glanced at Folly, who began to shift two small tables. Folly went down on his knees.

'Anything?' asked Ives.

'Might be. Just a minute.'

Ives felt the pockets of an old sports jacket. He drew the coat off its hanger, in order to examine it more closely. He took a soiled handkerchief, some string, a piece of sealing wax, a knife, and two keys out of one pocket, and dropped them on to the foot of the bed, watching Folly curiously.

Then he put his hand into the other pocket; and felt something cylindrical – solid, but not very hard. *There were three corks.*

'Folly!' he exclaimed.

'Come here a minute, will you?' asked Folly. 'I –'

'Corks!'

'Found 'em?' asked Folly, absently. 'I thought you would. But come and tell me what you make of this.'

Ives glared at the back of his neck, but joined him.

Folly was fingering a bare patch of carpet. It was not large, and looked rather as if it had been eaten by moths.

179

'Well?' asked Ives.

'Think of the marks upstairs, the cork, and the way that fire was started,' said Folly.

Ives tried to see the connection, but failed.

Folly straightened up, and gave him a lofty smile.

'My dear chap, you're tired – you would see what I mean if you weren't. That carpet has been eaten into by acid. The bench upstairs was eaten in the same way – so was the floor. Little drops of a corrosive acid fell at all three places, and the damage was done, quite irremediably. Don't you agree?'

'It *could* be,' conceded Ives.

'It almost certainly is,' said Folly. 'We'll need expert opinion, although all they'll be able to say is that it might have been, I suppose. Still, it's a reasonable conclusion. And somewhere, someone had to find out how long it took the particular acid they used to burn through a cork. Eh?'

'I suppose so,' said Ives. 'And it strengthens the case against –'

'Lee? *I* don't think so,' said Folly. 'I don't think so at all, Ives. I think it weakens the case.'

Ives fingered his jaw.

'It becomes so obvious –' Folly began.

'No, it doesn't,' growled Ives, in an angry and despairing tone. 'You may be nursing ideas of your own, but unless you give me a lead, I can't follow them. If you *must* keep things to yourself, all right, but *keep* them to yourself or else tell me the conclusions you've come to. I've been in this game long enough to know who's the better man but I've had twenty-five years at it, you know. In this particular job I've done the work, you've just taken the results and sifted them. It may be a holiday for you, but it's hard grind for me.'

'My dear fellow,' protested Folly gently, 'indeed, I appreciate all you've done, it couldn't have been improved upon. Now don't be upset – I *am* a little eccentric, you know, and I've been spoiled, perhaps.' He looked very earnest. 'If I've annoyed you, well, I'm really sorry. My mind's been so overflowing – like yours – and I either talk too much or too little.'

'You've found the corks and evidence of acid,' said Ives, already repentant, 'and to me that strengthens the suspicion against Lee and Pengelly.'

'Yes, of course,' said Folly, 'but – and you must do me justice – at dinner I was saying that there was another possibility, emerging from the one which I outlined to you. Simply, it's this: it's plausible that Nicholas Lee might have conceived and put this fantastic plot into action, but it isn't *likely*. I saw the possibility, and it occurred to me while we were talking that it was a brilliant idea, an *obvious* possibility, and that someone else might so have timed and dated the crimes to make it look as if they had sprung from this esoteric individual's mind. We have agreed between us that Bell may be the victim of a conspiracy. So might Nicholas Lee and Pengelly. And if they *are*, then someone *in the house when Dane was injured* is behind it. Rule out Pengelly for the time being, and whom have we left?' When Ives did not answer, Folly went on: 'One thing springs immediately to mind – a member of the family.'

Ives was so absorbed that he'failed to hear a sound at the door. To his astonishment, Folly put his fingers to his lips, slightly raising his voice.

'As I say, a member of the family. It is curious that Peter Marrigay's knife was used. Equally curious that Marjorie, should have suddenly recalled those details about her uncle, even more curious that the family should have agreed to tell us. One would think they would much rather keep such things to themselves, but – no, it concerned their Uncle Nicholas, and what do they care for him? *Nothing*,' breathed Folly.

'Well – ' Ives began.

'And the *family* took the decision to barricade the house, and prevent all outsiders from coming in,' said Folly. 'I have a suggestion to make about that, Ives – and I think you will agree that it's reasonable. If they wanted it to be believed that the danger came from without, what more natural than for them to act as if that were so, as if they completely trusted one another. We haven't discovered the

181

truth about the Marrigay family yet, but I would say that all the indications are clear – they are trying to push the blame on to someone outside the family. Don't you agree?'

'It's possible,' said Ives, weakly.

'Any one of them could, today, have put the hammer and tacks in a place where Pengelly would naturally handle them,' said Folly, 'and Pengelly, a very loyal servant, would say nothing to harm any one of them. There are other things to remember, too, Ives. We have only their uncorroborated statements about the incidents which appear to suggest they were attacked. There was a bullet in the tree; *was* it fired at Peter Marrigay? There was a trench in the road; *did* it nearly break Joyce Marrigay's neck? And I want you to see these things in conjunction with what I consider to be the most important question: *why* did the Marrigays suddenly unbarricade the grounds, what took away their fear?'

He paused, turned the handle of the door and pulled it open, and added in a deep, booming voice:

'Perhaps *you* can tell us!'

Joyce and Dane stood there.

CHAPTER XXIII

DISCOVERY

'Well, madam?' inquired Folly with the utmost politeness. 'Has your eavesdropping served you well?'

Joyce backed away, colliding with Dane who was just behind her.

'Or are you frightened of the truth? For I will tell you it is time that the members of this household realised that there must be an end to furtive, stealthy movements, to lies and half-truths. Murder has been done, and the murderer will be brought to book. So will his accomplices. And if you will pry at keyholes, can you expect us to think your motives pure and innocent?'

Joyce flinched at the accusation in his voice.

'So you are nonplussed, tongue-tied, your guilt – '

'We've had enough of this nonsense,' said Dane, quietly.

Folly glared at him.

'Don't be such a bombastic ass,' continued Dane, equably. But for the tension, Ives would have been amused. 'This *is* Miss Marrigay's home, you know. She has a right to be where she likes and do what she likes. As for eavesdropping and peeping through keyholes, your people have done quite enough of that themselves!'

'This is no business of yours, sir.'

'I made it yours,' said Dane.

'Alec, it's all right,' Joyce said.

'But it isn't all right. If Folly will bellow about the house, he must expect you and the rest of us to want to know what he's talking about.'

Peter appeared, rather suddenly. 'What's all the fuss?'

'He's wondering whether you lied about being shot at, whether Joyce lied about that trench in the road,' said Dane, 'and – '

'You will be good enough to leave explanations to me,' breathed Folly. 'Miss Marrigay – '

'*Is the Inspector here?*' Sergeant Owen was speaking breathlessly in the hall.

'Yes, *and* Folly,' said the constable.

'I must see them,' said Owen, hurrying towards the stairs, 'I've found – '

Then he saw Peter on the landing, and stopped.

Earlier that evening, Sergeant Owen had been facing the fact that he had not shone in this affair. The whole business had depressed, even humiliated him.

Ives faithfully reported to Owen practically everything Folly said – because Ives believed in giving his juniors every chance to follow a case step by step – and Owen had come to the conclusion that Folly was right about one thing; the biggest mystery was why Marrigay had suddenly opened up the house and grounds. And he might be right about the so-called reporter of the *Sunday World* being dead.

Although officially he was off duty, Owen decided to go to Marrigay. He stopped his car outside the *Marrigay Arms*, wondering if he could pick up anything from the people at the inn. Nothing useful was said, however, and leaving his car outside the inn, he had walked to the stile which led to Marrigay House, climbed over, reflecting again on the sudden decision to take down the barbed wire. It was curious that everything had started with Dane's arrival at Marrigay.

Nearing the house, Owen had heard a peculiar sound.

He stood still.

It was peculiar, in as much as it was night-time. Someone was trundling a wheelbarrow along a path. The sound was coming from the stables and outbuildings. Owen went round the back of the house, walking quietly, puzzled as to why anyone should wheel a barrow at nine o'clock at night.

The light from the kitchen window shone on Lem Pengelly.

A shadow loomed out of the darkness. Owen recognised one of the policemen from Marston.

Together they watched, unseen.

'What's he up to?'

'Only piling some more stuff over the dog.'

'Dog?'

'That brute that attacked the big fellow,' whispered the constable. 'Buried him behind the potting shed.'

Owen waited until Lem had gone off, wheeling the barrow, and then approached the shed. The constable was by his side.

'Who buried him?' Owen asked.

'The old man and his son.'

Soon, the wheelbarrow was trundled towards the sheds, and again Lem appeared in the light from the kitchen window. He was wheeling a load of stones and old bricks, and tipped them over the grave, then flattened them out with a fork. Owen stepped forward.

"Evening,' he said.

Lem uttered a startled exclamation. He stood rigidly, staring at Owen.

'Keeping yourself busy?' asked Owen.

'Must do something,' muttered Lem.

'That's right. How's your mother?'

'She's all right,' said Lem. He turned away, calling 'Good night', over his shoulder. Making for the back door, the constable, half-doubtfully, following him.

Deeply suspicious, Owen picked up the fork which Lem had left near the pile of rubble. He cleared the stones away, then dug into the loose soil. The earth had been recently turned, and it was not heavy going. He thought of the exhumation, and the dozen men who had been in the grounds – that was the way to handle a job like this. But now he had started, he might as well finish it. The dog wasn't likely to be buried *so* deep –

Well, it was deeper than he expected.

He was down two feet before his fork stuck into something and did not pull away freely. Owen put the fork aside, and picked up a spade. He cleared the earth away from the soft thing into which the fork had gone and then shone his torch into the hole.

Something glinted.

He bent nearer . . . and saw a button, attached to a coat.

'My God!' exclaimed Owen.

He turned and ran towards the kitchen, from the window of which the light was shining. The constable was near the back door.

'Anything the matter, sir?'

'Yes. Go into the kitchen. Tell them what you like, but don't let them out of your sight. Caution them, if needs be – no, tell Lem the Inspector wants to see him.'

Owen returned to the grave, aquiver with excitement, determined to make a job of it before reporting to Ives. He found the dog, on top of a man's body.

As he ran towards the house, he saw Colonel Marrigay looking down at him with a curious expression in his eyes.

'Now I think we know why Marrigay thought it safe to relax his precautions,' breathed Folly.

Leah and Lem were under guard in the kitchen. The rest of the household had been gathered into the drawing-room, and a constable was left in the hall, to report if any of them moved away from the room, or attempted to use the telephone.

By half-past ten, the body had been lifted from the earth and was lying on a bench in the potting-shed. The features of the dead man were quite clear. There was something familiar about the face, Ives thought, and Owen, still too startled to preen himself over his discovery, whispered that he had a feeling he had seen the man before.

After his one cryptic remark, Folly had said little and seemed content to leave the immediate arrangements to Ives.

Only when the body was on the bench and Folly had examined the ugly head wounds which had caused death, did Folly stir to animation.

'Well, Ives, we're certainly making progress now. I think we'll begin by asking Lem and his mother to view the body.'

But Leah's thin face and tight lips gave nothing away. She shook her head when asked if she had seen the dead man before. Lem stared at the face, and his mouth worked, but neither would he say whether he had seen the man before. He insisted doggedly that he had not known the body was there.

'He's lying, I'm sure he's lying,' Owen insisted, 'He was scared stiff when he saw me watching him.'

'You're probably right, Owen,' said Folly, benignly. 'This is indeed a good night's work – I shall have to put in a word for you with the Inspector!' he beamed. 'Peter Marrigay next, I think. He'll confirm the poor creatures' identity.'

'Confirm?' ejaculated Ives.

'Why, yes – I think I know who it is, Ives. Now don't accuse me of withholding facts, I started from the same point as you. True, I visited the Marrigay's London solicitors on my own, but I did tell you. And I went there for confirmation of an idea!'

'Look, I – ' began Ives.

'Now allow me a little triumph,' begged Folly. 'Just wait events. Send for Marrigay, will you? Oh – and have him watched afterwards. He will want to be on his own for a while, but I wish to know the moment he rejoins the others.'

Resignedly, Ives summoned Peter from the drawing-room.

Peter looked hard at the body; his face was blank, but he nodded when he straightened up.

'Yes, I've seen him before,' he said.

'Where?'

'He's the man who broke into the grounds, the day that Dane arrived,' said Peter. 'He called himself a reporter.'

'Had you ever seen him before that?' asked Folly.

Peter said 'No,' very quietly, but definitely.

Folly did not show any sign of disappointment, although Ives was sure he had hoped for something more helpful. Peter was not detained, but a man was sent to follow him. Folly was right in one prophecy, at least; Peter went to his study, not to the drawing-room.

Marchmant arrived while Folly and Ives were making a closer examination of the wounds in the back of the dead man's head. Owen came in on the police-surgeon's heels, carrying several of the tools which had been used to make the hole in the road. Folly said:

'One of these may have caused the wounds – what is your opinion?'

Marchmant examined the picks and axes, then the head wounds again.

'That's the lethal weapon, I think,' he said, pointing at a pick which had been scrubbed clean before the police had examined it. 'I'll have to make a closer examination, but there are several wounds in the skull which coincide with the shape of the pick. There are other minor injuries, caused by a different weapon.'

'Which came first?' asked Folly.

'Oh, the lesser wounds – they swelled up before he was

187

dead or mortally wounded. Is this getting you any nearer the solution?'

'Oh, undoubtedly,' agreed Folly, 'but we must be cautious – many are the pitfalls which confront the impetuous, eh, Owen?' He beamed. 'But we can deduce one thing logically – I have already referred to it.' He paused, as if he were aware that all of them were waiting on his words and was enjoying the suspense of his own making. 'I think we know why Peter and Joyce Marrigay felt that they could safely relax their precautions. *This* man was the danger. He once broke into the grounds. He pretended to be a newspaperman, but that was to deceive Dane, not Marrigay, who knew who he was. I think we shall find that later that night, this man was killed. Marrigay knew it, and the body was buried. Thus, the immediate cause of anxiety was removed, so the barbed wire and trappings were taken away.'

'It *looks* as if you're right,' said Ives.

'I don't see how it can be wrong,' Owen chimed in. 'It's masterly! You said look for a body, and here it is I – I give up! No wonder you've got a reputation!'

Folly blushed.

'He can't be wrong over this,' Owen repeated.

'Now, sergeant!' Folly wagged a reproving finger. 'Of course I can be wrong – I am not infallible. But if I am right, it helps us a great deal. Once we can discover who killed this man, then I think everything else will break open. And there is one other interesting thing – you know, *all* of you ought to have noticed what I mean.'

He looked at the body.

Ives rubbed his chin.

'I've been wondering,' he said. 'That nose – '

'A Roman nose, a Marrigay nose,' breathed Folly. 'The family likeness is marked. And there was talk from Uncle Nicholas about the senior Marrigay's infidelity, wasn't there?'

'What are you going to do?' asked Marchmant.

Folly beamed again.

'I think Marrigay will ponder over this and decide to

confide in his family and friends,' he said, 'that is where our eavesdropping comes in. I – '

A policeman approached.

'Colonel Marrigay's joined the others,' he reported.

Folly moved towards the door.

CHAPTER XXIV

CONFESSION

Peter entered the drawing-room, an unhappy smile on his face.

Marjorie jumped up.

'What did they want, Peter?'

Peter looked at them all in turn, Joyce was sitting absolutely still; Dane felt her rigidity. Roger's eyes glittered between bandages, Paula sat at ease in an armchair, knitting.

'I've just viewed a new body,' he said.

'Peter!'

Joyce shivered involuntarily, and Dane saw terror in her eye.. She moved a little away from him, staring at Peter.

'Are you joking?' demanded Roger.

'My dear chap, even I don't see anything funny in dead bodies,' said Peter. He smiled at Joyce. 'Take it easy, Joyce – it's not your doing, you know.'

She began: 'Is it – ' and broke off.

Peter nodded.

'What *is* all this about?' demanded Roger.

'Do you know who it is?' said Dane.

'Yes, I know him. You've seen him. The *Sunday World* representative!' Peter moved jerkily. 'You didn't think he was a newspaperman even from the beginning, did you?'

'Now look here – ' began Roger.

'At least I can tell you this story in my own way,' said Peter. 'All right, Joyce?'

'I – I suppose so,' whispered Joyce.

'The police are pretty sure to trace him, and once they do, they'll know what happened,' said Peter, 'so we may as well anticipate them. Joyce knows a little. I told her about it tonight. It goes back quite a while. We always thought that Mother and Father were an ideal couple. We were not quite right. Father had a mistress.'

'*Oh, Peter!*' gasped Marjorie.

'It needn't shock you as much as all that,' said Peter, with an edge to his voice. 'And we may as well face the facts. He had a child by this other woman – the dead man.'

'Upon my soul!' muttered Roger.

'During Father's lifetime, the son – our half-brother – was given an allowance. Just before his death, Mother learned about it. The allowance stopped. So our half-brother came here to protest. When Mother wasn't having any, he threatened violence. He so scared Mother and Uncle Nicholas that they took precautions. I was told about it soon after I returned. I strengthened the precautions. At the time, you see, I thought it was *only* this particular man. I could have taken the sensible course and reported it to the police, but that would have meant a scandal, and – oh, I wasn't in a normal frame of mind, anyhow. But after a while – especially after I'd been shot at and Joyce nearly had her neck broken – I wasn't satisfied at the way things were going. Our half-brother had not only threatened violence, he had shown he was prepared to carry it out. But once you've started a defence, there's a tendency to maintain it,' went on Peter, half-mockingly. 'It wasn't until you arrived, Alec, and the love-child broke in, that things came to a head. We now come to the difficult part of the story,' said Peter. 'I saw him to the gate and then our charming half-brother suddenly lost his temper and came at me with a knife. I dodged, picked up a fallen branch, and gave him a terrific clout on the head. I felt pretty dazed with the shock of it all, and when Lem came dashing up and told me the man was dead and I must get back to the house to establish an alibi, I went like a lamb. He said he and his father would bury the man behind the potting-shed that night, I wasn't to worry. It had been self-defence, he'd seen that. As usual I took the line of least resistance and left it at that. Weak? Perhaps. In character? Certainly. When you persuaded me to call in the police, Alec, I thought there was a chance that this wouldn't be discovered. From what the man had told me, I was certain he hadn't murdered my father, and that was the main problem.'

'You damned fool!' roared Roger. 'If you'd told the police everything, there'd have been no trouble. Lem would have testified that it was self-defence. You must have been crazy!'

'Possibly. Aren't we all a bit, at times?'

Paula stopped knitting.

'I shouldn't start a row now,' she said.

'But Roger's right,' said Peter, sardonically. 'I *was* crazy. I've been in a pretty odd state, you know, these few months since I got back to civilisation. For years taking a life here or there meant nothing – it was you or the other fellow, the only question was who got in first. But now I've got things back into proportion again and, in this case, I'm all for the truth and nothing but the truth.'

'You let old Pengelly be arrested – ' Marjorie said, in a shocked voice.

'Not for this particular crime,' said Peter, 'and in any case, I have only to tell the truth to get him cleared of any suspicion over the love-child. But there were other preoccupations. Father *was* murdered and the murderer was still at large. The love-child gave me a mouthful about that.' Peter paused. 'You see, I told him that if I ever saw him about again I'd break his neck, and he retorted that even if I killed him there'd still be the one to reckon with who'd got my father.'

'He was probably talking for the sake of talking,' said Paula.

'I didn't get that impression,' retorted Peter. 'He hated our guts – we were the legitimate children and got everything, he got nothing by my father's will and was never likely to get anything more. In such a mood, I think he would tell the

191

truth. And he wasn't a very good specimen, you know. I doubted – with that part of my mind which could still be logical – whether he had the brains to organise a terror campaign, which is what it amounted to. And as Mother was murdered and Uncle Nicholas nearly murdered *since* our half-brother died, we know that he was not uttering wild threats.'

'I'm not at all convinced,' sniffed Paula.

'What are you going to do?'

'Tell Folly,' said Peter.

Joyce shivered.

'M-must you?' asked Paula, in a quavering voice.

'Of course you must,' said Roger.

'You see, the adversaries are in complete agreement for once,' remarked Peter. 'What do you think, Dane?'

'You're right,' said Dane, in a hushed voice.

As he spoke, the handle of the door turned, and Folly appeared. He came in quietly, Ives behind him. Joyce stretched out her hand, and Dane took it and held it tightly. Paula put down her knitting. Yet at a moment when Folly might have been bombastic and gusty, he was quiet and reasoning.

'You are very wise, Colonel Marrigay. I was, in fact, about to charge you with complicity in this crime. You are prepared to make a statement?'

'Oh, yes,' said Peter. 'Now who's the eavesdropper-in-chief?'

'You are, perhaps, justified in making that retort,' said Folly, 'but it does not greatly matter. I – ' he broke off, for there were hurried footsteps approaching, and he frowned testily.

'Sir!' called Owen.

Folly looked into the hall.

'What is it?'

'Lem Pengelly has confessed.'

'*Confessed!*' cried Peter.

'About the body we've found,' reported Owen stolidly. 'He says the man attacked Colonel Marrigay, who knocked

192

him out. Pengelly took him to the garage. He came round and grabbed an axe, Pengelly hit him with one of the picks which was standing near, they had a fight and the man was killed. Then both Pengellys buried him.'

Peter said sharply:

'I shouldn't take too much for granted, Folly. The Pengellys would say black was white for the sake of the family.'

'*Did* you hit your half-brother with a stick?' inquired Folly.

'A bit of a branch, but – '

'Then the later story appears to hold water,' said Folly. 'I shall have to detain both of you for questioning, Colonel Marrigay. But before we leave, I think there are other things that we ought to clear up don't you?'

'I should say there are!' Roger burst out.

'I am going to take a somewhat unusual course,' Folly said, 'and take you into my confidence. You have shown that you now intend to tell the truth, you have fully explained some of the things which mystified us. But there remain three crimes unsolved. The murder of your father, of your mother, and the attempt to kill Nicholas Lee. Also, as you have pointed out, there is the probability that your half-brother was not the instigator of this campaign against you.'

Everyone in the room was watching him intently.

'I want to tell you what your Uncle Nicholas believes,' said Folly.

He told them, and also the method used for the murder of Mrs Marrigay.

He chose his words carefully, imprinting the picture clearly on their minds. No one moved or spoke.

'Now, do you place any credence in that story?' Folly asked, quietly. '*Was* your mother so bitter that she would take such a step?'

Joyce said quietly: 'I don't think so, do you, Peter?'

'No,' said Peter. 'I don't think she really knew the truth until just before my father was dead, and it was that discovery which aged her.' He spoke gently. 'In any case, she was murdered,' he pointed out.

'She – she *might* have started the fire herself,' said Marjorie in a muffled voice.

Peter shook his head.

'No, no. If she wanted to commit suicide, she wouldn't have chosen that way. We can't get away from the obvious, I'm afraid. Someone started that fire. I could have done it.'

Folly nodded ponderously.

'Joyce had the opportunity. So did Marjorie and Roger, or for that matter Paula and Tinker Bell. And when you come to think of it, Folly, you're getting warm. We know who fired at me, we know who nearly broke Joyce's neck, but someone who had access to the house put that revolver and the arsenic upstairs – '

Folly whispered, each word dramatically formed: '*How did you know what we found upstairs, Colonel Marrigay?*'

Peter shot a quick, startled glance at Joyce.

'Well?' boomed Folly. 'Who told you? How d'd you know?'

'I – I heard some of the police talking among themselves,' Peter said hastily, 'they – '

'You did not! Great care was taken to make sure that you could not know about that. Who told you, sir?'

After a long pause, Joyce stirred on the sofa.

'I did,' she said.

Until that moment, Dane had felt outside this inquiry, a spectator, watching the police and the suspects, now marvelling at and now amused by Folly's tactics and Peter's manner. He saw no danger to Joyce.

Now Joyce had smashed his complacency. The policemen, even Lem, seemed to be staring at her as if she were guilty.

How had she known?

Folly broke the silence in a quiet voice.

'Did you, Miss Marrigay?'

'Yes.'

'Then I must ask you the same question – how did you know what was in the imitation books?'

194

Joyce glanced up at Dane, and then looked away from him.

'I saw Alec looking at them. I came in from the village with Paula and went to my room to put my coat away,' she said, 'and heard someone upstairs. I knew it wasn't Pengelly, or Leah, who were both in the kitchen. I went up, and saw Alec standing in the room with the book in his hand. And then he found the gun.'

'I – see,' said Folly.

'Why didn't you tell me?' demanded Dane.

'I was bewildered,' said Joyce. 'I went downstairs and tried to think, and then you were hurt and Pengelly was arrested. I told Peter, and he advised me to say nothing about it – it didn't seem to *matter*,' she went on. 'It – '

Peter smiled at Dane. 'The truth is you discovered something which led to Pengelly's arrest. You had to tell the police. But there it was – you'd betrayed one of the family's loyalists. She couldn't talk to you about it.'

'Where *is* all this leading us to?' demanded Paula, pettishly. 'You seemed to have formed opinions about a great number of things, Superintendent.' She stared up at Folly challengingly. 'But I would like to point out that my husband is still in prison. You have no real evidence against him, *only* the fact that the knife was found in his laboratory, but – and Marjorie told you this, remember – Uncle Nicholas once had that knife. *And* on his own admission, he had been to the laboratory before joining the four of us, Roger, Marjorie, Tinker and me. He may have gone back there. Isn't that true, Jorrie?'

Marjorie nodded.

'He's cunning,' Paula went on. 'I've been thinking a lot about Uncle Nicholas. He was always so friendly and affable and ineffectual, but he didn't like being sneered at and slighted, and all of us did that to him sooner or later. *I* think that when he told you that cock-and-bull story about Mrs Marrigay murdering her husband and trying to murder him, he actually said a great deal more.'

'Why, this is most interesting,' said Folly. 'Please go on.'

'I'm going on all right,' said Paula sharply. 'It ought to

have sprung to your mind at once, after all you are a trained detective. I thought you were on to it when you were questioning us about the relationship between Mr and Mrs Marrigay.'

'Did you?' murmured Folly.

'I did,' said Paula. 'And now you've told us about Uncle Nicholas and his "suspicions" it's plainer still. If he knew so much about his sister, he almost certainly knew about the –' she hesitated, and then said with some embarrassment – 'love-child.'

'*Of course!*' breathed Folly.

'He may have been working with him!' murmured Joyce. Paula shrugged her shoulders.

'I suppose there's something in that,' Peter conceded. 'How long have you been thinking like this, Paula?'

'I've wondered about Uncle Nicholas for a long time,' said Paula. 'I know I may be wrong – but surely the police will be able to prove it one way or the other! It would be perfectly understandable for Nicholas to hate the lot of us. Supposing you bring Leah in,' she added, unexpectedly.

'Why?' demanded Roger.

'I think I see why,' said Folly. 'Yes, perhaps it is a good idea. Will you –' he turned to Ives.

No one spoke while Ives was out of the room. Paula was no longer knitting, but leaning back with her eyes half closed. Dane thought: 'She's fighting hard for Tinker' and he was stirred by admiration of her calmness, by the fact that she had said so little and thought so much. This was Paula's moment.

Leah came in,

She looked immediately at Peter, and there was appeal in her expression. Her eyes were a little frightened, even anguished. She stood quite still, holding her hands in front of her, tightly clenched. Her husband and son were under arrest because of their loyalty to this family – and still she appealed to Peter for guidance.

He crossed to her side, and put a hand on her shoulder.

'Answer everything the Superintendent asks you, Leah,'

he said, 'it must all come out, everything you know or suspect. It will help old Pengelly and Lem. Do you understand?'

'Ess – sir.' Her voice was thin and sibilant.

'I want to know – ' began Paula.

'*If* you please,' interrupted Folly, glaring at Paula. He may have seen the quick look of dislike which Leah sent towards her. 'Now, Leah, believe me when I tell you that the police will be quite fair towards your husband and your son.'

Leah gave a submissive little nod.

'In fact we want to be fair to everyone,' said Folly. 'You don't like Mr Bell, do you?'

She shook her head.

'Because you believe he had something to do with the death of Mr Marrigay?'

She nodded.

Paula gripped the arms of her chair tightly.

'Who suggested that he had?' asked Folly. 'You didn't *know* anything about it, did you?'

'Madam said – it was no natural death,' said Leah.

'Ay, yes,' said Folly. 'And she mentioned – '

'She couldn't have named Tinker!' cried Paula.

'Will you be quiet!' roared Folly, and Paula subsided, shaking with anger. 'Now perhaps we can get on,' said Folly, altering the tone of his voice as he looked at Leah. 'And Mrs Marrigay mentioned Mr Bell, did she?'

'She didn't – name anyone.'

'*Ah!*' breathed Paula.

'But you and your husband thought Mr Bell was responsible. Why?'

'They quarrelled.'

'About money?'

'Ess.'

'You and your husband heard them?'

'Ess.'

'Who else heard them?'

'Mr Lee,' said Leah, drawing in her breath.

'Was your suspicion only because of the quarrel?'

197

'No.'

'Then why was it?' asked Folly.

'Mr Nicholas said – ' Leah paused, and shot a glance at Paula. 'Mr Bell had poisons.'

'*Aaahhh!*' Paula could control herself no longer. 'You see – that's all there was to it! And Nicholas didn't explain it to them – oh, no, he was far too cunning, he just suggested it, knowing that the suggestion would grow into suspicion and the suspicion into certainty.'

Folly said: '*Please*, Mrs Bell. Now, Leah, you have no reason whatsoever, apart from that, to suspect Mr Bell?'

The old woman shook her head.

'And none of you saw Mr Bell with the gun – or with a knife – or with Mr Nicholas's tools?'

'No.'

'Now, Leah, listen to me,' said Folly. 'A few days ago a man was killed – tell us exactly what your son told you, please.'

'Tell the truth, Leah,' Peter advised.

She told them exactly what her son had told her. She knew where the body had been buried. She herself had suggested burying Thor there, because she thought it would explain why the earth had been freshly turned. As she talked, Paula sat back with her eyes closed.

Dane thought: Had Nicholas tried to throw the blame on Tinker Bell?

Had the old man sufficient cunning?

Leah finished, and Folly thanked her gravely.

'There is just one more thing I want to know,' he said, 'and you will be careful how you answer, I'm sure. Do you know who the dead man is?'

She looked at him evenly.

'Ess.'

'Who?'

'The master's son,' she said.

'Who told you?' asked Folly.

She gave the slightest twist of a smile.

'Would I need telling?' she said, 'knowing him so well.

But Mr Nicholas, he told us. We pretended not to know.'
She gave another little secretive smile.

'It all seems to come back to Uncle Nick,' said Peter. 'If only we could explain the fire.'

'That was started some time before it broke out,' Paula said, 'that would be easy enough – wouldn't it, Superintendent?'

'Oh, yes,' said Folly.

'And there's something I haven't told you because Tinker didn't want it said until he could be *sure*,' said Paula in her steady, deep voice. 'Nicholas was very interested in spontaneous combustion a week or two ago. He'll deny it now, of course. He was always taking an interest in something or other, and chemistry fascinated him. Tinker told him what text books to read.'

'Did he then!' exclaimed Folly.

'I've no doubt that Nicholas Lee has done all this,' said Paula. 'I've always thought him unbalanced – haven't we all?' she demanded. 'Buried in those sinister myths, it's just the kind of thing that would appeal to him. There's been evil in this house since that man first came here.'

'How right you are,' sighed Folly. 'Evil – it has been in the very air. Yes, and the case against Nicholas Lee is very strong. I think we'll tell them, Inspector, they have a right to know – don't you agree?'

'I'll leave it to you,' said Ives.

'Thank you. Then, my friends, here is the evidence against Nicholas Lee. That he had access to the laboratory and the material. That he showed interest in spontaneous combustion. That in the pockets of his coat we found corks like that used to start the fire. That his carpet was burned by acid. That he could have poisoned Mr Marrigay, and could have poisoned himself. That he was seen with the knife with which the bullet was taken from the tree. That he owned the tools with which the road was dug up. That he bought the dogs and named them, and that he knew the dead man for what he was. A powerful array, as all of you will agree. And there are other things. We are told he influenced the Pengellys against Mr

Bell, he certainly ran away when the police were first brought in. He was mocked and laughed at because of his eccentricities and his hobby, and such a man might consider a slight a mortal insult. And yet, you know, in spite of that formidable list, I am *quite* sure that the murderer – or shall I say an accomplice of the murderer, is in this room *now*.'

CHAPTER XXV

FOLLY POINTS A FINGER

'You *can't* mean that!' cried Marjorie.

'Confound it, you've just made out a case against Uncle Nick!' growled Roger.

'Don't point at me,' said Peter.

'Peter!' exclaimed Joyce.

Only Dane and Paula sat silently, looking at the fat man. Paula's lips were set into a thin line and her eyes were frosty, while Dane looked blank – he felt helpless and lost, for he could not follow Folly's reasoning. It had seemed certain that Folly was going to accept the evidence against Nicholas Lee, which to Dane seemed overwhelming; but the detective looked at them in turn, without smiling.

Ives moved restlessly across the room.

'I do mean that,' said Folly.

'Since you've put most of your cards on the table, what about the trump?' asked Peter.

'I do not think this facetiousness is suited to the occasion,' said Folly.

'You're suggesting that one of us has framed the old man,' said Peter.

'I think so, yes,' said Folly. He glanced at Ives. 'Inspector, *you* tell them why I am so sure that it could not have been Uncle Nicholas – not all of it, at least.'

Ives spoke in a voice in which gratification was sternly

held back:

'Mr Lee could not have been responsible for the attack on Mr Dane. The staircase was deliberately rigged to make him fall.'

Joyce gasped.

'Yes,' said Ives, looking at her steadily. 'It was done deliberately and quickly, while Mr Dane was examining the things he found upstairs. And it was done, knowing that Pengelly would be suspected. The saw was cleaned of prints and put into the kitchen, where Pengelly would naturally see it and put it away in its proper place. That was a foul trick – for anyone in this house – to try to blame Pengelly.'

Dane was looking at Joyce; *could* the obvious conclusion be the right one?

'And Nicholas Lee could not have released Thor,' said Ives. 'Once the staircase incident pointed to Pengelly, the release of the dog would appear to be explained. Oh, Pengelly was meant to be a victim. Don't you agree, Superintendent?'

'Fully,' said Folly.

'Joyce,' said Marjorie, in a horrified voice, 'you knew Alec was upstairs, you – '

'Supposing we have less of this casting of suspicion upon others?' suggested Folly, acidly. 'Major Hurst – you are in debt, are you not?'

'What the devil do you mean?' roared Roger.

'I'm asking you a simple question,' said Folly. 'Is it true that you are in debt?'

'I'm up to my eyes in it, but if you think – '

'I am establishing facts,' said Folly. 'You have a motive for wanting your wife to inherit from her mother, then, but – *you* were not in the house when Mr Dane was hurt. You could not have put the string on the stairs.'

'What the hell are you driving at?' demanded Roger.

'I am trying to get the facts and someone in this room knows the truth,' said Folly. 'Your wife – '

'If you suggest that she – ' began Roger, striding forward.

'Now don't be silly,' rebuked Folly, 'you will not make any progress by ferocity. You cannot deal with me as you once

201

dealt with your brother-in-law – a *very* remarkable outburst that, if I may say so. I will repeat, your wife was here. And your wife "remembered" at a very convenient moment, that she had seen Uncle Nicholas with the knife.'

'Why, I'll – ' began Roger in a strangled voice.

'You will stay where you are,' said Folly, distastefully. 'I have more to say yet, we have more to discover. Mrs Hurst, be good enough to answer my question. Did you know about your half-brother?'

Marjorie raised her hands.

'*Did* you?'

'Don't answer him!' snapped Roger.

'Y-yes,' sighed Marjorie.

'Thank you,' said Folly, 'we are now making progress. Major Hurst, *why* are you in debt?'

'I – '

'*Why are you in debt?*'

'Oh, it's my fault,' cried Marjorie, 'it's not Roger's, I – I paid him – '

'Paid whom?'

'My – my half-brother.'

'Ah-ha!' exclaimed Folly with deep satisfaction. 'We are beginning to get the truth. It seemed to me that if this miscreant failed to get money from Mrs Marrigay he would try elsewhere. So, he came to you. He gave you to understand that your mother did not know the truth, no doubt.'

'Yes,' said Marjorie.

'And you paid him much more money than you could afford, to ensure his silence?'

'Oh, I know it was silly, but I thought it would hurt my mother so much if she knew.'

'Yes, indeed. And did you give this money away with your husband's knowledge?'

'Of course!' cried Marjorie.

'That was very generous of Major Hurst,' said Folly in a silky voice.

'There wasn't anything else to do,' said Roger, gruffly.

'This money was paid in large sums – sums at least much

larger than you could afford,' Folly continued. 'It is, therefore, possible that an inheritance would prove extremely attractive, and – '

'If you want to believe that, I can't stop you,' said Roger. 'May I inquire if you also believe that Marjorie set the dog on me ?'

'No, I do not,' said Folly, 'and that is why I do not think that you or your wife are concerned. So, we are narrowing down the suspects. Now, Miss Marrigay.'

Dane stood up.

'If you will sit down – ' began Folly.

'When I have asked you what you think you are achieving by this rigmarole,' said Dane, sharply. 'Why don't you tell us what you think – '

'But I *am*,' said Folly tartly. 'And you will be surprised, perhaps, to know that I have thought a great deal about you, Mr Dane. The remarkable coincidence of your arrival, your association with Miss Marrigay, suggesting an earlier acquaintance although you have never admitted to such, the fact that she had the opportunity – '

'Oh, don't go on!' cried Joyce.

'Let him,' said Peter, slowly.

'I shall go on whether I have your kind permission or not,' said Folly. 'I shall examine this situation closely and carefully. You, then Mr Dane, first brought this affair to the official notice of the police, and as the half-brother was not a resident here, may well have got to know him *and* Miss Marrigay. You obtained apparently unlimited time from your daily duties. These are interesting facts, are they not ? It is easy to imagine collusion. You would naturally feel that you were quite safe from suspicion, as you were apparently a new acquaintance. You could, however, have been informed of everything that went on here, including Nicholas Lee's eccentricities and, not being a wealthy man but having an ingenious turn of mind, might have persuaded your accomplice, Miss Marrigay – '

Joyce jumped up. 'Alec – don't listen to him! Alec – darling – I didn't tie that string. I wouldn't hurt you, oh, whatever else I do I wouldn't hurt you!'

Dane turned towards her, and there was a light in his eyes.

Folly said: 'I agree, Miss Marrigay, You, therefore, are ruled out.'

'Leaving me,' Peter said, mockingly.

'Before I deal with you, sir,' said Folly, 'I will tell you of one thing which I discovered in London and with which I have not even acquainted Inspector Ives. After I heard from Nicholas Lee of this change in the affections of Mr Marrigay, this infidelity, I set out to find whether it was true. And the means at the disposal of the law are many. I traced this half-brother – that is why I suggested we *might* find a body, Inspector.'

Ives said: 'Oh,' in a muffled voice.

'But I discovered something else – there were *two* children of the liaison. The man now dead, and – '

Paula jumped up. 'No!' she cried.

'Yes,' said Folly, in a stern voice. He pointed straight at Paula. 'His name was Bell. Your husband. Your husband, who had also been in receipt of an allowance from old Mr Marrigay, who had persuaded Mr Marrigay to lend him ten thousand pounds on a note of hand alone, but who was not satisfied, who – '

'No,' repeated Paula, in a strangled voice.

'Oh, but this is true,' declared Folly. 'And there was a quarrel, was there not – sharp and fierce, but hardly over a loan which had been made some years before. No. The truth is that your husband was working with his brother. Your husband asked for more money from Mr Marrigay, and threatened to disclose the truth if money were not forthcoming. But Mr Marrigay was adamant. Your husband poisoned him, putting arsenic into a dose of *Kaylene*, believing it would be easier to deal with his widow. But she suspected someone within the house. For when she thought the danger was from outside, she opened her door, so that she could call for help. But when the guests were here, she locked her door – she locked it, as she believed, on murder.'

Paula's knitting dropped from her hands.

No one moved.

Folly went on gently:

'And let us examine the circumstances. You were here during the first fatal week-end, Mrs Bell. Your husband had the poison and the chemicals needed for the fire. He carefully built up suspicion against Nicholas Lee and, when *you* saw that might not succeed, you tried to divert suspicion to old Pengelly. *You* were out when the dog was released – it was on a Tuesday, a clever mythological touch. The evidence is clear that you tied that piece of string But there is more. There was mud on the stairs. Some came from Pengelly's boot, mud of heavy consistency. There was other dirt, from the gravel of the drive where *you* had been walking.'

'Joyce was out there!' said Paula in a grating voice.

'Oh, yes,' said Folly, 'I would expect you to point to someone else. But only you tried to turn suspicion towards Nicholas Lee. And there are other little things which Lee will remember. He had that knife when he came to London, but it was stolen from him. You gave Lee the arsenic tablets when he visited you, knowing he was an arsenical subject, having more arsenic in his body than the average person. How clever – how easily that could be made to look like attempted suicide! Here, tonight, you again tried to blame Nicholas Lee. I have no doubt that the story of the burglary at the laboratory was false. The assistant whom you dismissed will be able to tell us that Nicholas Lee's interest in spontaneous combustion was doubtless suggested by you to him. You put the corks in his room, the arsenic and the gun in the books. You and your husband "experimented" with acid in his room and in Pengelly's – oh, suspicion was to drip everywhere,' said Folly. 'There is yet another thing. On the days of the attacks here, your husband went to Salisbury. His brother visited him there, received instructions, and came back and carried them out. How neatly it all fits in,' said Folly.

'Can you prove all this?' demanded Roger.

'My dear sir!' remonstrated Folly. 'I would not make such assertions without having proof. Of course it can all be proved. Inspector, perhaps you would care to make a formal charge against Mrs Bell.'

'You *can't* prove it!' cried Paula.

'Oh, but I can,' said Folly. He took a cork from his pocket. 'This came from a stock at your husband's laboratory. It has your fingerprints on it. It was placed in Mr Lee's coat *after* he had left for London.'

Paula swayed as Ives made the formal charge.

Paula had made a statement, admitting so much that the truth was beyond dispute. She was sent, under escort, into Marston, and Ives and Folly left the house together.

As they were getting into the car Ives asked:

'*Are* her prints on that cork?'

'I haven't the faintest idea,' said Folly, blandly. 'Corks do not take fingerprints very easily. You don't condemn me, do you?'

'I marvel at you,' said Ives.

'Thank you,' said Folly, as if bowing to an ovation. 'There are small matters that were doubtless done by the first half-brother. Removal of the "Beware of the Dog" notices and the poisoning of the dog. We shall never be really sure, but we have the major truth.'

Joyce and Dane sat in the pavilion at Lord's, watching Peter Marrigay batting with an ease which earned the deep admiration of the crowd. The sun glinted on the engagement ring on Joyce's finger.

Dane was smiling.

'I can't help thinking about it,' Joyce said, tentatively, as if such happiness had to be paid for.

'It has a better side,' said Dane slowly. 'It forced Peter to come right out and face up to things – and look what it's done for him. Oh, good shot!'

The ball flashed through slips, and deep third man chased unavailingly after it.

'Yes, that's true,' said Joyce.

'And it did another thing,' said Dane. 'Peter and Roger

get on perfectly well now, I doubt whether they would have ever seen eye to eye without this business. There was evil, you know, it was weighing all of you down. Now –'

He stopped as someone touched his shoulder.

He looked round and saw Roger, who was bending low.

'Had to come,' whispered Roger, in a carrying boom loud enough for everyone nearby to hear. 'A boy. Both fine. Wonderful, isn't it?'

'Oh, that's grand!' cried Joyce.

'Hush!' whispered Roger, in an anguished but delighted voice, 'we don't want to tell the world!'